THE HEAP

THE
HEAP

A NOVEL

SEAN
ADAMS

wm

WILLIAM MORROW

AN IMPRINT OF HARPERCOLLINSPUBLISHERS

THE HEAP. Copyright © 2020 by Sean Adams. All rights reserved. Printed in the United States of America. No part of this book may be used or reproduced in any manner whatsoever without written permission except in the case of brief quotations embodied in critical articles and reviews. For information, address HarperCollins Publishers, 195 Broadway, New York, NY 10007.

HarperCollins books may be purchased for educational, business, or sales promotional use. For information, please email the Special Markets Department at SPsales@harpercollins.com.

FIRST EDITION

Designed by Fritz Metsch

Library of Congress Cataloging-in-Publication Data has been applied for.

ISBN 978-0-06-295773-3

20 21 22 23 24   LSC   10 9 8 7 6 5 4 3 2 1

For Emma

THE HEAP

JOIN THE DIG!

THE FALL OF LOS VERTICALÉS!

Los Verticalés! A marvel of modern architecture! An achievement in nontraditional urban planning! A car-free, elevator-enabled society! The city that grew up rather than out, defying directional norms until the day that it could no longer! It stood nearly five hundred stories tall, bustling with life and excitement. Today its mountainous remains cover twenty acres of desert land. The relief effort will be colossal.

And YOU can be a part of it!

THE GREATEST RECYCLING PROJECT THE WORLD HAS EVER SEEN!

In collaboration with artisans the world over, all nonhazardous materials from the Los Verticalés Dig Site will be reclaimed and reused. This will not be an exercise in mindless rock moving! Each Dig Hand will be made a curator of debris, a prospector of diamonds in the roughest of rough! Each pitch may reveal a potential work of art! You will not simply dig; your efforts will make the world a better place!

DIG FOR SURVIVORS!

Radio disc jockey Bernard Anders was such a touchstone of life inside Los Verticalés that residents often called him "the Voice of the Vert." Today he is recognized as something different: the only confirmed survivor of his former city's collapse. His location? Unknown! Miraculously, Bernard and his equipment survived the fall. For ten days, he sat silent. Then, he tested his microphone and saw the levels rise: another miracle! He continues to broadcast to this day from a dark hole somewhere deep within the wreckage, taking calls from his legions of devoted listeners and watching the days tick by on his soundboard's digital clock while he awaits rescue.

Will yours be the shovel that uncovers him?

THE LATEST IN DIG-RELATED TECHNOLOGY!

With Bernard's survival playing out on the radio came the knowledge that some of the Los Verticalés Dig Site must be electrified. But fear not! The city's "founding father from afar," Peter Thisbee, has personally developed a set of shockproof gear for this purpose, including boots, overalls, and special ConductionSens shovels that will alert Dig Hands to any live electrical currents by way of a whistle built into the shaft. Experience firsthand the new era in digging!

ALL TYPES NEEDED!

Not cut out for the pitch-and-heave life? No problem! The Los Verticalés Dig Effort is an enormous project, requiring workers of all skill sets, including drivers, office support staff, supervisors, site managers, event planners, service industry and retail staff, and so much more! If you want to be involved, you *will* be involved!

AN EXCELLENT COMPENSATION PACKAGE!

Though all positions are classified as "volunteer," Peter Thisbee has established the Los Verticalés Relief Foundation, which will generously provide each worker at the Dig Site with a fully weatherized camper, a rehabilitated bicycle, and a small living stipend. And best of all, the beautiful desert views come free of charge!

So, what are you waiting for? Join the Dig, and help make a better, more beautiful tomorrow TODAY!

I

THE

DIG

EFFORT

FROM *THE LATER YEARS*:

NEIGHBORS

Though many of us in Los Verticalés were surrounded by other units, there were precious few we considered "neighbors." Residents in the first layer of inner units rarely cavorted with those in the outer units across the hall. Yes, all windowless condos were outfitted with UV screens that streamed a view of the outside and could "re-create 92 percent of the window experience," but that 8 percent of variation—and moreover, the difference in wealth required to afford an outer unit versus an inner one—accounted for an entirely different lifestyle. The inner unit located behind another inner unit was an even greater mystery. Depending on hallway layout and traffic patterns, two units backed against each other, separated by only a wall, might be a twenty-minute walk apart.

Our truest neighbors, then, were those on either side of us, but these too could be forgotten, especially among the inner units. If there was one benefit to UV screens, it was that they could be configured any way we liked. The manual that came with them included a note from Peter Thisbee himself, urging us to place them only on walls where one might "traditionally find windows" to avoid "directional disorientation." Almost no one followed these guidelines. Instead, we placed them where they best suited the room, and even though we understood the artifice, it was not uncommon to hear a bump in the next unit and step to the UV screen to look out.

We never considered those who lived above or below us because we never heard them. The engineers chose the densest possible flooring materials to foster a sense of community. Each floor worked like a neighborhood, the stairwell and the elevator serving respectively as the highway and the high-speed rail, connecting distinct urban districts. We never considered the possibility that someone a level up or down from us might affect our lives in any meaningful way. This is ironic to think about now, because it was not our neighbors across the hall, or next door, or behind us who were our end. When the Vert collapsed we killed those who lived under our feet, while those above, in turn, killed us.

Or, not "us," exactly, but everyone else.

AN APARTMENT

ORVILLE SAW it happen out of the corner of his eye: saw Hans pitch his ConductionSens shovel into the rubble, saw him stumble forward and fall, both man and tool disappearing out of view.

And he had to admit, it was just a bit cathartic that it should be Hans. Hans, who all morning had been overexerting himself, or more accurately, overexerting his display of just how much he was exerting himself, putting more energy into the theatrics of each pitch than into the physical effort of the pitch itself. It was ridiculous, shameless showboating. There were only three of them—Orville, Lydia, and Hans—working this patch, so who was he trying to impress?

No, Orville decided, it was more than just ridiculous, actually. It was offensive. Especially with Orville right there. Because, let's be honest, if there was one person who should be allowed a little dramatic display every now and then, it was him, Orville, given that he worked under a denser psychophysical burden than anyone else in the Dig Effort. But did he play up his circumstances for sympathy? No. Never. Orville siphoned all the jittery energy he derived from his personal turmoil directly into the work of his shovel. He might even have called his devotion to the task at hand monkish, if monkishness did not preclude its own acknowledgment.

The pep in Hans's step did make sense, at least on one level. He had, that morning, led his first orientation session for the new Dig Hands, and apparently it had gone well. "They're hungry!" Hans said. What he didn't mention was how few newbs there were. When the three of them had gone through the same session ten months ago, the leaders had had to split people into five groups, there were so many. Nowadays, the influx of volunteers had lessened to a steady trickle. Orville imagined a group of between two and seven people. He wondered if Hans had mentioned him as a way of endearing himself to them, if he had paused dramatically as he explained Bernard's situation to say how much this weighed on him personally, given that he worked with Bernard's own brother, Orville Anders.

But Orville wouldn't hold a hypothetical against him. Truth was, Hans was one of his only friends on the Dig, and more importantly, he was now a man in need. Orville threw down his own ConductionSens shovel and scrambled the fifty or so feet up to where Hans had been. Lydia did the same.

In the rubble, they found a hole. Lydia loosed the flashlight clipped to her overalls and shined it down. Hans sat up on a laminate wood floor not too far below.

"I'm okay," he said. "Landed on my tailbone, but I'm okay."

"Is it a radio studio?" Lydia asked.

Hans turned on his own flashlight now, cast it around, shook his head. "Living room."

Lydia gave Orville an apologetic look. It was a look he'd grown familiar with, one he appreciated and hated at the same time for how thoughtful and yet pitying it was. Then the two of them crouched down and eased their way in.

Hans was right: It was a living room. A whole intact apartment, actually. There was no power, so there was no air-conditioning, but it still felt nice compared to the heat of the Heap's surface.

Hans went into the kitchen with his flashlight and checked the fridge. "Got beers in here," he said. He tossed a can to Lydia, one to Orville, then took one for himself. The beers, like the apartment, possessed a coolness by contrast. The three of them sat on a leather couch and drank.

"It's a nice place," Hans said.

"No windows, though," Lydia said.

Hans cast his flashlight around. Among a preponderance of photographs showing Shanghai street life, he found a cracked UV screen. "Yeah, that'd be a tough sell."

Orville finished his beer quickly and got up.

"You getting a refill?" Lydia asked.

Orville shook his head. "Gonna check out the back."

He left them there and made his way down the hallway into the rest of the apartment. Away from the hole Hans had made, the darkness increased. He found a bedroom, his flashlight illuminating a queen bed, more UV screens on the walls, and an abstract painting above the headboard. They should take it up. Send it to the Sale. No reclamation necessary. It might be valuable enough to bring in some good money. He'd deal with that later, though. Across the hall from the bedroom was a frosted glass door. The bathroom, Orville predicted, and he was right. What he didn't predict was finding a body in the shower.

He walked back to the living room, got another beer out of the fridge, and told Hans and Lydia, "Get on the two-way with boss. Tell him to bring the doctor. We got a dead."

WAITING

"WE'RE FUCK near the far side over here," boss said on the two-way. "Will be a minute. Can you wait?" Of course they could. So they waited, Orville, Lydia, and Hans, sitting in the living room, sipping their beers.

"Well, that explains the smell," Hans said at length.

Orville and Lydia chuckled before falling once again into silence. It was a sick joke among Dig Hands to talk about the smell, not because it was funny, but because to them it wasn't anything. A dead could compost itself for months in a sealed-off space and still go undetected by three intruders, even as they casually had a few beers, breathing through their noses with abandon. Orville understood, logically, that it was ridiculous he needed to see it to know it was there, but even now, after its discovery, he could detect nothing of its odor.

Smell was the first sense to go on the Heap. Before the sun bleached your eyesight, before the grip of your Conduction-Sens reduced your hands to ten points of numb leather calluses, before the basic flavorless provisions of the produce tent could blight away large swaths of your palate—before any of this, your nose went haywire, a defense mechanism to guard against the bouquet of death that hung in the air.

It was a mass grave, really. They found deads all the time, most of them less intact than the one in the bathroom. Hell, often there was no telling the difference between some poor crushed dead and food waste until you found a bone. And it wasn't just the bodies. The sense of deadness went well beyond that. The whole place was an overnight ruin.

Which was all to say: As they waited for boss and the doctor to arrive, Orville felt neither nausea nor heebie-jeebies from being in the apartment with the decomposing body, or at least not the standard heebie-jeebies. Perhaps a more existential heebie-jeebies, a phantom heebie-jeebies, emanating as much from outside as from within. It wasn't being there, waiting. It was being there with Hans and Lydia. Their motives had always been different from his, and these moments seemed to amplify that.

Lydia had political ambitions. She'd come to the Heap to get her foot in the door in case CamperTown ever set down roots. Hans was a photographer who'd hoped to capture a unique way of life through the lens of his camera. Orville came here for his brother. They might bond over their equal levels of nonsuccess—Lydia served on the Committee for Better Life in CamperTown but hadn't made any meaningful political connections, Hans had taken no more than ten photos since his first week, and Orville had yet to unearth Bernard—but for Orville, it was personal.

Whenever they found a body, especially an intact one, he could feel the other two watching him closely for signs of emotional distress. Which he did feel, of course. Even just a moment ago, despite knowing instantly that it wasn't Bernard, Orville still felt the urge to climb out of the living room, scramble down to his bike, and turn on the portable radio he had hooked to his handlebars, just to be sure Bernard was okay, as if this dead stranger might signify more death to come among the rubble. And what kept him from doing so? Not composure, but a rule, his rule: no listening to Bernard during the workday, lest his brother's entrapment be reduced to background noise. But Hans and Lydia's silent scrutiny when he rejoined them on the couch displaced this distress, rendered it abstract, so that Orville found himself

not feeling anything in particular, focusing instead on trying to embody just enough physical discomfort to read as a
good brother-in-crisis.

At any rate, it was a relief when boss and the doctor
arrived.

The doctor made his way to the bathroom. Not a minute
after he'd disappeared down the hall, he was back. "It is my
professional opinion that the deceased fell victim to conditions of the collapse. For example, maybe he bumped his head
really bad when the whole building gave way around him."

This was a good enough explanation for now. Orville and
Lydia moved the dining table under the hole in the ceiling to
work as a step stool. Then the doctor put on his gloves, threw
a pair to Hans, and the two of them took the body out to the
medicart, struggling only briefly with the handoff to get it
up and outside.

"Where'd you guys get those beers?" boss asked. Lydia
shined her flashlight toward the kitchen.

The doctor had a lab in the makeshift shipping-container
hospital where they did tests to establish identity in order to
keep the Victims Log up to date. Protocol said tests were to
be done as quickly as possible following a dead's discovery,
but when they came back a few minutes later, the doctor said,
"Got him loaded up and going to let the sun dry him out a
bit. He's been going sour in here for a while. What's another
hour, right?"

Then there were five of them, sitting in the dark, drinking.

"So this is how they lived," said boss. "Guess I never realized how normal it would look."

"Don't care for the lighting," said the doctor, squinting to
look around the room.

The walls groaned slightly, and the apartment shook
for a moment. Hans stood up, alarmed, but boss held up his
hand. "Just a shift."

"Felt like a big one," Hans said.

"That's because we're inside it. Relax. This place held up this long. It's not like it's about to be crushed now."

Orville paced the floor back and forth once, then a second time, stomping hard and listening for anywhere it sounded hollow.

"What're you doing?" Lydia asked.

"Looking for where to dig."

"Whoa, whoa," said boss. "Who says we need to dig right here?"

"That's what we do," Orville said. "We dig."

"Yeah, but there's plenty of digging to be done elsewhere. Why don't we make this a sort of employee lounge? A place where people can come to take a load off after a long day, you know?"

"Should we send a memo around CamperTown?" Lydia said.

"Nah," said boss. "Let's just keep it a thing of 'if you find it, you can use it,' you know? What do you think about that, doc? Sound good?"

"Sounds great," said the doctor, coming back from the fridge with two more beers, both for him. "Our own little hideout."

CALLING IN

RUBBLE DISPLACED by the week's digging so impeded the path around the Heap that Orville, going against the flow of traffic toward CamperTown, eventually ceded the packed ground for raw desert. It irked him, and not just because he had to pedal harder to get to the phone bank. It meant tomorrow would be a sort day. Orville understood the task's purpose. The stuff had to go somewhere if they were to make any true progress in the cleanup. But for Orville it meant a day without digging, a day further from finding Bernard.

And it could be a long day at that, if you ended up getting cornered by a Displaced Traveler out walking around. One of them had come to the sorting station a few weeks back and taken an interest in a piece of stainless steel. Hans made the mistake of positing that it belonged to the elevator door, nothing more than a passing comment really, but the guy totally tweaked. No, he'd said, it couldn't be a piece of the elevator door because of how reflective it was, and then he got into some reverie about how there was a distinct, "almost beautiful" sense of camaraderie you felt packed in an elevator, even if you didn't know anyone. Hans tried to calm him down by saying he could relate, having ridden in packed elevators himself, but that only exacerbated the situation. The guy insisted that in the Vert it was different, "insisted" being a polite way to say it. Fact was he got real worked up, almost to the point of violence, and Orville even considered announcing who he was—or whose brother he was—but he couldn't tell if that would help the situation or only prolong it. Luckily, Lydia was able to get him off their backs with a lie about someone finding a fully intact urinal up the path, but not before he'd wasted an hour of their time.

There was no need to get all angry about that again, though. For all he knew, tomorrow would go smoothly, and besides, his day wasn't over yet.

Once the bike traffic thinned, Orville retook the path and turned on his radio.

"I'm doing a report in school on the effects of darkness," said the caller, a young girl by the sound of it. "What would you say the effect has been on you?"

"Not great," said Bernard.

If Orville listened all day maybe it would be too gradual to notice, but like this, tuning in each night, he could hear it: the slow deterioration of decorum as Bernard inched closer to a breakdown.

To be fair, at least this question was original. Most of the time it was the same thing over and over again, new listeners interested in the necessities. Where do you get your water? "There's a trickle running down the wall," Bernard claimed. And how do you avoid starving? "Rats come through sometimes. What I do to them, it's not something I want to talk about. I put a hand over the mic, so you don't have to listen." If you spend long enough in a dark hole somewhere saying the same things over and over again, you're bound to lose your patience.

"How would you describe your state of happiness, on a scale of one to ten?" the girl asked.

"I don't know," Bernard said. "Does a four sound too high? Look, I need to go."

"No, wait, I have—" But Bernard hung up before she could finish.

Orville coasted into the phone bank, parked his bike, and turned the radio off to avoid feedback. There was no one else there—hadn't been since about the third month of the Dig Effort, after which time those with lives and families beyond the Heap began to thin out. These days, all that remained were the connectionless, even the newbs, or maybe especially the newbs. Despite this, Orville still walked all the way to the fifth and most private phone to dial in.

"Orville!" Bernard said. "I'm so glad you called." He started their conversation like this every day, then, as usual, launched directly into what he wanted to talk about: "I was just thinking to myself, did Mom ever choose favorites between the two of us? And then I got to thinking, if she were alive today, how would my current predicament affect which son took the top spot? My first thought: It would definitely shift things in my favor. Tragedy points, you know? Or a redistribution of emotion by necessity. I need her support more than you do."

"Seems natural," Orville said. The phone bank had no roof. The sun beat down, and already he could feel sweat gathering in his inner elbow and between his ear and the receiver.

"Well, but hold on," Bernard said. "That's my *first* thought. Second thought is: I'm not doing anything. Yes, it isn't my fault, but the fact remains that I'm just here doing nothing. Except broadcasting. And that's the real problem. If Mom were alive, she'd hear me, all day, all night, doing nothing. It would make my not doing anything seem almost active. You, meanwhile, would be up there with your shovel. You'd call her, right? But probably not every day. She could only guess at what you were doing, and her imagination might paint a stark contrast between us: me, actively lazy; you, unknowably hardworking. Not to mention, you're digging down to me, but I'm not digging up to you. So, technically, you're doing more for the family than I am. Therefore, advantage you."

"Could be a draw," Orville said.

Bernard sighed. "It's not fun if it's a draw, Orville. For the sake of conversation, let's discount the possibility for draws, okay?"

"Okay," Orville said.

"Third thought," Bernard said, then went into it, but Orville had trouble following. Since they'd begun these talks shortly after Orville arrived—it embarrassed him that it had taken a whole two weeks to realize that he too could call in and talk live on the air with his brother just like everyone else—Bernard had grown more and more philosophical. They didn't speak of concrete memories, but instead about some theory of their sibling dynamic.

Back when Bernard first got offered the job at WVRT they'd talked briefly about what he could expect there: a windowless apartment; a scrambled sense of time; recycled air. "People think of it as a city within a skyscraper, but to me it sounds more like living in a giant airplane," he'd said. When Orville asked him why he would go somewhere like that, Bernard talked about how disheartened he'd grown at his current station: the studio was woefully out of date, the station manager inept and nepotistic. He told Orville about the powerful antenna this new station would install, the potential for worldwide fame—strange to think about that now. But he spoke halfheartedly. It was a prepared response. He grew more excited when he mentioned he'd spoken to a real estate agent and could sell his house at a profit. Or about how the commute would be short, on foot, that he'd bring his car but barely use it, thus saving on gas. No snow. No heat waves. Life would be predictable, and Bernard wanted it that way.

This was one way in which Orville and his brother were similar: their desire for simplicity allowed them comfort in discomfort, as long as it was predictable enough. Orville benefited from it now. He never grew tired of digging, never felt the walls of his miniscule camper closing in, just as he imagined Bernard had never grown bored of crowded hallways and fake windows.

But this didn't explain exactly how Bernard had grown into such a deep thinker. Maybe the straightforwardness of his time inside Los Verticalés had freed up some headspace, thus allowing (or even necessitating) a more anthropological approach to life, an approach that naturally would only be augmented by the dark, where, without anything to observe or anywhere to go, he would have no choice but to look even further inward. Orville couldn't be sure. He'd only begun to think this all through recently. Their initial conversation about the move had registered as little more than the requisite phone call to family that precedes a major life change. It was an act of covering one's bases. When you weren't close to your brother, you did what you could to avoid being blamed for that lack of closeness, which meant keeping each other abreast of the big things. That day on the phone, Orville had said only, "Huh," then remained quiet until Bernard ran out of steam and the call, mercifully, ended.

"Not to mention the pressure on me," Bernard said now. "Could you imagine, if every time I opened my mouth I had to consider the fact that our mother might be listening?"

Orville stayed mostly quiet now, too—he spoke as little as he could and never cut his brother off—but not for expedience. Bernard spent all day allowing others to dictate the flow of conversation. Orville wanted their time to be special. He gave Bernard the reins, and Bernard took them.

"It would be a lot," Orville said.

This didn't always leave Orville satisfied. There were days when he felt like nothing more than a receptacle. If someone else could've called, someone else Bernard had known before he moved to the Vert, it would be no different. They were acquaintances, really. Orville supplied only the most tenuous connection to Bernard's life before the darkness. He provided no kinship, only an accelerant to his brother's thoughts. In this way, these calls, even Orville's presence at the Heap, could be considered little beyond a symbolic gesture. He dug each day, hoping to save Bernard, but so did everyone else.

"I don't know if I could handle it," Bernard said, "not being able to say whatever I want. As far as I see it, that's the only way I'm not constrained right now."

Orville didn't want it to be like that, another exercise in covering his bases. He wanted to want to be there. He wanted to cherish these conversations. He wanted to find a way to get closer to his brother, to start their relationship anew, or, God forbid, end it on a high note. Orville tried not to think about that second possibility. Bernard had survived in the rubble for so long. It seemed like he could live forever down there.

"Now imagine this," Bernard said. "Not only is she alive, not only is she listening, but she's here. Not here-here, but up where you are in . . . what is it called again?"

"CamperTown," Orville said.

"Right, she's in CamperTown. So now it's not only me who has to watch my words. It's you, too." And he was off again, on something about how people are the people around them, and something about the fabric of being. Bernard seemed to be enjoying himself, and that was what mattered.

If Orville felt like nothing more than a receptacle for Bernard's thoughts on the bad days, he had to admit, on the good days—like today—he didn't feel much different. He merely found pride in feeling that way, in allowing his brother the freedom to pursue these trains of thought without interruption, until they eventually came to an end. This was why their conversations always ended the same way, today being no different.

"And what's new with you?" Bernard said. And Orville, the proud receptacle, said only, "You know. Same old. Just digging."

[5]

FROM *THE LATER YEARS*:

STRUCTURES OF POWER

Despite possessing a municipality's population, Los Verticalés was, in the eyes of the law, an elaborate condominium. We weren't bothered by this at first. Many of us believed all the "city" talk to be a sales pitch. But as our numbers continued to grow, we noticed something problematic: Without being a true city, we could not have a true city government. Many major positions such as head of security and building manager were hired by Peter Thisbee, not elected. That left only the condo board, but even then, the choice felt inevitable. Anthony Mitner, who lived in an outer unit on the wealthy fifty-sixth floor (high ceilings) and owned a chain of juice bars local to the Vert, had served as the condo president for as long as any of us lived there. The same went for his fellow board members, other wealthy resident business owners. Whether they'd been democratically elected due to their success and then bought by Thisbee or if he'd hand-picked them at the outset and pulled some strings to get them instated we couldn't be sure. Regardless, the point stood: even though he didn't live in the Vert, the real power lay with Thisbee.

Making matters worse were the condo president elections themselves. At some point, feeling helpless to effect any change in leadership, we began to treat the annual pre-election meet-

ing (occurring in the first-floor concert hall and simulcast to amphitheaters throughout the Vert) as a sort of variety show. Twenty residents would announce their candidacy each year, but instead of speaking about how they would improve life in Los Verticalés, they instead performed. Sometimes they danced. Sometimes they sang. There were stand-up routines, magic acts, spoken-word poetry. Once, a woman from one of the floors close to the ground did a routine with her three trained schnauzers and a number of hula hoops that we still cannot exactly describe except to call it "mesmerizing." Each year, though it was never explicitly stated, whoever tallied the second-most votes (after Mitner) was deemed to be the winner of the contest and enjoyed several months of celebrity treatment.

Only once did a true political challenger arise. Rolinda Jacobs, inner-unit naturalist and expert in "sustainable low-light indoor agriculture," stepped up to the stage and actually spoke the way a candidate might. She argued for a more democratic approach to governance, with delegates from each floor convening once every two months to discuss how to make the Vert better for all who lived there. She also proposed a radical housing shake-up, including a standardized condo price to keep outer units from only being available to the wealthiest of residents. This would be impossible to enact, of course, but that seemed beside the point. Truly, it seemed all she wanted was to highlight the inequality rampant within our walls.

Many believed Jacobs had a chance against Mitner, but shortly before the final vote could be tallied, she rescinded her candidacy. Months later, a fourteenth-floor unit with a large deck opened up. Jacobs moved into it and could be seen beginning construction on an ambitious container garden. Rumors abounded: that she wasn't anywhere near the top of the waiting list for such a unit, nor could she possibly have afforded it; that she'd never even wanted to be the condo president, and it had all been a power play; that, in fact, the whole thing—her campaign, her backing out, the perceived corruption—all of it was orchestrated by Thisbee to sow doubt that a real opponent to Mitner would ever come forward.

But after a few weeks, we forgot about her intrusion into our lives. It had been fun to taste true politics for a moment, but the fact was we missed the singing, the dancing, the schnauzers.

6

THE COMMITTEE FOR BETTER

LIFE IN CAMPERTOWN

"I WAS going to talk to the doctor about borrowing a wheel-chair," someone said.

The conference trailer fell silent. This had been the rhythm of their meetings ever since the topic had turned to Thisbee's approaching visit: One of the seven members of the Committee for Better Life in CamperTown spoke up, then silence, then another spoke up, silence, each point entirely separate from the last. Only the occasional flare-up of a tangential argument could bring anything resembling a flow to their conversation.

Lydia looked to Chairperson Gil. He only nodded as if the need for a wheelchair were self-evident. "Okay," he said. "That sounds good."

Which was a lie. It didn't sound good. It didn't make any sense. It had come in response to the suggestion that perhaps it would be a good idea to take Thisbee around the Heap proper, to show him the Dig Hands at work. It was the first proposed alteration to the actual tour route in some time, and the first time anyone had thought of including sites beyond the Assistance Sector. All previous iterations had involved only the hospital, a cubicle building, and a few of the various utility bodegas—for the repair of shovels or bicycles, the sewing of overalls, etc. Initially, there'd been

plans for a larger ceremony, where Thisbee would give a
speech. Thisbee's people nixed this, so the plan changed.
There'd be a wine and cheese reception at the tour's conclusion in the old school bus that had been converted into a
library. Then they received word that Thisbee would be arriving early in the morning, so the plans changed again: it
would be just a cheese reception. Cheese was a crucial part
of many breakfast dishes, was the justification. Omelets, for
example. Or a bacon, egg, and cheese sandwich. It was right
there in the name; no one could argue against that (though
some concerns were raised, not by but on behalf of James, a
Committee member who was lactose intolerant).

Nobody ever considered taking Thisbee through Camper-
Town, which frustrated Lydia. But the one time she'd suggested
it, there'd been zero enthusiasm from any of the members or
Chairperson Gil, the apparent tour guide, so she'd dropped it.
A walk through CamperTown with someone not attuned to its
intricacies would be bland, and the tour was going to be bland
enough already. Lydia had since taken on the role of intellectual defensive artillery, shooting down nonsense as best she
could.

"I'm sorry," she said, "but why do we need a wheelchair?
Is he injured?"

"There's just a lot of walking to do is all. And it might be
a bit much for him to handle . . ."

"He can walk like the rest of us," said someone else.

"We don't walk around the Heap," Lydia said. "We ride
bikes."

"We could rig the wheelchair like a chariot," said the
woman who'd made the initial suggestion, "and someone could
pull him on a bike."

There followed a cacophony of voices, some angry, some
less so. "Maybe we could just give him a bike." "He gave us
our bikes." "No, I worked for my bike. There's a difference."
"That's a good idea: instead of us working to please him,

maybe he could do some work to please us." "Might do him some good, experience what it feels like to sweat." "I'm sure he sweats plenty." "Not like we sweat!" This last comment was punctuated with a fist brought down gavel-like onto the table, resulting in a new silence, more brooding than before.

When Chairperson Gil first announced Peter Thisbee's impending trip to the Dig Site and the Committee for Better Life in CamperTown's responsibility of planning for it, Lydia had been relieved. Committee meetings up until that point had been a rudderless exploration of complaints. Such as: How small could a thing be and still be complained about? And the follow-up: How far could devil's advocacy go? The answer, in both cases: there were no limits. Thisbee's visit would at least give them a focus, Lydia thought. She was wrong.

Despite his long absence from the public discourse concerning the Heap (and the discourse itself seemed mostly absent these days), Thisbee remained a conduit for opinions that were as vehement as they were half-baked. The ones expressed just now in the trailer were a microcosm of those from the days following the collapse. Some spoke as if Los Verticalés were his child and he needed to be treated as a man in mourning. Others called him a tyrant and claimed Los Verticalés to be some sort of sick social experiment. Thisbee himself kept a low profile during that time, neither embracing the former nor denying the latter. This worked in his favor.

The debate eventually contorted in upon itself, grew circular. Those who sought to condemn Thisbee as the sole responsible party for the collapse had to then acknowledge him as the one who gave the residents of Los Verticalés a chance to live the life they truly wanted. Those who sought to praise him had to reconcile that he'd allowed a structure so precarious as the Vert to exist in the first place. As passion for the subject cooled, Thisbee, by way of a statement from his legal team, announced that, despite the sale agreement not requiring him to do so, he would be "purchasing" back each destroyed unit from the owner's next of kin. He also offered families of the victims airfare to come to the site in order to scavenge for their loved ones' belongings. The payouts from the condo sales were accepted; the invitations were not. A mere two days after Bernard began broadcasting, Thisbee put forward a set of detailed plans for the Dig Effort. Again, he released this only through a statement from his lawyers. They would clear the site, reclaim what could be reclaimed, and sell what could be sold to build an as-yet unspecified monument in honor of Los Verticalés. After this, his name receded from most Heap-related discussion. If there was a figurehead for the operation, it wasn't him. It was Bernard.

Lydia had done her homework on Peter Thisbee. She admired many things about him, but this she admired most: his willful invisibility. Had he affected more bravado along the way, he might now be moored in a never-ending loop of explanations and justifications. Instead, he had established an important precedent. His silence did not mean he was not hard at work. If anything, it conveyed the opposite. He broke the silence only to announce—or have someone else announce—bold action. He sought only to lead, not to be seen doing so. This in turn allowed him to keep leading in the face of disasters, such as the collapse.

Lydia sometimes considered herself a kindred spirit: she kept a relatively low profile, despite her aspirations. Then again, she wasn't working on Thisbee's level. She wasn't even in charge of the Committee for Better Life in CamperTown. And she let herself wallow in the figurative muck more than she imagined Thisbee might.

For example, this sweat talk, a recurring theme whenever they discussed Thisbee, born out of some weird desire to be everymen in the face of a supposed plutocrat—it bothered her. Lydia was the only Dig Hand on the Committee, which meant Lydia was the only one with a right to be exhausted. These other people? They could take whatever they felt was exhaustion—whatever they *mistook* for exhaustion—and shove it up their asses. That would be difficult, though, considering their asses were safely cradled by chairs (and, Lydia imagined, probably growing rapidly larger) all day—in their Supply Distribution Bodegas, or the always-empty Heap Visitors' Information Center, or whatever the hell white-collar-as-fuck bullshit administrative jobs they worked on the Heap's periphery. Her ass, meanwhile—despite being least worthy of the aforementioned up-shove of faux-exhaustion—was out there on the Heap all day, unprotected save for her overalls.

Lydia put her hands in her lap, under the table, so no one could see them quaking. She took a deep breath. In moments like this, as her inner frustration nearly reached a point of outerizing, she had to remind herself: her serving on the Committee was a choice, just as it had been a choice to come to the Heap, just as it had been a choice to work as a Dig Hand.

Chairperson Gil looked at his notes. "I think we're going to have to table the wheelchair talk for now," he said. This was where Gil excelled, in the use of "table" as a verb. "Anybody have anything else they want to bring up?"

"Abandoned camper," mumbled Benjy.

Benjy looked about a hundred years old and awoke only as each Committee meeting concluded, with some trivial parting thought. He worked the gate, which basically meant he sat in a booth at the entrance to CamperTown, collecting signatures from outside service workers and delivery people who came in. He was supposed to keep things in order, to know who came and went, but if you asked him, he'd shrug and say, "Check the logs."

"I'm sorry, someone abandoned their camper?" Gil said. He put his pen to his notebook, excited by something worthy of report and requiring little discussion.

"Nope. Out beyond West CamperTown in the desert. Same one I brought up a couple months ago. Real eyesore. Dented. Base half buried in sand. No paint, just tin. Looks tacky but also reflective. Nearly blinds me every time I try and watch the sun set. Not to mention the hooligans. See lights going out there late at night. Once a month, like clockwork. Would love to see it go."

Chairperson Gil nodded and replaced his pen on the table. "I mentioned that to Mr. Thisbee's people already, and they assured me he would consider removing it."

"Maybe we should just move it ourselves."

This was Lydia. She spoke casually, with no ire or spite. It was not a demand, barely even a suggestion. And still, Chairperson Gil looked at her with a mixture of fear and disbelief.

"If Mr. Thisbee's people say they're considering it, we need to believe they're considering it," Chairperson Gil said. "We must go through the proper channels."

7

THE DISPLACED TRAVELERS

AFTER THE meeting, Lydia made her way to the far end of CamperTown, where the Displaced Travelers lived in a number of large RVs parked in a circle, giving them a private courtyard. From above, Lydia imagined it would appear tumorous, a bulge growing off the otherwise neat grid of campers. Inside, it felt like another world. They'd strung a thick net of Christmas lights between the RVs and set up café tables of muted shades of pink, green, and blue. On each, a potted flowering cactus. There was something resort-like about it. Lydia couldn't help it: whenever she came here, she was acutely aware of how she smelled. But the Displaced Travelers never judged her.

An enclosure, Lydia had thought the first time she'd seen their little settlement. These were the few residents of Los Verticalés who'd been away at the time of its collapse, and they'd managed, even living on what was essentially a campground, to create something that felt interior. As much as they had once lived in Los Verticalés, Los Verticalés lived in them. This was why Lydia came: to learn about the ant farm from the ants themselves. The inner workings of the Vert remained, for most, a foreign language. Lydia's visits to the Displaced Travelers gave her a vocabulary few others possessed. If she could gain fluency, she might use it to better make her case to those who could speak it, like Thisbee, and exclude those who couldn't, like the Committee, when the question inevitably arose: What happens next for CamperTown?

Lydia saw it like this: CamperTown was the bizarro Vert. Campers were too small to really live in full-time, which meant communal spaces would be necessary. Instead of a city confined by walls that grew up rather than out, it would be a sprawling open-air city that grew forever out and never up. It could be beautiful, Lydia thought, the perfect antithesis to Los Verticalés and yet with the same allure: a uniqueness of life that only those within could understand, a true sense of community. This, more than Thisbee's promised monument, would be the real tribute to the city that came before. That was why Lydia never imagined building CamperTown into something recognizable. She didn't want to replace the campers with houses, to widen and pave the paths until they were standard streets. She wanted it to stay itself. In this way, her desire to get involved with local politics was maybe not so political at all. She wanted a part in governance only insofar as it allowed her to build a place unlike any other. *I'm really more of a societal engineer than a politician*, she'd say, if anyone asked. But nobody had, and the truth was, at present, she was neither.

Lydia stepped into the courtyard and found that, as usual, the man with the glasses and the mustache was outside. He sat cross-legged at one of the café tables, smoking a cigarette.

He nodded at Lydia. "How's it coming?" He had to shout to be heard over the roar of the RVs' engines. The Displaced Travelers ran them almost all day for the air-conditioning.

Lydia stood behind the chair across from him but stopped short of sitting down. "How's what coming?"

The man motioned with his cigarette in the direction of the Heap. "The whole thing."

"It's coming," Lydia said. She crossed her arms, then uncrossed them because it felt like closing herself off, then recrossed them because maybe closing herself off was right after all.

The man eventually motioned to one of the RVs. "They're in there."

Some of Lydia's defensiveness had to do with him, specifically. He was even more of an enigma than the rest of the Displaced Travelers. He possessed a disassociated quality she couldn't read, a paper-thin sadness. The others were bitter. Their being here was proof enough. Being alive, Lydia understood that they'd managed to squeeze some extra money out of Peter Thisbee, probably enough that they could live anywhere. But they chose to stay, and to spend their time cataloguing their former lives.

Their reasons for being away at the time of the collapse were unanimously involuntary—mostly business trips and funerals—and they spoke of their survival with disdain, as if jealous they could not be there for their city's crowning achievement. They sated themselves with a sense of duty. If they had outlived their neighbors, it was only so they could tell the collective story of Los Verticalés at its greatest height. They titled the project *The Later Years*.

The RV the man indicated was set up like a newsroom: desks everywhere, a Displaced Traveler typing furiously at each one. Lydia cleared her throat, and the clatter of typing came suddenly to a stop.

"Oh, it's you," one of them said, the woman working closest to the door. She stood from her desk and extended a folder to Lydia. The rest resumed typing. The folder looked thicker than usual.

"You've been working hard," Lydia said.

"It's not hard," the Displaced Traveler said. "It's our lives."

Lydia nodded. When she'd first heard about the project, she'd thought up an elaborate lie—about being an editor in the past—to get a copy. She didn't have to tell it. She didn't have to tell them anything, actually. The Displaced Travelers didn't seem to care. They neither delighted in sharing their work with her nor showed any concern that she never reported back with her thoughts. Their focus never erred from the writing itself. They allowed her access simply because it was the quickest way to get rid of her.

On her way out, by way of thanks, she said, "Probably a sort day tomorrow."

The typing ceased again. This time it did not immediately resume.

8

FROM THE LATER YEARS:

MEDIA

We were, technically, under the umbrella of an outside news-paper, an outfit from a town nearly two hours away. After covering with much bewilderment the initial construction of Los Verticalés, though, they left our community alone, returning only on slow news days to file vague articles about our continued growth. They did this "reporting" entirely from the exterior, if they even came at all. Some residents claimed that in the days before some of these articles ran, they'd received phone calls from unknown men or women asking, without any explanation, for the current floor count. Meanwhile, the radio station provided us with only basic day-to-day knowledge— things we needed to know, such as elevator issues, broken lightbulbs, snow days, and hallway and stairwell closures. For the more substantial matters, such as the controversy surrounding Rolinda Jacobs, we relied on a series of print news sources within the Vert.

First, there was the Unobstructed View. *A full-color news weekly distributed to every residence within the Vert for free, it so favored the luxurious outer units that many inner residents felt its delivery each Friday to be an insult. It covered almost no serious developments, instead focusing on cutesy feel-good stories: a balloon released from a child's grip whose path across the sunset held a rapt audience among west-facing condos; a kitten that slipped out a window, climbed onto a ledge, and nearly fell to an untimely death before being successfully coaxed back inside and given fresh milk; the latest in grills; flower-box trends; the ten best cocktails to enjoy with a summer breeze; etc. It contained so much fluff that even its intended outer audience barely skimmed it. In the inner hallways, copies were gathered without being opened and redistributed to local papier-mâché artists.*

Beyond the Unobstructed View, *several subscription papers offered a more substantive product. These varied in a number of ways. Some discussed Vert-wide issues, while others focused on areas as small as a single floor or two. They also differed in their allegiance. A few favored the windowed, but many dedicated themselves to the plight of the windowless, their tones ranging from quietly disappointed to radically charged. There arose a problem here as well, though; while the writers employed by these papers often lived in the inner units and thus understood the issues they faced, the papers themselves required a high level of capital to get off the ground, and therefore were almost all owned by three or four wealthy outer-unit entrepreneurs. Thus, the reportage lacked true bite as the papers were allowed to point out as much strife as they pleased, but were discouraged from distributing blame.*

This provided an opening in the market for cheaply produced newsletters. Released on an irregular "as needed" basis, these simple leaflets adhered to no formatting guidelines or length requirements, being sometimes as short as three pages and other times as long as eighty. They essentially functioned as companion pieces to the subscription papers, not so much reporting the news as correcting any misconceptions in it and, furthermore, reacting to it with opinionated essays. As such, their anonymous writers cared little for journalistic integrity and saw no issue using strong language and hyperbole.

The very existence of these newsletters thrilled inner-unit evangelists. They charged no formal subscription fees, but each issue included an ad telling readers where and when to leave "donations" that could cover the expenses. Perhaps it would be in a custodial closet on the 37th floor, or inside a specific napkin dispenser in a diner on the 153rd floor. For this reason, inner residents who received them never shared a newsletter with anyone they were not certain they could trust, lest the money be stolen or confiscated by security. Even more mysterious were "the Printers": a tree of volunteers who each made a negligible number of copies at their workplaces before passing these off to other volunteers who did the same, until, without a single one of them making more than ten copies, there were enough to distribute to the entirety of the readership.

Despite the secrecy of their operations, everyone knew about the newsletters, even those in the outer units. Among themselves, they would often chuckle and mockingly shush each other, feigning fear that "one of their essayists" might be lurking around the corner. Occasionally one of them would joke that they should start their own newsletters to give voice to their true feelings, and everyone present would laugh. But the laughter would be uneasy, and the initial joker would not be able to hide his apprehension. Truthfully, the outer units possessed a fearful respect of the newsletters. They showed a level of cunning and initiative that made even the wealthiest outer resident uncomfortable. Moreover, the newsletters could not be controlled, and that was a phenomenon with which those with windows had little experience.

9

A SPIKE

ORVILLE NEVER would've imagined that a very public call to his brother would be a pivotal part of a nightly four-part recharging process. But he couldn't deny it: talking to Bernard gave Orville hope. The shower that followed upon getting back to CamperTown (step two) provided him with refreshment. An additional benefit of the call: by the time he got back, there was barely a line out front of the shower tent. Then he'd usually sit out on his Adirondack chair and clear his mind while the sun set (step three) before heading to The Bars (step four), where the rowdiness of the other Heap workers would reinforce the cooperative nature of their work. Orville always welcomed this reminder. He didn't get crazy or anything, only ever had a beer or two. He didn't even branch out socially, choosing instead to keep the same company as during the day. Hans and Lydia were all he needed. They understood that his desire to remain mostly anonymous didn't mean he wanted to be alone. Being there at The Bars with them each night, he felt comfortable.

And he was looking forward to another comfortable night when he stepped out from his camper—his clothes fresh, his skin smooth and free of grime—and found one of his Adirondack chairs occupied by a man in a white linen suit. He sat there, staring at his watch until the camper door clicked shut, bringing his attention to Orville. The man stood quickly, smiled, and held out his hand to shake. His teeth were the same shade of uninterrupted white as his pants, and his hair was neatly combed to one side, uniform in color, unbleached by the sun. If it weren't for the sweat gathering on the man's temples, Orville might've believed him to be a magazine ad come to life.

"Mr. Anders," the man said.

"Orville. You can call me Orville." Orville reached out and took the man's hand. It felt like silk, and the man flinched just barely at his touch.

"And you can call me Hal," said the man. "As in Hal Cornish, of Sundial Media." He waited for a moment, as if this information would mean something to Orville. "We're the ones who've been sending all the letters."

"I don't go to the mail station much," Orville said. "Nobody does, really."

Hal Cornish blinked. "So, you have no idea who we are?"

Orville shook his head.

"Or why I'm here?"

Orville shook his head a second time, and to his surprise, this seemed almost to delight the man.

"Well, that's no problem," said Hal Cornish. He took a moment to arrange the chairs so they faced each other, and then motioned for Orville to sit as if he owned them. Orville remained standing, so Hal Cornish did as well. "I'd be happy to give you the complete rundown. What we're offering is a wonderful opportunity. We're aware that the Dig Hands work on a volunteer stipend system, is that correct? We can give you much more than that, and for just minutes of work each day! Imagine! For less time than it takes to—"

"Whatever you're selling, man, I'm not buying it," Orville said, holding up his hands. "Last thing I want is more work, doesn't matter what it pays."

"But that's what I'm telling you: this wouldn't be any more work," Hal Cornish said.

"Then why are you paying me for it?" Orville grinned. "Or is it just because you're such a nice guy?"

The man sighed. "Let's start again. I'm Hal Cornish, of Sundial Media. 'The sounds of the desert and beyond.' Our holdings are vast, but all you need to know is that we own 103.1 WVRT. So, do you want to hear what I have to say or not?"

Orville stopped grinning. The man had maintained eye contact with him since he'd first stepped outside. It had felt at first like a simple sales trick. Now Orville wilted under it. "I'm sorry," he mumbled. "I didn't realize. I thought you were trying to scam me."

Hal Cornish smiled and took a seat, gesturing again for Orville to join him. This time Orville complied.

"No scam, Mr. Anders. This opportunity is very much real, and available to you and you alone. Let me explain."

Here's what he told Orville: Following the collapse, Sundial had been shocked to see 103.1 up and broadcasting. Its range—nearly the entire United States, Mexico, and down into South America—wasn't a surprise. They'd originally installed a special high-power antenna some miles from the city, hoping that one day, when Los Verticalés stopped growing upward, they'd be able to haul it to the roof, the antenna's strength and city's height combining to make a signal that could be heard around the world. But that Bernard and his equipment were able to survive the fall? Who could have expected that? Problem was, it was a nothing station. All Bernard could do was talk and take calls and talk some more. Not that exciting, right?

"Wrong!" said Hal Cornish.

Two months after the collapse, when it became clear that any rebuilding effort would take years, Sundial began thinking about transferring the antenna to another station, replacing it with something lower power to broadcast no farther than CamperTown. (Hal Cornish spoke as though their decision not to shut it down entirely despite the financial loss was the noblest of charitable acts.) But first, they decided to look at the numbers. The results were surprising.

"Good?" Orville asked.

"Better than good," Hal Cornish said. "Through the roof!"

They'd been thinking about it all wrong. A man stuck in a hole broadcasting involuntarily might not be entertainment, but it provided listeners with a fresh perspective, a truly distinctive radio experience. Just the mundane details of Bernard's strange subterranean existence were tantamount to the juiciest of drama.

"I went down to Chile recently," said Hal Cornish. "All the kids there are buying ham radios. They want to tune in to hear the 'Hole Man.' That's what they call Bernard down there: 'Hole Man.'"

"Huh," Orville said.

"But here's the kicker." Hal Cornish leaned forward and reached into his white linen jacket, pulling out a piece of paper. He unfolded it for Orville. It was a chart. The x-axis read *Average Listeners*, the y-axis, *Time of Day*. A jagged line crossed the page—rising up in the morning when Bernard woke, fading at night as he went to sleep. The only interruption a single sharp spike. Hal Cornish pointed to it.

"This is you."

Orville stared at it. Sometimes when he indulged a deep, dark part of his ego, he imagined himself as a sort of urban legend among the other Dig Hands: the family member of the trapped survivor, who dug just like them, who sweated just like them, who made significant their daily work. Because if all he did was fart around with a shovel, then that was all there was to do, end of story. It was gratuitous, imagining himself as the engine of the entire Dig Effort, yet the chart confirmed something even stranger: Orville was a celebrity.

Hal Cornish folded the paper, replaced it in his jacket, and held his hands out, palms up, in front of him. "Two brothers, struggling to connect through layers of earth," he said, looking from his left palm to his right, as if one were Orville and the other Bernard. "It's fresh, yet timeless. Who doesn't have a hard time keeping in touch with their loved ones? Maybe for everyone else, the rubble is a metaphor for a time zone, a lifestyle choice, a deep-seated grudge, or a botched best-man speech. Doesn't matter. Point is: Listeners can't get enough of it. Even down in Chile."

"Does it really sound like we're struggling to connect?" Orville asked.

Hal Cornish laughed. "Don't worry about that! It's not a problem." He took a deep breath. "What *is* a problem is revenue. This is where the opportunity comes in. We've got advertisers that are hungry for a piece of this pie, but we've got no way of getting their messages to Bernard. We could call in each morning, obviously, relay them that way, but we've got data that shows that level of transparency doesn't play well. So, working through Bernard isn't feasible. But you? You're out here. You're accessible. So, here's how it'll work: We get some sponsors for 'Brother Talk,' or whatever you want to call it behind the scenes, they send you some words to say, you slip them into conversation, a check is cut, everyone's happy. What do you think?"

Orville sat there, speechless. It felt like the punch line to a joke, for this revelation of Bernard's (and by extension his) fame to culminate in a request for advertising help. He felt a surge of something rise in him that he realized was anger only when it reached his fingers and they clenched into fists.

"I don't think Bernard would like that," Orville said as calmly as he could. "And honestly, I don't feel comfortable with it myself."

Hal Cornish's smile faded. "I was worried you were going to say that," he said. For a moment his voice sounded almost menacing, but in the next, it softened once again. "But hey, you wouldn't be here moving rocks all day if you weren't a bit of an idealist. So I get it. Still, worth a shot, right? We'll move forward with our plan B, so to speak. Just know that we mean no hard feelings with this, and the offer stands, no matter what." Hal Cornish stood, took a business card from his breast pocket, and held it out. "To get in touch."

Orville remained seated. Getting up would be following Hal Cornish's lead, and he didn't want to give him the satisfaction. He took the business card and turned it over in his hand. It showed the man's smug face, smiling the same smile as the real one standing over him. Orville just wanted him to leave, but if he opened his mouth, he didn't know what he might say.

Hal Cornish leaned down and lowered his voice. "Orville, you're going to want to hold on to that. Trust me."

Orville felt like a child being gently reprimanded. Still, he refused to look up from the card and, eventually, Hal Cornish left.

Inside his camper, there was a compartment: the love seat cushion opened like a trunk. Orville hadn't realized it until he'd been living in the camper for a month. Now he used it to stash a lot of the clothes it never got cold enough to wear. He opened it and set the card inside. It was the same as throwing it away, he told himself. He hadn't been intimidated by someone who wore a white linen suit. Not a chance. In there, it would be out of sight and, Orville hoped, out of mind.

THE BARS

THE BARS was actually a single open-air bar, called "The Bars" by virtue of the fact that, aside from the small stand that served as the bar, it was just an area of ground demarcated by a makeshift steel rod fence. It was the only drinking establishment in CamperTown and as such was always packed.

Lydia ordered a whiskey and made her way to their normal corner. The crowd buzzed with conversation around her, and walking through it, she felt like an orange needle sliding across FM frequencies. Most of the noise registered as discordance, but occasionally topics cut through with almost daunting clarity: collapse theory and collapse theory rebuke; the impending sort day; whether anyone's shovel struck power. She nodded at people she knew from one place or another, but didn't engage. Like Thisbee, she was a doer, not a figurehead.

Orville was late, and Hans was talking to a woman nearby, some newb from his orientation session, apparently. Lydia couldn't hear everything they were talking about, but she gathered that Hans had mentioned he was a photographer, because the conversation ended with the woman insisting, "I've got to see some of your pictures!" and an exchange of camper locations.

"Guess you'll have to finally unpack your camera," Lydia said when the woman left.

Hans dismissed her with a snort. "I have photos."

Lydia had been to Hans's camper only once, when Hans

had invited her and Orville over for dinner. That was early on during their time at the Dig, before they had accepted that the campers were not entire homes; rather, they were essentially bedrooms, and therefore inhospitable to casual company. Lydia didn't remember any photos hanging up, but when she related this to Hans, he only said: "I keep them stashed away so they don't get ruined by the sun. Anyway, even if I took photos, I wouldn't have anywhere to develop them."

"The apartment we found today," Lydia said. "What about that?"

She could see that Hans had not considered this, and she wondered if she had finally unlocked him. Hans spoke frequently about his ambitions while doing little to see them through, which would've been fine if he didn't so often bemoan his struggle in achieving them as if it were on par with hers, in both scope and effort exerted. Only when he spoke did she realize he'd actually been searching for the best way to dismiss the idea. "A man died in there, Lydia. It wouldn't feel right."

They were interrupted by a card going around. A guy named Spud had gotten caught in the day's nasty Heap shift. Broken leg, bruised ribs. "Could be worse," said the man who handed the card to Lydia. When she took hold of it, he didn't let go but shifted his grip to graze her knuckles with his thumb. His breath was thick with rum. "Could be *much* worse."

She pulled it out of his hands, ripping it just slightly, and signed. Hans took it next, then handed it into the crowd behind them.

"Hypothetical question," Lydia said, watching the card weave from person to person. "Let's say you were in charge of planning a visit for a very important person, and you had to remove one thing from CamperTown to make it look less like a pile of garbage. What would it be?"

"Is the entire Heap off-limits?" Hans asked.

"Yes."

"Then I'd say . . . that camper. The one in the desert."

"Exactly," Lydia said. "It's so easy. You dig it out of the sand, rent an object mover, and haul it off. But Gil seems to think he has to wait until he gets permission from Thisbee's people to do it. As if they care about some weird busted camper. I don't even understand how he ended up in charge of the Committee, or why it has to be the chairperson who gives the tour."

"Should be you," Hans said.

"No shit."

"Or me," Hans said. Lydia turned to him. Just the brief reliving of the day's meeting left her feeling worked up. Now she was ready to unload on Hans, to finally deliver a monologue about passion and realism, how the former withers without the latter, or corrodes from within, leaving, after time, a convincing-looking shell that is still just that: a shell. And so if Hans didn't get realistic about his level of determination and un-ass the metaphorical couch on which he sat to actually do something, he might find doing anything worth doing to be impossible without a large-scale rebuild.

But when she looked at him, he grinned. He meant no harm. It was a joke. "Look, I know this is everything you've been hoping for since you got here, but I do run the orientation sessions. I could teach Peter Thisbee a thing or two about ConductionSens shovels."

Lydia still buzzed sharply inside, ready for confrontation, but managed to say, "Orville might get lonely out there without us."

"He could come with me," Hans said. "And you too, I guess. It could be a family affair."

Lydia laughed at this, feeling her adrenaline subside. There might be nothing Orville would want less to do with. It didn't matter that Peter Thisbee had founded the city in which his brother once (and, actually, still) lived. Thisbee wasn't going to pick up a shovel and pitch in, and therefore wasn't worth Orville's time.

But then something occurred to Lydia, and she buzzed anew.

§

THE CROWD at the bar, though no different from on any other night, left Orville feeling itchy. How many of these people listened to him? He monitored those around him, waited for someone to cast a glance in his direction. But as he slipped past some people, bumping into others, no one paid him any attention.

He was like his brother in this way. According to Lydia, the Displaced Travelers said barely anyone in the Vert knew what Bernard looked like. When the story came out about his discovery, only a few papers ran a photograph: a small, blurry picture from one of his first radio jobs. The others used radio-related clip art. This likely would've pleased Bernard to see. Throughout his whole career, he'd always wanted to be a voice, and only a voice.

The radio up at the bar was tuned to him now. A caller asked in a gravelly voice, "Do you have a pillow?"

"No, no pillows down here," Bernard said.

"That's crazy," the man said. "Where do you put your head at night?"

" 'That's crazy,' " mimicked Nina, the bartender. " 'Where do you put your head at night?' "

Orville watched the two newbs nearby look at each other in disbelief, confirming through eye contact what they'd heard. It was what everyone went through when they first got to The Bars, hearing Nina speak in a voice so unlike her own and so entirely like someone else's. Next, they'd mention it to someone who'd been around longer, at which point the newb would find out that Nina had done some voice work in the past. After that, they'd bring this information back to Nina—"Did you ever do cartoons?" they might ask. "Or commercials?"—and receive nothing more than a cold glare.

Orville had forgone this final bit when he'd arrived, and as such, Nina had always shown him kindness. Tonight, she brought him a beer and asked him if everything was okay. "You look distracted," she said.

"Just had to deal with an unwanted guest at my camper," Orville said.

"Another Dig Hand trying to sneak into your bed?"

Orville laughed in spite of himself. He wondered sometimes if she flirted with everybody, or just him. "No. Not from the Heap at all. Entertainment industry."

Nina gave him a confused glance, but she was already on the move. It was crowded and she was too busy to pretend to care for long. Orville felt stupid for saying anything as he muscled his way through the crowd to find Hans and Lydia.

"You're later than usual," Lydia said when he arrived.

"You know, it was the craziest thing," Orville started to say. Before he could go on, he noticed a young man—a kid, really, no older than early twenties—standing just in his periphery, staring at him with a smile that seemed to apologize for its own dumbness. It was standard that everyone got a little dressed up to go to The Bars, but Orville could tell instantly from the crispness of his blazer and tie: this was a newb.

"Orville Anders?" he said. Orville nodded, thinking of the spike on the ratings chart. Would this be his first autograph request? The kid only held out his hand. "Terrance Stanley! I've just arrived at the Heap this very morning, and I wanted you to know that I will be devoting my every shovel thrust to uncovering your brother!"

While he spoke, the kid looked between him and Hans. So it was confirmed. Orville was a part of Hans's orientation speech.

"I appreciate that, Terrance," Orville said. With the extra

company, he didn't feel comfortable discussing the offer he'd received, and opted instead for cliché Bars talk. "Anyone strike power?"

Lydia shook her head. Hans quietly burped.

"Strike power?" Terrance asked.

Hans, a bit drunk, put his arm around the boy and pulled him fully into their group. "Electricity!" he said.

"Surprised you didn't cover that in your session, Hans," Orville said.

"No, no, we did!" Terrance stammered. "I just hadn't heard it called that. 'Strike power,' like 'strike oil.' That's why we use the special ConductionSens shovels, to know if a part of the Heap carries a charge."

Hans shot Orville with a finger gun. "See?"

"And then we can leave that part alone," the kid added proudly, "and find somewhere safer to dig." Orville laughed and Hans hung his head. Terrance looked from one man to the other, deeply concerned. "What?"

"It's not about a safety hazard," Lydia explained. "The shovels are made to protect us from the shock. We want to strike power. Bernard's broadcasting, so he's got power. If we strike power, there's a chance that we're close to Bernard."

"When's the last time someone struck power?" Terrance asked.

"Nobody's ever struck power," Orville said. He could see it on the kid's face as he spoke the words: the slow realization of just how much work this would all be.

Hans seemed to notice it too. He downed his drink quickly. "Time for a refill. Anyone else need anything?" Orville held up his fresh beer and Lydia shook her head. "Fine. Suit yourselves. Terrance, join me?"

They disappeared into the crowd, a relief to Orville. This might even be better. Lydia, more than Hans (and definitely more than some newb), would understand the assault on his integrity that Hal Cornish's request constituted. She would know that even asking him to use his standing as Bernard's brother for any amount of gain was manipulative and wrong. And he was ready—ready to tell her what had happened and have her recoil in disbelief and say, "Christ, Orville! I'm sorry! That's so fucked up!"—but Lydia spoke first.

"Orville, I need a favor."

"What?" Orville said.

"I need you to ask to be the one who shows Peter Thisbee around," she said. "I know that's probably not something you'd want to do. But you won't have to. I'd come with you and do all the talking. You'd just have to walk around and seem interested."

"You want me there for moral support?" Orville asked.

"No. Or, yes and no. It's just . . . you know this tour is important to me, right? But I can't just stand up in the next Committee meeting and say, 'You're all going to listen to me from now on.' Because I'm a nobody. But you? They'd have to listen. You're Bernard's brother!"

Orville stared at her a moment, then turned and looked around at The Bars, looked at the crowd of other Dig Hands, the same ones he saw every night, save for the newbs. Out past the fence, through the hazy dusk, he saw the outline of the Heap looming. He could discern no meaningful change in its shape since his first week here. It remained steadfast in the face of the Dig Effort. The Heap was, in a very basic sense, Orville's greatest obstacle, yet its worst feature—its immovability—also provided him with something to emulate: a radical stoicism. He tried to channel the Heap now, and failed.

"Did you all get together or something, to remind yourselves of that?" Orville's eyes remained on the horizon. He lifted his beer to his mouth, but lowered it without taking a drink.

"What?" Lydia tried to look where he looked, as if this might provide some answer. "'You all'? It's just me."

"It's not just you," Orville said. He spoke low and sharp. His thumb scratched absently at the beer label, which tore, softened by the bottle's perspiration. "It's you, it's Hans, it's . . ." But Orville found himself suddenly greedy. To introduce new information, like Hal Cornish, into the conversation would provide Lydia an out. ". . . everyone. They—you—all seem to have reawoken to the fact that I am Bernard's brother—"

"Orville, what's this about?"

"—And that my being Bernard's brother might be something you could profit off of."

" 'Profit off of'?" The shift in Lydia's tone was slight but significant, a transition from pleading unintentional insulter to the insulted. Orville's thumb stopped carving up the label. He turned back to Lydia. She looked at him coldly.

"I was just asking," Lydia said. "You can say no."

"Then it's a no." It was a last-ditch effort to regain the control he'd had, but it came out sounding so petty and stupid that he took a quick swig of his beer, as if to wash out his mouth. Here he was, just an hour or two removed from a conversation in which a man had tried to commodify his relationship with his trapped brother, and he was the one left looking like a piece of shit? He didn't deserve this, and he blamed everyone: the man, Hal Cornish, obviously, but also Hans for using him in his orientation speech, Terrance for interrupting their night, Lydia for making such a selfish request, and him for not being able to help himself.

There was only enough time for Lydia to mumble, "Fine," before Hans and Terrance rejoined them, swaying a bit more than before.

"Shots," Hans explained. Then to Orville, "You didn't tell us: What was the crazy thing that happened to you on the way here?"

"Oh, it was nothing, really," Orville said. An awkward silence fell over them that almost seemed to mute the noise of The Bars at their backs.

11

FROM *THE LATER YEARS*:

TIME CHANGE

While each subscription paper and newsletter portrayed condo president Mitner negatively at times, none could claim he ignored us. Indeed, he took our feedback in stride and proved himself to be a dynamic problem solver. If anything, the ambition of his solutions often far surpassed any response we expected. Take for example the issue of traffic. It was a complaint levied anywhere and everywhere. We discussed it constantly. We devoted the first ten minutes of every dinner party and every coffee date to complaints about our journeys through the crowded narrow hallways to get there. We called the radio station, whenever the line was open, to outdo each other with stories of not one, not two, but three elevators passing by, filled to capacity. We even complained within the traffic itself, bonding over our frustration with one another's presence.

Finally, it grew bad enough that it needed to be addressed. The commonly proposed solution involved a high-speed elevator and a widened hallway. The latter half of this caused much debate. Those in the inner units thought it palatable as long as the expansion only involved a downsizing of outer units. The outer units, meanwhile, argued for an even encroachment. After all, they said, the two kinds of unit were, when you really thought about it, mostly equal. Yes, their units, equipped with windows, did not require the inferior live-broadcast UV screens of those on the interior, but glass panes and outer walls made for higher utility costs. Hadn't they paid enough already, the outer units argued? (No, the inner units believed, they had not.)

In a cryptic press conference, Mitner announced there'd be no widening of the hallway or high-speed elevators, because his own (as of then unspecified) solution to the problem required no construction. This came as a relief. It made the issue of congestion less political, we thought. We were wrong. The solution drew an even starker contrast between inner and outer units, essentially dividing them into two entirely separate populations.

What Mitner did was this: He took the live broadcasts that ran on the UV screens and added a slight delay each day for a month until the inner units were an entire twelve hours behind the outer units. Operating in two different time zones meant cutting hallway congestion in half: the inner residents would be a few hours from waking up as the outer residents made their way home from work.

Everyone hated it. The outer units complained that the inner units made more noise than necessary during their daytime hours out of spite, while a popular newsletter ran a vitriol-filled op-ed with the headline "The Making of the Mole People." We all made it clear that we expected a reverse of the policy as quickly as possible.

Instead, Mitner doubled down. He began to isolate groups of inner units throughout the Vert, reversing some delays, adding to others. Soon, the outer units—there were fewer of them than the inner units—all ran on "true time" while an inner unit might be in any number of different time zones. The result was not a population divided in half; rather, Mitner, whether he meant to or not, had developed an entirely unique twenty-four-hour culture.

Did we have criticisms? Were some of us upset? Yes, of course. But Mitner had made things so complicated that we had too much to sort through, and by the time the dust settled, we had to admit: We liked the newly asynchronous nature of

*our lives. For one thing, it lent the Vert a sense of internation-
ality. We found cities around the world with which we shared
our waking hours and decorated our condos in allegiance to
them, followed their sports teams, sometimes even learned
their native language.*

*More importantly, it gave us a sense of pride in the Vert
itself. We had for so long simulated traditional urban living
within an enclosed structure. Issues arose—for example, how
would we hold a street fair in a hallway?—and the work-
arounds for these issues resulted in certain Vert-specific
quirks. But while we celebrated these things as if they defined
our lives, they weren't dissimilar to the logistical problems related to terrain or zoning all other cities face. The scrambling
of our collective sense of time finally provided us with something unimpeachably different, and unimpeachably "us." Our
restaurants developed a kind of egg-rich cuisine that could be
consumed for breakfast, lunch, or dinner by the steady stream
of patrons arriving at all hours of the day. At our offices, we
watched as our coworkers came and left around the clock, enjoying the perpetual osmotic sense of morning hopefulness
and end-of-day relief. And if, for whatever reason, we could
not sleep at night, we simply stepped out of our condos into
a bustling world of people at various points in their days, a
world never too loud and never too quiet, a world never empty,
a world that felt exciting, alive, and volatile, and safe.*

12

SORT DAY

NEXT MORNING, en route to the Heap, Lydia saw the Displaced Travelers making their way through CamperTown. They were barely a few rows of campers away from their air-conditioned RVs but they'd already begun to sweat. The woman who'd handed Lydia the pages yesterday gave her a cursory nod. Lydia checked to make sure nobody had seen before she returned it. It wouldn't look good for her if people knew she'd been the one tipping them off about the sort days.

Sort day was grueling enough work, and the Displaced Travelers only made things worse. They stopped at each sorting station they came to and demanded to see whatever objects had been deemed salvageable on the pretense that the objects might've belonged to them, but they rarely took anything. It was nostalgia they were after. They didn't care for furniture or for art, but a hallway sign or an unearthed railing from the stairwell could send one of them into a seemingly endless reverie, during which they would invoke their dead friends and neighbors just enough to keep conscientious Dig Hands from outright ignoring them. Like *The Later Years*, it was an exercise in remembrance that served only them. Through her disclosure, Lydia merely hoped to endear herself to them. She didn't take any pride in slowing down the Dig Hands' progress.

She, unlike Orville, liked sort days. For starters, sorting required more thought. Then there was the unwritten sorters-keepers rule: that any Dig Hand who found something intact

in the rubble could keep it. Nothing valuable enough to pull
in any significant cash, but maybe a card table or a nice stool.
Even if it was something you didn't need, there was always
a chance to pawn it off to an Assistance Sector worker for a
couple of drinks at The Bars.

Really, though, Lydia liked sort day because it provided
a change in perspective. Life on the Heap could start to feel
pretty isolated after a while. Keep digging and it's easy to
forget that your ConductionSens shovel isn't an extension of
your arms, that shifting rubble isn't just what bodies do, that
there's a world beyond not covered by a massive pile of wreckage. Sort days reaffirmed their connection to the outside, because sort days were less about the Dig Effort and more about
the Sale.

In terms of actual logistics, things pretty much went
how one might expect: All the Dig Hands assembled in their
teams around the Heap and went through the debris loosed
by the Dig, picked out the intact stuff, and sorted the rest
into piles based on material—wood, tile, drywall, etc.—so
that it could be shipped out and used in reclamation projects.
Nobody knew exactly what happened from there, whether
the scraps were sold, in bulk, to artisans to do with as they
pleased, or if Thisbee's people contracted them and sold their
finished products. Then there was the question of what exactly constituted an artisan in Thisbee's mind. In one of
the pamphlets they'd all received during orientation, there
was fine print that identified those eligible for materials as
"individuals or entities determined to use them in projects
where their visual appeal will surpass that of their current
state." These parameters, many believed, were soft enough
to include anyone from sculptors to contractors to those who
ran recycling centers. Even with this loose definition, some
still wondered if the Sale could possibly generate enough
money to fund the Dig Effort, or if there was a better option
they hadn't yet realized. Lydia had once heard the Displaced

Travelers debate the merits of tunneling under the Heap all the way down to the parking garage, where, possibly, floor upon floor of barely driven cars sat unscathed—"But not unstained," one Displaced Traveler had said, with a sly grin—ready to be sold. Lydia had proposed it to boss, but it would take a major team, and besides, why bother? The Sale seemed to be doing well enough.

Suffice it to say, Lydia enjoyed this idea of there being some greater order to what they did (however vague it might be), so Lydia enjoyed sort days. Or Lydia usually enjoyed sort days. This one? Not so much. It was Orville. She could tell as soon as she parked her bike that he was still in a mood about the night before. Which was fine, because she was too.

"See, this would make a great photo," Hans said. He'd found a statuette of a building in Dubai and had placed it next to a scuffed jewelry box. He took a large chunk of concrete from the junk pile and laid it just off from the statuette. "No, there. That encompasses everything. Beauty and destruction."

He stepped back and framed it with his fingers. He could've just as easily brought a camera.

Orville looked at neither Hans or Lydia. "You check inside the box?"

Hans did now and found a rusty necklace that he presented to Lydia with mock romance.

"It'll look great with your overalls," he said.

He meant it as a joke, of course. But it was a joke that Lydia didn't care for, given the latent misogyny of presenting jewelry to the only woman present. And really, Hans wasn't the problem. It was just that, in that moment, he was a tiny part of the bigger problem of life on the Heap, which was a certain hairy-balls machismo that some men seemed to feel was their right as soon as they laid hands on a shovel and put their strength toward something charitable. She hated it, hated their dumb jokes that she was expected to ignore, their limp-dick chivalry for which she was expected to be grateful. Yet despite all this, she didn't want to give Orville the satisfaction of seeing her lose her cool, so she tried to say, "Thank you," in a way that was not too bitter, and yet did not invite further conversation.

Orville had basically called her an opportunist, but that wasn't what hurt. Lydia *was* an opportunist. She could admit that. If anything, it frustrated her that opportunism was so maligned. There was all sorts of advice about what to do with lemons, but as soon as you had lemonade, you were supposed to just sit back and be content. To parlay the lemonade into something more was to cross a boundary between ambition and greed.

What hurt was that he had so quickly dismissed her. Lydia understood that working with Orville meant her own motives for being at the Heap would always come second. She sought personal gain, whereas he sought to help his family, to save a life. This was the basic math of virtue, and she'd never thought of Orville as selfish. At least, not until now: not until she made one tiny request that would cost him so little and help her so much, and he had swiftly cast it off and taken offense to it.

It was as if he didn't realize how much she and Hans did to make him comfortable each day. They worked alongside him, they paid their respects to Bernard, but they also allowed him to just be one of them most of the time. They coddled him by not coddling him. Lydia always thought that he knew this, and yet at the first suggestion that he do something for one of them, he turned into a one-man show of gloom. Lydia could've laughed at the theatrically sullen way he inspected each piece of detritus before putting it in its appropriate pile, if she weren't so peeved.

She almost hoped the Displaced Travelers would come by; it would at least be a change of pace. But they never showed up, not before the three of them had finished for the day and gone to relax in the buried apartment.

Boss and the doctor were already there. The beer in the fridge was gone, and they each had a bottle of white wine. Their eyes looked tired in the fuzzy light of the electric lantern they'd brought. "Under the sink," boss said, and Hans went to get a bottle.

"Hey, settle a bet," the doctor said. "Snakes: Can they go backwards? They can, right?"

"I never said they couldn't," boss said. "I just made the point that, given the circuitous path they take everywhere— like, slithering—that the concepts of forward and reverse are nonmeaningful. When would a snake ever have to back up?"

"In a dead-end, snake-size tunnel," the doctor said.

Boss put a hand to his forehead in disbelief. "And what the fuck tunnel would that be?"

"Maybe a tunnel for snakes that someone didn't finish," the doctor said. "Like at a zoo with funding issues." Then he turned to Orville and Lydia. "So?"

"I don't know much about snakes," Lydia said.

Orville shook his head. "Me neither."

"Jeez, what a somber bunch we got here," said boss.

"Tell them about the fan," said the doctor. "That'll cheer them up."

"The who?" Orville said. For a moment, his mood seemed to change. Not that it lightened. To Lydia's ear, he sounded livid.

Boss laughed. "Take it easy! It's funny."

He explained: the delivery guy who brought liquor to The Bars—"He's a friend of ours," the doctor said—had, on his drive in that morning, seen a man out in the desert digging. "It was a couple miles past the casino, coming this way," boss explained.

"If he's such a fan of digging, why doesn't he come help us out?" Hans called from the kitchen.

Boss threw up his arms, still holding his wine. Some sloshed out, but he didn't notice. "Who knows! But how weird is that?"

"Pretty weird," Lydia said. Orville nodded.

Boss didn't appear satisfied. "Oh, c'mon! That's all you've got to say? What's going on with you two?"

"Nothing," Orville said.

"Nothing I understand," Lydia said. Orville made a noise like a huff and Lydia turned to him, ready for whatever he had to say, just as Hans came back with a bottle of red wine and three glasses. He set them out on the coffee table and poured each to the top. Lydia took hers and downed it in three swigs. Just because Orville was acting the sourpuss didn't mean she had to sit there and wallow in his self-importance. "I've actually got some stuff to do," she said. "See you all later." And with that, she got up and left through the hole in the ceiling.

IN THE ASSISTANCE SECTOR

LYDIA MADE good time getting around the Heap, but as soon as she got within the Assistance Sector itself, she had to slow down and eventually get off her bike. The narrow roads that wound through the assemblage of mismatched temporary buildings were too crowded with fresh-off-the-clock workers to ride, despite it being quarter to five. Lydia rolled her eyes at this internally before remembering that she herself had stopped working some time ago to drink wine in a dead's buried apartment. She just hoped Gil hadn't left for the day.

This was where all aspects of the Dig Effort beyond the actual digging were handled. There was the shipping-container hospital on one end, and the Large Coveted Object Moving Rentals building on the other, bordering the unincorporated desert. The space between was packed tight with huts, bodegas, and the big, ugly hangar-like "offices" full of cubicles in which desk jockeys carried out a number of bland, yet apparently necessary, administrative tasks.

It was walking distance to CamperTown from here, so Lydia caught some looks on account of her bike. Mostly, though, the Assistance Sector workers ignored her. They walked in groups of two, three, four. They gossiped, told jokes, vented, all of which Lydia picked up only through context clues. She recognized few of the names, and all their day-to-day processes were disguised in colloquial shorthand.

It fascinated her to see them like this, to see what being tired looked like for them. They suffered no soreness, no fading endorphins, no sun sickness. Theirs was a sedentary tired, a tired born of boredom, and boredom was an intellectual issue. To be bored and productive showed some proof of untapped intelligence. Lydia had sensed this pride before. In Committee meetings, to one another, it was "the Sector" or the "Business District," but when they talked to Lydia, a Dig Hand, they made sure to pronounce its full five syllables: "you can find me in the As-sis-tance Sec-tor." The Dig Hands showed no such respect. They called this place the Ass.

Lydia didn't go so far herself. She'd arrived with the skills and education to land a much cushier position, yet opted to work on the Heap. It was more authentic. Moreover, it sounded more authentic, and that sort of thing mattered when you had aspirations like Lydia's.

In front of her, three men walked side by side, creating a slow-moving wall. "Why have an ink-use protocol if you're not going to follow the ink-use protocol?" Lydia heard one say. The others mumbled something sympathetic. Space opened for Lydia to get around them, and she sped up, nearly knocking straight into the Displaced Traveler with the glasses and the mustache coming the other way.

"Afternoon," he said to her as he passed. Lydia turned to see where he was going, but he quickly disappeared into the crowd, and Gil's storefront was already in her sights.

That Chairperson Gil manned an office supply bodega was both perfect—a man so fearful of confrontation working in such a deferential position, subservient to the subservient— and perfectly ironic—a person with political power, however small, being so insulated from almost everyone he represented. Not that Chairperson Gil didn't have his heart in the right place. He wanted good things for CamperTown. He just needed a little help when things got messy. And that was what she intended to offer him: a little help.

The crowd had thinned to a few stragglers when she found him, locking up. This was good, not just because he was still here, but because it gave them some privacy.

"Gil," Lydia called.

With his back to her, Gil flinched and dropped his keys, managing somehow to catch them and fumble them into his pocket in a motion both awkward and impressive. He turned to her. "Lydia! What a pleasant surprise! How was sort day? Find anything nice? I heard last time someone found eleven ottomans in one place. What could the story have been there? A furniture store? Say, anyone find any end tables? I've been putting my books on the floor, which is fine, but it really doesn't look too nice. Piles of books everywhere, you know? Like some sort of absent-minded professor!"

Lydia had spoken to Gil outside of meetings enough to expect this: when in situations where he no longer had the power to table things, he evaded any confrontation by offering a charcuterie of disarming pleasantries. She would have none of it.

"Gil," she said, "I want to propose a trade."

Gil forced out a nervous chuckle. "What could you want from me?" He did a flourish with his hands to indicate the bodega behind him. "Post-its? Thumb tacks?"

"A favor for a favor."

"Oh, Lydia, I don't know if—"

But Lydia had only just settled on what she was going to say on the way over. She couldn't let Gil get her off script. She spoke loudly, drowning him out. "Here's the deal: The busted camper isn't just an eyesore. It's an embarrassment. It's no big deal most of the time, because it's just us around here. We're used to seeing junk. Junk is our way of life out on the Heap. Trust me, I know. I climb all over it every day. But a person like Peter Thisbee? He wants order, cleanliness. We wouldn't all be here if he didn't."

Gil's face quivered just slightly, and Lydia couldn't tell

if he was trembling or on the verge of shaking his head in disapproval, only he couldn't bring himself to do it. His hand absently tapped his pocket, jingling the keys inside in a subconscious SOS. "I need—"

"To follow protocol. I know," Lydia said. "Because why have a protocol, if you're not going to follow a protocol? You're the chairperson for the Committee for Better Life in Camper-Town. You need to do things by the book. But I'm just a lowly Committee member. There's not as much at stake for me." This was a lie—as far as Lydia was concerned, there was plenty at stake—but she had to paint the right picture. "I can feign ignorance of the rules, rent an object mover, and just drag that piece of junk out into the desert. I can even drag it back after they leave, if you want. But while they're here, it'll be out of sight."

"They don't want it moved," Gil muttered.

"That's what they said? That they don't want it moved?" Lydia stepped closer, spoke lower. "Or did they say they'll get back to you about the possibility moving it?"

"It's not really my job . . . to question . . ."

Gil was breathing heavily. He couldn't finish his sentences. He would topple at any moment, Lydia could tell.

"Trust me on this, Gil: With people like Peter Thisbee and his team, it doesn't matter what he said. He'll get here, he'll see that old camper, and he'll say, 'What the hell is that doing out there?' And you know whose problem it will be? Not theirs, that's for sure. Not even when it's them who dragged their feet. No, Gil, it'll be your problem. But I'm willing to make it go away." She paused here, took another step closer, made sure her tone was cool and reasoned, and delivered the final word: "And all I ask is that you allow me to accompany you as you show Peter Thisbee around."

"They put me in charge for a reason!" Gil shouted. They stood there for a moment in silence, both of them shocked by the outburst, until Gil could catch his breath.

"Sorry. Really, I'm sorry. I shouldn't have raised my voice like that. It's just—Lydia, you're a valuable member of the Committee, but Mr. Thisbee trusted me with this position, and this tour, exactly because he knows I won't do anything too cavalier."

He seemed to be waiting for Lydia to say something, even just to acknowledge that she'd heard him, but Lydia had no words. All this time, she thought that Gil knew, deep down, that he was not doing a good job, but it turned out he really thought this was what "they" wanted: this cowering, useless approach.

"Well, I need to be getting home to my camper," Gil said at last. "I'll see you at the next meeting, I hope."

Lydia nodded. "Of course," she said. And though the buildings of the Assistance Sector didn't stand very high, providing a giant swath of sky impeded only to her left by the looming mass of the Heap, Lydia felt suddenly trapped.

PHONE TROUBLE

DESPITE IT being early, Orville still rode as fast as he could toward the phone bank. He didn't stick around the apartment much longer than Lydia. Her obvious attempt to one-up him had left him feeling raw. She "actually" had things to do? As if *he* didn't? Ha! That was enough to make him laugh. Or laugh sneeringly. Or just sort of vocalize a sneer that resembled laughter as little as possible, because laughter was a happy thing and if there was one way Orville didn't feel right now, it was happy.

As he rode, he turned the radio on. "I run a window-washing company," said the caller. "What tips should I pass along to my employees for if they're ever involved in a collapsing building scenario?"

"I think it'd be a lot different for them being outside of the building," Bernard said, "than if they were inside like me."

"What about if they were washing the windows in a courtyard?" the caller asked. "Would that be comparable?"

No, Orville didn't feel happy at all. What he felt was betrayed: betrayed by his quote-unquote friend who'd spent their entire quote-unquote friendship plotting ways to use him to get to some dipshit entrepreneur, who, by the way, just happened to be the one whose bright idea it was to build the megatower that would eventually collapse and entrap his brother.

Was this maybe an overreaction? Did he really think this had been the entire basis of their friendship, this desire to use him for personal gain? It didn't matter. It felt good to feel mad after a day of more passive sullenness. And anyway, the call would help. It always did.

Orville stood up and pedaled harder. As he crested a hill, the phone bank came into view. A truck was parked next to it, yellow caution tape drawn around poles driven into the ground at the bank's four corners. Coasting to a stop and switching off his radio, Orville saw a man down on one knee working on a phone with a screwdriver. He wore a light blue uniform, pit-stained, and a dark blue hat like a train conductor's, wet with sweat around the edges, but not up to the salty white line left by perspirations past. *Starlight Telecom* was stitched into his work shirt, just above his breast pocket.

Orville got off his bike and stepped up to the caution tape and called out: "Excuse me, can I ask what you're doing?"

The man did not stop working. When he answered, he spoke like each word was of equal importance. "Yes. You can ask that. That is your right as an observer of what I am doing, but it is not my duty to respond to it. Nonetheless, I will, but I want it to be understood that my doing so in this case is a personal decision, not a professional one, and as such, further questions will be dealt with on a case-by-case basis, at my discretion. At any time, I may cease to answer questions, given that my job is to do what I am doing, and not to answer questions about it. Do we have an agreement?"

Orville stood, dumbfounded by the response for a moment. "Yeah, okay, sure."

"Then I will tell you what I am doing. What I am doing is decommissioning this phone bank."

"Decommissioning? Like, shutting it down temporarily?"

"You are partially correct," the man said, "in regard to your definition of what decommissioning means. Shutting it down is the part that is correct. There is no requirement within its definition that a decommissioning must be temporary."

"So you're shutting it down for good?" Orville asked.

The man returned the screwdriver to his tool belt and retrieved a wrench. "Yes, and I want to add: you seem to be asking these questions in rapid succession, and though we did not agree on a predefined rapidity with which we would exchange information, I do feel you are not honoring the nature of our agreement, in that you seem to be expectant of a response rather than hopeful for one."

Orville was too distraught to pay the man's formality any attention. He took hold of the caution tape and gripped it tight. "But, you can't do that," he said. "You can't shut the phone bank down. People need that!"

Now the man threw down the wrench and stood to face Orville. His words grew angrier, but the uniformity of his emphasis remained the same. "Though, as I have made clear, it is not a requirement of my position to speak with you, you will forgive me for being a man of personal and professional pride, and therefore, against my better judgment, I will address the two wrongful assertions you have made in the order you have made them. First, you have told me that I cannot decommission this phone bank, but, sir, I absolutely can do that. In fact, I am in the process of doing just that. In further fact, it is essentially the only detail of my position, that I be willing and able to decommission phone banks when contracted to do so. Were I called upon by someone to recommission this phone bank immediately upon completing the decommission, I would be well within my rights to tell that person, 'No, sir. I am employed for decommissioning only.' It is possible, like my decision to address your questions, that I would recommission the phone bank out of the goodness of my heart, given that it would merely require me to do the steps I have done in reverse order. Although, to be quite honest, your abuse of said goodness of said heart would likely result in my being less generous in the future. Are we clear on the first point?"

"Yes," Orville said, "but why—"

The man clapped his hands to silence him. "No! Your questions are over! Moving on to the second point, that people require this phone bank. This, like some other things you have said, is only partially true. Our data—which I am not required to review, but which I do review, another illustration of how I go above and beyond—shows that this phone bank is used just once each day to call the same number. Therefore, your use of the word 'people,' as in the plural of 'person,' is downright fallacious, whereas your use of the word 'need' is debatable at best."

"But that's me!" Orville cried. "That's my phone call. You know, on the radio—"

The man shook his head as harshly as he spoke. "No, sir, I do not know 'on the radio,' as I am not concerned with radios, only phones. And speaking of phones, now is the time I will terminate this conversation and return to decommissioning this phone bank."

Orville couldn't believe it. "So you're just going to—"

"And speaking of phones," the man repeated, slower this time, "now is the time I will terminate this conversation and return to decommissioning the phone bank."

With that, he turned, picked up his wrench, and resumed whatever task he'd been working at before. Orville stood there for a moment. He considered ripping the caution tape and addressing the man with his fists, but it wasn't worth it. Orville would work through the appropriate channels, or so he thought.

ALL ALONG THE HEAP, I

BOSS SAT in his camper, sipping brandy by himself. He would not go out to The Bars tonight, had not been in quite some time, and he felt good about that. He used to be one of those people who go out and get blitzed at every opportunity, but no more. He was turning a corner, wising up. Did it show? Did he look like a more mature, less erratic man than when he'd first arrived at the Heap? He got up and went to check the mirror hanging next to his bed. The answer was no. He looked terrible, actually, all weathered and tired. His face seemed almost inflamed. Like a bee sting. As in a bee sting singular. Like how a bee sting might look through a telescope. (No, microscope.) But how? Having a little wine, then some brandy—was that really enough to make him look so bad? Except, hold on, that wasn't all. Didn't he also pour a little brandy in his coffee in the morning? And hadn't he had a beer with his lunch, locked in his office? Or was it two beers? Did he finish the bottle he'd had with the doctor? Did they open another? Was there some whiskey in there somewhere? His memory was a waterlogged map. He remembered some things clearly, but other moments came to him smeared and unspecific. Why did he feel so tired if he slept so much? His life was a puzzle, but he couldn't solve it, not now. Thinking of his fatigue invoked a fresh wave of it. His eyelids dipped, blurring his already blurry vision. He finished his brandy in one gulp, then poured himself another to have in bed.

Ꙭ

NINA POLISHED the bar, preparing for the night. Usually
it was hard. Her patrons waited patiently enough at the entrance, but they were held back by nothing more than a steel
rod gate. Even if she turned her back to them, she could feel
their presence, and it would cause her to rush. Today was
different. Today she polished slowly, her thoughts surrounding her like a membrane. They weren't particularly complicated. She could distill them down to a single question: Why
couldn't she keep herself from doing the voices? She knew
the answer: because she was who she was. Voices had been
her life. How could she stop here? Still, she should've been
more careful, less obvious. She could have satisfied herself
by adopting a new voice when she first got here. Nobody
would've known it wasn't her real voice, except her. But it
was too late to think about that now. Not to mention, did she
even have a real voice at this point? She often tried to remember how she'd spoken before she'd met Strom and joined the
Vocalist Cartel, but there'd been so many voices since then.
Not that whoever Orville had mentioned—someone from the
"entertainment industry"—was a Cartel member, necessarily. The potential scared her, though, which was okay, maybe
even a good thing. It had been a long time since she'd left
them. She was out of practice. A little bit of extra fear might
be what kept her alive.

Ꙭ

TERRANCE HAD woken that morning with a hangover, but
he'd made a promise to himself the day before to get up early
and take a long circuitous route through the then-empty
Assistance Sector on the way to his dig area as a way of getting to know the place. And it was on this ride that he saw the
café, wedged between two long buildings that seemed to be

offices of some kind. It was just a stand, really, with a counter and a few stools out front, but Terrance loved it as soon
as he saw it. Nearly an hour before work got started, there
were only two men there, both with simple white diner
mugs that they sipped from occasionally. They spoke neither to each other nor to the barista who sat reading a book
inside the stand itself. Terrance decided in that moment that
he wanted to become one of them, a regular. They would
sit together, enjoying the quiet camaraderie, which maybe
over time would become less quiet. They'd start by greeting each other with a nod, then a word, then maybe names
would be exchanged, then maybe a good-hearted jab or two,
say, for example, if one of them had clearly come that morning from a lady's camper (in this fantasy, Terrance hoped
it would be him), until eventually they, all three of them
(Or why not four? Why couldn't the barista join in?), would
build up an intricate set of inside jokes, at which they could
be heard laughing all the way from CamperTown. But Terrance had already had two cups of instant coffee that morning, and he didn't want to overcaffeinate. So he noted the
closing time—five o'clock, the same as everything in the
Assistance Sector—in case he needed a little pick-me-up on
the way home before heading to The Bars that night.

The day was certainly exhausting enough to warrant
one. He arrived at his dig area at 8:45, hoping to get started
with the sorting early out of fear that the mixture of hangover and inexperience would slow him down, making him
a burden to his team. The two other Dig Hands he worked
with showed up a half hour late and began sorting without
a word of greeting. Around lunchtime, one of them put the
better part of a perfectly nice enamelware dining set into
the pile of unusable garbage. When Terrance pointed it out,
the guy started in on something about dust, about how there
might be certain types of dust in the debris that could be
dangerous to consume. It was suspect, Terrance thought, and

at odds with what he'd learned at his orientation meeting. "Remember, we are just the initial sorters," Hans had said, "so always round up, in terms of estimated value. It's worse to waste what might be a valuable piece than waste a minute of someone's time down the line." But the man seemed so dead set on arguing that Terrance simply let it go. He left at a quarter to five, racing toward the Assistance Sector. On the way, he saw two of the weird people who lived in the RVs—he forgot what everyone called them—nearly come to blows over what looked like a dented push mechanism from an emergency exit. Fighting through the crowd of departing workers to get to the café before closing, Terrance arrived at 4:53. And found the barista—a different one—lowering a chain gate over the stand. "I was going to buy a cup," Terrance said, to which the barista replied, "We're closed." Terrance pointed to the sign displaying the hours, but the barista only shook his head. "It's bad for your sleep cycle to drink coffee this late anyway." This was only day two for Terrance and he would not become jaded yet. Still, he couldn't help but notice a pattern: the use of some pseudo-intellectual explanation to smooth over laziness.

Back in his camper, he drank a cup of instant coffee out of spite and decided he would never return to the café.

꙾

ORVILLE RODE away from the phone bank even faster than he'd come. Not to escape it. He wanted to work up a fresh sweat. An orchestra of hysteria tuned itself inside him, drowning out the distant whistle of betrayal he'd felt since the night before. Orville wanted to open his pores and release the noise.

Who would he complain to about the phone bank? Boss? Or was this something bigger? Did he need to get in front of the Committee for Better Life in CamperTown so they might raise the issue to Thisbee? Both courses held equal potential for drawn-out scatterbrained shittiness, and all Orville really wanted to do right now was scream. The irony occurred to him then: Bernard was the exact person Orville really wanted to talk to about not being able to talk to Bernard. It was the first time he wanted control of the conversation, the first time that his dilemma wouldn't sound petty compared to Bernard's. This affected them both. And, in fact, it was affecting them both at that moment. He hadn't thought about that. What was Bernard doing on the air?

Orville slowed down and turned the radio on. He expected silence, Bernard's soft breathing. Instead, his brother seemed to be explaining something to someone: "—that's just the way it is between siblings, though. It's shallower than friendship, yet so much deeper. Do you understand what I'm talking about?" Orville ceased pedaling altogether and squeezed the brakes. He skidded to a stop and stamped his foot down. Somewhere inside him, in that split second before the response came, he knew what he would hear, and yet, when he heard it, his whole body felt weak. "Of course," said the caller.

And the voice was a perfect impersonation of his own.

II

THE

VOCALIST

CARTEL

[16]

FROM THE LATER YEARS:

BASE EXPANSION

To *allow for continued upward construction, the base of the building (a word we rarely used after our first few months there; it seemed so trivializing) required expansion. This made for an interesting problem: lower floors being built outward meant the conversion of certain outer units to inner units. Though covered in each unit's purchase agreement and easily predictable, this invariably took the targeted residents by surprise. Compounding the issue: Inner units were valued at significantly less than outer units. Therefore, to sell one's "innerized" unit and move to one of the newly built outer units on one's own floor (or a floor above) required a considerable financial hit. A few particularly wealthy lower-floor outer residents did exactly this, but for many, it simply was not possible.*

The transitional months were a trying time. First, the filling in and replacement of their former windows with UV screens often left residents feeling light-headed and congested. Then came the time zone reassignment. Since the initial time scramble, the condo board had accelerated the process so it could be completed within a single week for those new to inner life. To make up for the disorientation such a quick change could cause, businesses within the Vert allotted each formerly outer-living employee five paid days off for "sleep modification time." Longtime inner residents scoffed at this. Extra leave to adjust to the conditions they'd always known? What they might do with a week of free time! Making it especially infuriating: few innerized residents even took their allotted days. They resisted the change. As the time began its shift, they taped cardboard over their UV screens and continued to live on "true time" so the coworkers they'd long shared a shift with—other outer residents—would not know of their ill luck.

But everyone knew. The signs were clear enough. The skin of an innerized resident, with no exposure to sunlight (real or artificial), took on a sickly paleness. They squinted more. They guzzled coffee, looked at their watches constantly, and took their lunches precisely at noon, as if fearing that a few minutes earlier or later might be just enough for the time change to seize them. They wandered the halls that connected the newly constructed outer units on their floors and introduced themselves to the new residents as their neighbors just a few doors down. "On this side," they might add, their voices just a little too loud and desperate.

The clearest indicator of their new status, though, was how they spoke of the population they were set to join. The outer units discussed the inner units the way winning sports teams often talk about their lesser opponents: with more condescension than disdain. The concerns of the inner units were cute. Their antics showed passion that might make them, the outer units, jealous if they didn't see, from their elevated position in society, its frivolousness. This changed after innerization. The innerized resident spoke of the inner units with blatant disgust, as if inner life were a festering open wound on the otherwise healthy body of the Vert. Mostly they spoke this way to their (not yet realized to be) former compatriots of the outer walls, who answered such tirades with a sad smile or a forced laugh. Only occasionally, when the denial of their situation ran so deep as to completely demagnetize their moral compasses, did they march into the innermost hallways to shout insults and threats to all who passed by.

You might imagine that there would be repercussions for this. Perhaps someone would call security. Or maybe, being outnumbered, the innerized resident would be thrown to the ground by an angry mob and beaten until unrecognizable. But no: if ever the inner units enacted violence on such an unwanted visitor it was in self-defense. Truth be told, they relished such tirades. They knew the hate speech to be temporary. Soon, the angry innerized would cave. He would uncover his UV screens. He would fall in line with his new time zone. He would adjust his hours at work. In other words, he would become a full-blown inner resident. Not only would he apologize, profusely, to anyone he offended during his transition; he would look on his former life with confusion and anxiety. He would be sickened by the privilege he once enjoyed and speak out against it more than any of them who'd been there, windowless from the beginning. He would become, in some ways, the ultimate inner resident.

17

THE GATE

THE NEXT morning, Orville went to the gate. He took a spoonful of instant coffee and ate it, chased it with some water, and got on his bike, rushing through the Ass, which stood all but empty. It was rare that he came this way at all, and especially rare that he was out this early. On another morning, it might've been something special, something that reconfirmed his commitment to all this—a positive lens through which to view an area he avoided, an abrasive place turned peaceful.

This morning, Orville could feel no such thing. Or worse, he *could* feel it, but only long enough for it to become a wholly formed feeling and thus a better meal for the parasite of dread inside him. This parasite had already eaten his sense of relief the day before, when he got home from the phone bank, shutting the door behind himself and collapsing on his bed. It ate the few moments of normalcy at The Bars later that night. Even the moments of iciness between him and Lydia were consumed; it wouldn't allow him the respite of lesser shittiness. His sleep the parasite ate in pieces, so that Orville drifted off and reawoke several times throughout the night feeling tense and confused. He knew now why people often had trouble sleeping when they felt terrible. It wasn't a punishment; it was a defense mechanism. Doom stretched across eight restless hours was better than a concentrated burst of doom upon waking.

Orville had decided not to tell anyone anything about

what was going on until he himself could get a better idea, and the first step toward doing so required checking the logs. What he expected to find there, and how he would use this information, was something he planned to figure out on the way over. But the trip was shorter than he anticipated. He arrived before the sun had fully risen.

The gate marked where the paved road, Access Avenue, ended, giving way to the Dig Site's packed dirt paths. The lifting barrier was controlled from within a booth next to it, although it was mostly symbolic; without a fence around CamperTown, it wouldn't be hard to circumvent. Orville coasted up to the booth, a cubed hut with windows all around, and found it empty. On the side facing the road was a built-in intercom system with a long narrow microphone snaking inside, and an empty nameplate holder embedded in the glass. On the desk sat a large binder.

In his rush to get out the door and do something, Orville had not considered the basic logical question of when the gate actually opened. Feeling stupid and defeated, he turned his bike back toward the Ass and, luckily, saw the old man walking in his direction. Orville offered a weak wave that the old man didn't return. He took short steps and kept his head at an angle, as if someone had once told him never to take the ground for granted. It felt like ten minutes later that he finally arrived.

"Sorry, I know it's early," Orville began, putting down his kickstand and dismounting his bike, but the man ignored him. Instead, he entered the booth through a door in the back, sat at the desk, slipped his nameplate into the holder— *Benjamin*, it read—and said . . . something.

"What?" Orville said.

The man spoke again, and again it came out garbled and inaudible.

"I can't understand," Orville said. He tapped the glass, pointing at the intercom system. "Maybe lean in closer?"

Benjamin shook his head. He slid open a side window. "Can't. It's too loud. Listen." He put his face closer to the microphone. "Hello, hello," he said. It came out clear and at a reasonable volume, but Benjamin recoiled, cupping his ears. "See what I mean?" he said through the window.

Orville nodded, because it seemed like the only thing to do.

"Anyway, what I asked was, coming or going?" The old man didn't look at Orville. His focus instead was on unwrapping a napkin, revealing two pieces of buttered toast. He lifted one to his mouth and took a bite.

"Actually, neither," Orville said. This finally gained Benjamin's full attention. He met Orville's eyes, still chewing. Orville tried to clarify. "I mean, I just—" But the old man held up his hand, continued chewing for an impossibly long time, swallowed in a way that looked almost painful, and then, in a gesture that Orville could not help but admire, took another bite, at which point the process repeated itself.

"So, neither?" Benjamin said, finally.

"It's about other visitors," Orville said.

Benjamin slid the binder from the table and angled it out the window. "Have to check the logs for that."

The binder was so cumbersome, Orville had to set it down on his bike seat to flip through.

"Chronology not guaranteed," Benjamin said behind him. "Dropped it yesterday morning. Damn click mechanism opens up. Pages all over the floor. Assume they didn't lose their order, but can't be sure."

Orville flipped all the way to the most recent page, and there it was: *Charles Gilmore, Starlight Telecommunications.*

"This guy," Orville said, holding the binder up in front of the window. "What was he here to do?"

"Telecommunications work."

"That's what he said?"

"No." Benjamin tapped the window, indicating the binder page. "That's what he wrote down."

"But what does that mean, do you think?" Orville asked.

"Something with the phones, maybe," Benjamin said.

"Like what?"

Benjamin shrugged. He'd begun working on his second piece of toast by now.

Orville returned to his bike with the binder and flipped back a bit. The pages had gotten more mixed up than Benjamin had realized, and it took him some time to find *Hal Cornish, Sundial Media*. He repeated the same process with Benjamin, asking him why Cornish had come, but again got nothing.

"Something about media, I guess," Benjamin said, reading the name for what appeared to be the first time.

Orville tried his best to keep calm. "What does that even mean?"

"News reporter, maybe," Benjamin said.

"He's not a reporter."

"Maybe they're making a drive-in," Benjamin said through a full mouth of toast. "But for bikes. Ride-in, I guess."

Orville stared at him. "A ride-in theater? Is that something you heard about, or are you just guessing?"

"Just guessing," Benjamin said. "If it's not that, heck if I know. I'm not very savvy on that stuff. Media, I mean."

"So do you have any idea about the people who come through?" Orville said. He shut the binder and shoved it through the window, not waiting for Benjamin to take it. It fell on the floor with a thud, but didn't open. "Or do you just let whoever wants to drive right into our community as long as they have a name to write down?"

The old man sat up straight now. "You need to watch it," he said, pointing the crust at Orville in an authoritative way.

He was right. Orville did need to watch it. Yes, the man was inept, but none of what was happening was his fault.

"Sorry," Orville said. "I was hoping . . ." But he didn't know how to finish. What had he hoped? That there would be no record of any of these comings and goings? He didn't need that to prove something nefarious was going on. A man was pretending to be him on the radio. That they'd gone through the appropriate channels only made it worse, really. They felt comfortable enough to hide in broad daylight. They felt like this was their right.

Benjamin seemed intent on hearing a full apology. He'd crossed his arms, still holding the last bit of toast so that it poked out from under his armpit.

"I . . . I've been dealing with some guests that haven't been exactly welcome," Orville sputtered finally.

This provoked something unexpected. The old man nodded knowingly. "The flashlights. Out by the broken-down camper," he said. "They flash in my window too. Every few weeks. Don't know who it is, but don't care for it. Not one bit."

Orville had no idea what the man was talking about, but he said, "Sure," because it was the easiest way out of the conversation.

§

A SHORT time later, he met with Hans and Lydia at their dig spot along the Heap. Hans began climbing the debris. Lydia followed, but Orville called after her. She turned, looking expectant. Of an apology maybe. An explanation. What Orville said instead was, "Is there a way to make a special request? For the casino shuttle?"

18

MEET WITH A PURPOSE

THEY HAD agreed to meet twice a week in the time immediately leading up to Peter Thisbee's visit. This plan was proposed back when they thought there would be a festival, with
events and decorations. That the event had been downgraded
to a simple tour early in the morning rendered these extra
meetings unnecessary. Yet, since canceling them would require Chairperson Gil to actually take action, Lydia found
herself in the conference trailer for the second time in just a
few days, among the collected members of the Committee for
Better Life in CamperTown.

The only thing that made it feel different from their regular meetings was the absence of Gil. While the other members discussed how long they had to wait before they could
leave, Lydia gave herself over to fantasy. Maybe he wouldn't
show up. Maybe she would eventually stand up and say, "Gil
has left us, and friends, we must view this as a gift. It's time
to get to work," and the others would sense in her the spirit
that Gil lacked. Or maybe Gil would arrive, pale and solemn,
and announce that he'd been shown a better way to lead, not
mentioning Lydia by name but looking straight at her as he
spoke, his gaze so firmly set on her that the others took notice.
At the very least, maybe he would come and, out of spite, lead
an organized tour-planning session wherein they made up
for time wasted in meetings past.

The crux of each possibility was that, though Lydia had
failed to bargain her way onto the tour with Thisbee, her

confrontation would bring about some change. And it did, just not for the better.

Chairperson Gil's arrival twelve minutes late elicited a collective groan from the room, the decided-upon threshold for guilt-free departure being fifteen minutes. He carried a large book with a white cover, on which a title was printed in simple black font: *Meet with a Purpose.* It looked like a prop from a movie where someone worked in an undefined corporate role. Lydia sat a few seats away, so she couldn't be sure, but she was fairly certain there was no author name.

"Okay, we're going to try something different," Chairperson Gil said. Unlike how things played out in her imagination, he managed in one sweeping glance around the table to make eye contact with everyone *but* Lydia. This all hinged on avoiding further confrontation—Lydia realized as much even before he explained the plan: they would break off into pairs and discuss the topic at hand.

A moment passed, in which Chairperson Gil smiled at them enthusiastically—likely a tactic discussed in *Meet with a Purpose*—before someone asked, "What's the topic?"

"Oh, right . . ." Gil took a small notepad from his breast pocket, placed this on the table alongside his book, and cleared his throat.

"Got one," Benjy said, before Gil could speak. "Gate traffic. Too busy these days. Maybe we could do possible solutions?"

"That's a great idea," Gil said, "but why don't we table that one for a later meeting, and focus on the tour for now. As we all know, I'll be leading it, but I want you all to feel like you're along for the journey too. Although you won't be. But you can be in spirit, by helping *me* come up with the best way to represent *us.*"

The mission of each pair: to best describe the role that the Committee for Better Life in CamperTown played in CamperTown life. Lydia ended up with a woman named Janelle who worked in some sort of bike allocation and repair position. Janelle was known for having painted her camper bright yellow. "Because that's just the kind of bitch I am," she'd often say as an explanation.

Gathered at the end of the table, Janelle took hold of the pen and the paper Gil had supplied to the two of them. "Always grabbing the pen," she said. "Classic me."

Lydia thought Janelle was leading up to offering her the pen, but Janelle did not offer her the pen. All around them, the other pairs' discussions wove together into an unintelligible white noise that insulated each conversation.

"So," Janelle said, biting her lip in mock concentration, "what do we do?"

"We build support structures to keep our unique community exactly that—unique—while streamlining and simplifying all necessary policies and procedures."

Janelle squinted at Lydia, as if seeing her for the first time. "Did you just come up with that?"

"I like to think about these things," Lydia said.

"I love it." Janelle began writing. "'We . . . build . . . support . . .'"

"Wait," Lydia said, "I want to keep that one."

Janelle laughed. "Keep it? But it's perfect!"

Lydia reached out and as calmly as she could stilled Janelle's writing hand. "It's," she said, "mine."

The look on Janelle's face transformed slowly from confusion to a knowing smile. "I know! You got it from your friend, didn't you?"

"My friend?" Lydia removed her hand and was relieved when Janelle didn't resume writing.

"On the radio."

"I've never called in to Bernard," Lydia said.

"The other one," Janelle said. "The brother. Someone said you know him."

"Orville," Lydia said. "We're on the same dig team." She really didn't know if she meant it as a slight to Orville for his recent bout of gloominess or if she wanted to protect her personal relationships from Janelle, whom she'd decided—only officially in that moment—she didn't like.

"I figured maybe you'd been inspired. They're always talking about such clever stuff," Janelle said. "Well, the underground one is. The one up here's not much of a talker. Though he has been a bit chipper lately."

"He has?" Lydia tried to hide her surprise.

"Yeah, last couple days, he's started saying more. Not a ton, but it's definitely a change." Janelle leaned in. "What's the deal with that? There something going on?" She spoke as though they, the two of them, had some stake in Orville and Bernard's relationship.

"There's always something going on," Lydia managed, a complete nothing statement, but Janelle nodded, satisfied.

Lydia couldn't tell the truth, which was that she rarely listened to Orville's calls to Bernard. It felt too weird, and besides, when she did tune in, Orville rarely said anything meaningful, if he said anything at all. But now, apparently, he'd grown more talkative? In the days coinciding exactly with the downswing of his mood? Orville didn't seem angry at Lydia personally anymore, but that didn't make it any easier to be around him. He rarely spoke, seemed to avoid eye contact, and the only time in the last few days he'd said more than two words was to ask about a form so he could go to the casino during the day. Lydia had told him, as dryly as she could, that she'd look into it, but even this assurance was met with a mournful nod, as if the trip were some involuntary burden.

Communities were made of people, Lydia thought, with different faces for different situations, and complicated inner lives. It was important for people in power to always remember that.

For the remainder of the meeting, she and Janelle tried in vain to come up with something definitive to say about the

Committee. They weren't the only ones. When Gil brought them all back together and asked for what they'd come up with, he was met with silence.

"I guess with a name like the Committee for Better Life in CamperTown, it's pretty self-explanatory," he said finally. And then the meeting was over.

19

GREATER FORCES

ORVILLE FOUND himself once again starting his day in the Ass, his second visit in less than a week. It wasn't as early as it had been when he made his trip to the gate. He sat on the bench under the beach tent that served as the "bus station." The shuttle itself was kept in a little makeshift garage just down the road, but it couldn't get out through the morning rush. Orville kept his head down, embarrassed by how he looked waiting for a bus to the casino before nine in the morning, and nervous for the day ahead of him.

It had taken a couple of days for Lydia to figure out which form he needed and get it processed, but she'd done it, which was more than he probably deserved after how he'd been acting. He'd already decided: tonight, he would tell her and Hans everything. The sense of potential relief kept him going. Without this unburdening to look forward to, what came between then and now—the trip to the casino, the call—might be too much to handle, and so he found himself thinking about that rather than what he planned to say, or how he planned to bring some conclusion to all this.

Eventually the crowds thinned out as the Ass workers made their way into various drab structures, and the shuttle could make its way to him. The driver opened the door. "Casino," he called out, as if there were more than one destination or one person waiting. Orville got in.

The ride up Access Avenue was just like the one he'd taken in, except in reverse, and the shuttle was smaller than the bus they'd chartered for the newbs back then. When you signed up for the Dig Effort, you were connected with a specialist who helped assist your move to CamperTown. Primarily, they helped you sell your car (if you had one). This, they argued, benefited everyone; the various construction vehicles and supply trucks needed uninhibited access to the Heap, and the money from the car could serve as a cushion for workers to support themselves until their first stipend paid out. Really, though, Orville always suspected that it was to make sure the people who came were serious. You couldn't just drive off when you felt like it; if you agreed to come, you were in it. He couldn't tell how well it had worked.

On the horizon, Orville saw the massive antenna. The sight of it must have given Bernard chills when he first came to Los Verticalés. Orville had thought about this when he arrived at the Dig Site, and he thought about it again now. He wondered what Bernard might be talking about, but the driver didn't touch the radio.

A few miles into the drive, Orville noticed moguls out in the desert, each one a mound of displaced sand next to a hole. At the last one, the smallest, he saw a man leaning on a shovel, wiping his brow. It was the fan boss had told him about. Orville couldn't help but snort.

※

IN THE windowless casino, surrounded by machines that dinged and flashed so loudly and so frequently it felt like they were trying to make up for there being only about three or four people present, Orville discovered that the only thing he couldn't put a coin into was a pay phone.

He went to the front desk. "You got a phone I can use?" he asked the young woman working there. He was told no, the desk phone was not for public use.

"However, each of our rooms *is* outfitted with its own private phone." The woman said this as if it were a feature, not an expectation. Orville had spent his accumulated stipend payments on almost nothing but the bare essentials. He was reluctant to get a room he didn't need, but seeing no other way, he eventually agreed.

Inside, it looked so clean, Orville felt nervous walking on the carpet. It was a fairly standard hotel room, yet compared to his camper it felt as expansive as a gymnasium. He sat on the edge of the bed and, for a moment, basked in the pure quiet of the room. A click sounded, and then the air conditioner switched on, turning the space arctic.

Orville took a deep breath, retrieved the business card from his pocket, and picked up the phone.

"Mr. Anders," Hal Cornish said after his assistant had patched Orville through. "I'm so glad you called."

"Didn't make it easy," Orville said. "You want me to call, then you shut down all our phones."

"I was wondering how they managed to keep you off the radio."

"You don't even know what your people are doing?"

Hal Cornish seemed unperturbed by this. "These things are complicated. Where are you now?"

"I'm at the casino," Orville said. "I had to get a room."

"We'll cover that," Hal Cornish said. "I know these past few days must've been difficult for you, but I want you to think of this as a partnership. As long as you're reading the ads, you're keeping Bernard on the air. One thing that *will* have to change: You'll have to check your mail. Every day would be preferable, in case we have to change things up at the last minute, but I'll send you an overview at the beginning of each week, so you can start thinking about what you want to say."

"Whoa, whoa," Orville said. "I'm not calling to concede."

The line went silent for a time. "Say again," Hal Cornish finally said.

"I'm not agreeing to any part of this," Orville said.

"You went through all this trouble, of getting to the casino, getting the room, and"—Hal Cornish took a deep breath here—"you're not interested in considering my offer?"

"That's correct," Orville said.

"Then why are you calling, Mr. Anders?"

This, Orville was not ready to answer, but the words came to him. "I'm calling to tell you to stop. Because if you don't, I'll be forced to take action, actions that you won't appreciate, do you understand?" Orville couldn't help it. He felt so incredibly cool in that moment that he had to hold the receiver away from his mouth to catch his breath.

Hal Cornish did not seem impressed. "I'd say if there's anyone who's having an issue understanding, it's you." He spoke lower now. "Orville, what you're doing—holding out, threatening—it's dangerous. You have no idea who you're dealing with."

Orville laughed, or forced himself to laugh. The excitement had jumbled everything, and he didn't know what was real and what was his own play-acting. "You're going to send your people after me?" he said.

"Stop calling them that!" Hal Cornish's voice came out in a hiss, but there wasn't menace in it. Orville had prepared himself for some level of menace, quiet or otherwise. This sounded a lot more like fear.

"Stop calling them what?" Orville's hand gripped the soft maroon duvet on the bed.

"My people," Hal Cornish said. "These people are not mine."

"Well, whose people are they?"

"Nobody's. This is what I mean. You don't understand. I thought you'd get it—I thought they'd *make* you get it. That's something they're good at, reminding you that there are greater forces at play here. But you remain obstinate. You think this is another issue you can solve with a shovel and some muscle, when it's no such thing. Wait, you haven't told anyone about this, have you?"

"I might've," Orville said. It came out cracked and nervous.

Hal Cornish breathed a sigh of relief strong enough to be picked up by the phone. "So you haven't," he said. "I'll be honest, Mr. Anders, this is the only good news you've given me this whole time. Keep it that way, for your sake and for the sake of your friends. In return, I won't say anything either. I won't talk about this call, about your threats, about anything."

"Talk to who?"

Hal Cornish ignored him. "Please call back soon, Mr. Anders," he said. "But don't waste my time like this again. It's bad for both of us."

He hung up before Orville could reply.

❧

LYDIA HAD asked him how long he needed to be at the casino for. "Whole day?" she'd said, and agreement seemed least likely to raise suspicions. So Orville had a good several hours before the driver would be back to pick him up. He could do any number of things not possible in CamperTown. He could watch television. He could gamble. He could take a nap on a large bed. He did nothing. He didn't even open the blinds. The hotel room remained a detached cube of what should have been comfort.

The greatest temptation was to call Bernard, but he didn't do this either. He kept thinking of what Hal had said, or moreover, how he'd said it, his fearfulness, which stoked Orville's own fear now. He paced the room for a time and tried to make sense of it, tried to remember the exchange differently, to retrofit it with something other than terror. He wanted to convince himself of the ridiculousness of a radio station threatening him like Cornish had. He failed. The phrase "greater forces at play" loomed in his mind, though what that even meant, Orville had no idea.

Eventually, the day passed, and it was time to get back on the shuttle. Outside the casino, Orville felt blinded by the desert's brightness. The driver pulled up after a moment and opened the door. "CamperTown," he called out. Again, Orville was the only passenger.

This trip, the radio was on, low at first, so that Orville could barely make out Bernard. Someone seemed to be asking about the smell, a fairly common refrain, to which Bernard responded as he normally did: he'd gotten so used to it, he couldn't really say much. "It's just what life smells like for me," Bernard said. "Look, I actually have to go." A stillness attacked Orville's throat, holding down the breath.

To make matters worse, the driver reached to the radio and turned up the volume. One of their many listeners, apparently.

"Orville!" Bernard said. "I'm so glad you called. I was thinking, you know how yesterday we talked about how things might change, if our places were reversed: me out there, you down here?"

But Orville didn't know. How could he? He hadn't been listening. The first day of his replacement he'd waited only a moment before switching the radio off in disgust, and since then he'd been too nauseated by the whole thing to try again. Now he'd have to hear the conversation regardless.

"Of course," said Orville on the radio. The real Orville tried to practice his breathing, an attempt to block out the man pretending to be him. He slid closer to the window, watched the landscape with a forced intensity. After a time, the mounds of cast-off sand appeared, then the holes in the sand, but the fan too had gone home for the day. A little while later, he saw the antenna again. It taunted Orville.

His name was on the request form, but who knew if the

driver even read it. He didn't seem bothered by Orville Anders being a passenger and speaking on the radio at the same time. Hans and Lydia knew he was away, but they couldn't be certain when he got back. The flagrance of it all perplexed Orville, just as it had at the gate. The ease with which the truth could be uncovered almost seemed to ensure it would not be. The difference between then, when he'd checked the logs, and now, listening to himself talk to his brother, was the weight of Hal Cornish's words. It was not only that anyone who looked could see what was happening; it was the fear of what might happen if they did.

As they pulled into CamperTown, the conversation came to a close. "And what's new with you, brother?" Bernard said.

It was here that the imposter broke from Orville's own approach: "I was thinking of building a fire pit outside my camper, and did you know that Maverick Bricks offer the best price per brick of any major brick manufacturer in the continental U.S.?"

"It's an ad," Orville said to himself, in the shuttle.

The driver turned down the radio, met Orville's eyes through the rearview mirror. "What was that?"

Orville could only shrug. It wasn't an appropriate response, but what was he supposed to do? Speak?

STUCK INSIDE

IN THE conference trailer, Gil said, "On the little piece of paper, you'll write the single most important word to describe what we do here." He collected these and wrote the words on a white board.

"Now," Gil said, "on the other piece of paper, the full-sized one, I want you to write an explanation of your role within the Dig Effort without using the words on the board. This should"—Gil looked down and read directly from *Meeting with a Purpose*—"help us better synthesize our places in the project."

The inclusion of words like "Dig," "Organize," and "Work" rendered the exercise mostly impossible, but Gil still smiled and thanked each person as he collected the results.

⸎

"SEE, NOW this is a photographic moment," Hans said. "This is what people want to see." It was a lucky day. They'd uncovered some couch cushions and laid them down on a door wedged into the rubble. They sat on it, eating lunch.

"Win anything?" Lydia asked.

It took Orville a minute to realize it was a question for him. "What do you mean?"

"At the casino. Did you win anything?"

For a moment, he was returned to the hotel room. He looked over his shoulder, expecting to see Hal Cornish emerging from some unseen cavity, a contract in his hand.

Turning back to the others as casually as he could, he shook his head. "Nope. Didn't win anything."

"Don't feel bad. The games are all rigged," Hans said.

"They really are," Orville agreed.

§

"AND WHAT'S new with you, brother?" Bernard asked.

"Well," said the imposter, "I tore my work gloves, and Bernard, you know I don't have time for stitching. So I applied a little bit of Tuff Glue and I haven't had an issue since."

§

IT WAS three in the morning and Lydia couldn't sleep. She left her camper and walked through CamperTown, to its edge. The moonlight glinted off the empty camper far out in the desert.

She stared at it for a long time, dreaming of its removal, before she sensed movement to her left. Her eyesight had adjusted enough to see the figure winding its way through the campers, but she could make out no specific details. Whoever it was, they hadn't seen her. Lydia decided to follow at a distance. They seemed to be making their way along the final row of campers all the way to the desert on that side, but stopped next to the entrance of the Displaced Travelers' camp. They left the Christmas lights on in the courtyard all night, and in the dim glow, Lydia saw who it was: the man with the glasses and mustache.

Lydia walked back to her camper wondering what else happened after she went to bed.

§

"AND WHAT'S new with you, brother?" Bernard asked.

"Actually, more than meets the eye," said the imposter. "Not to get too graphic, but perspiration can certainly be an issue when you're digging all day like I am. It pools up in all sorts of unfortunate places, and can cause some serious chafing if you're not careful. That's why I've invested in a pair of No Sweat Undies. They don't absorb sweat. They don't wick it away. Bernard, they make it like the sweat was never there!"

AT FIRST, Orville rode out to the phone bank to listen to his radio. He couldn't stand near the phones. They'd put up a more permanent fence around the whole thing and even hung up a sign: *Attended by Starlight Telecom.* This ritual brought him no solace, so he started just going home. He kept the radio low and pulled his bike inside so no one could tell he was there, not that anyone other than Hans and Lydia even knew which camper was his. Each day, Orville feared some sign that his brother's relationship with his imposter had somehow grown stronger than theirs had ever been. Each day, no sign came. What little relief this might've provided Orville was counteracted by shame. The consistent shallowness of the conversations only reminded Orville of the shallowness of their relationship—a shallowness, Orville worried now, that was entirely his fault. Orville could grandstand internally all he wanted about playing the listener, about finding Zen-like pride in being a receptacle for Bernard's thoughts, but the impersonator's performance was an unnerving reflection of Orville's despondency. The man pretending to be him exhibited no emotion until the end, when it came time to read the ad, at which point his energy increased tenfold. If there was anything impressive about the conversations, it was Bernard's ability to carry on despite getting so little in return. Orville wanted to blame this on some defect in the impersonator, but he knew he couldn't. This person was a pro.

❧

GIL COULDN'T remember if the process was called web-
bing or spidering or what. "It's basically where you write
one word in a big bubble, and off of that big bubble, you
draw lines connecting to smaller bubbles, each with a word
related to the big bubble word," he said. "We're going to do
that about something important here at the Dig Site. But
with a twist! We're going to think of our big bubble word,
but we're not going to write it down. We're going to leave
the bubble empty in the middle, so that, when I shuffle
them up and hand the pages out, it'll be your job to fill in
someone else's big bubble." He looked down at *Meet with
a Purpose*. "This should help us see how different people
process different things." He didn't bother mentioning how
this related to the tour.

"Little bubbles," Benjy said, his pen poised at the blank
page. "How many?"

"I'd say four, minimum," Gil said.

Lydia did eight. One of the little bubbles said "synergy"
in it. Another said "outcome-driven." She handed it in. The
little bubbles on the page she received read: "Big," "Pile,"
"Of," "Stuff."

❧

SOME VENDORS came in and held a street fair in Camper-
Town one evening. Orville followed the crowds to it. Every
stand showed a new product, every product one that the imposter had hawked on air. Orville made eye contact with each
salesman, trying to see if they'd been sent to taunt him. He
waited for one to cast him a devious look, but nobody even
glanced at him. They were too busy selling.

Later that night, at The Bars, someone tapped Orville
on the back. He turned to find Terrance. "Thanks for the
tip," he whispered with a wink and a smile, reaching down

to snap the waistband of his underwear, peeking out from under his jeans.

❧

WITH EACH passing exercise, Lydia found herself further knotted in a living riddle. It went like this: She should quit the Committee for Better Life in CamperTown because it did not serve her ambitions, but joining the Committee for Better Life in CamperTown was the single step she'd taken to serve her ambitions. So, if she left, she would have done nothing, but if she stayed, she would continue to do nothing.

Lydia began thinking of the conference trailer as a void.

❧

"AND WHAT's new with you, brother?" Bernard asked.

"Bernard, I'll be honest," said the imposter, "it can get mighty uncomfortable with doing the bathroom stuff when you're out there on the Heap, which is why I carry Carson's Mighty Wipes with me at all times. They're mighty clean."

Orville sat up in his camper. The impersonator had made two mistakes. He'd said "there" when he'd spoken of the Heap, an implication of his not being "here," and he'd affected too much of a country bumpkin accent in order to play up the product's name. There came a pause on the other end of the line. Bernard noticed, Orville knew it! Or perhaps he'd known it all along. Perhaps he could see through the fake Orville from the start, and he'd been waiting for the perfect moment to strike him down, to tell the world—because the world was listening, all the way down to Chile—of the man's fraudulence.

"That's great, Orville," Bernard said. "You've been so talkative lately. I really appreciate hearing what's going on with you."

Orville lay back down. None of the tension in his body released.

It had been three weeks since his replacement. There were times throughout when he wanted nothing more than to share this with someone, to be given a shoulder to cry on. This superseded shoulders now. This required necks to grip with his callused hands, eyes to be goopified by the pressure of his thumbs, skulls to be reduced to miniatures of the Heap beneath the pressure of his boot. Orville wanted revenge, greater forces be damned.

21

FROM THE LATER YEARS:

PARKING

Everyone arrived at Los Verticalés with the same concern: that life inside its walls would prove too claustrophobic. Even after a comfortable year or two, this feeling still lingered, and therefore, so did all our cars. We couldn't sell them in case we did decide to leave, so they occupied spaces in a constantly expanding underground parking garage, ready to take us back into the greater world at a moment's notice.

This readiness was facilitated by an enterprising resident, Hannah Quin. She founded a company called QuinCare and hired several attendants. Their job: to keep cars clean and functional. Rust wasn't an issue, but dust was likely to gather inside and out. More importantly, QuinCare attendants drove every car two laps around the garage each week to ensure everything was in good working order. Once a month, Quin drove her own pickup to the nearest town to fill up fuel canisters, which she used to replace the gas burned during these short go-arounds. This was one of QuinCare's founding principles: "A full tank is a happy tank."

It was a brilliant business model. We each paid so little for QuinCare's service that we barely noticed the deduction each month. But multiplied by the number of cars, it was rumored that QuinCare might've cleared somewhere in the high six figures each year. To make it even more lucrative, Quin had

buried in the fine print of the contract a clause stating: "It is un-
derstood that QuinCare may, from time to time, employ your
vehicle as a temporary residence." Which is to say: they slept
in the cars. Nearly everyone employed by QuinCare sold their
condos within the first month of operation. Quin bought them
all gym memberships (at a discounted company rate) so they
would have access to showers and bathrooms. Their only ex-
pense was food.

But Quin wasn't done yet. She expanded the business even
further. The tightness of our living space made certain illicit
behaviors psychologically unfeasible. The hallways buzzed
constantly with people. A visit to a married lover's condo, for
example, would mean subjecting oneself to droves of witnesses
upon entrance and exit. The dozen or so hotels within the Vert
provided no help either: they served the few visitors to the Vert,
but subsisted primarily on giving inner families a taste of the
outer life. As such, their hallways also teemed with familiar
faces. The parking garage, by contrast, was large, dark, cav-
ernous, and contained many "temporary residences" that Quin
rented out to cash-paying customers.

When we found out our cars served as hourly motel rooms,
it angered us, naturally. Quin (or Madam Quin, as some of
us had begun calling her) offered a simple solution: a fee. We
could pay an additional fee each month to ensure our cars never
served as temporary residences. (She never admitted outright
what she was doing, which made it all the more infuriating.)
She had the market on car upkeep cornered, so we paid it. Or
some of us did. Others did not, and allowed their cars to con-
tinue as dens of sin.

We eventually forgot about QuinCare's initial set of ser-
vices. The parking garage became accepted as the red-light
district of Los Verticalés. Those who frequented it grew bolder.
We'd be riding the elevator, perhaps even a crowded one, and
a stranger would begin talking to us. The conversation would
be innocent enough, maybe even pleasant, not necessarily

flirtatious. At some point, the stranger, without a break in conversation, would subtly reach his or her hand to the control panel—and they always stood by the control panel; that should've been the giveaway—and let it hover over the P *button. To accept the invitation, we simply needed to nod.*

22

PERSONAL BUSINESS

LYDIA HAD finished her whiskey and soda long ago, but she didn't want to get another one, so she stood with Hans in their usual corner of The Bars, eating the ice cubes.

Hans had made a comment about how the dazzling sunsets they'd been experiencing lately would make a great photo series, then quickly explained that he meant for another photographer. He personally hoped to capture something gritty and real, something that more accurately portrayed the life they lived, not to mention the deaths—the *tragic* deaths—of those whom they often uncovered. "Probably in black and white. This"—he dismissed the sky over the Heap, all wild oranges and reds, with a casual gesture of his hand—"is nature photography."

"You're not a nature photographer," Lydia said.

"Not if I can help it!"

"No, Hans. It wasn't a question. It was a statement," Lydia said. "You're not a nature photographer. You know how I know that? Because nature photographers take photos." Lydia crunched down on an ice cube hard to punctuate the statement.

Hans took a sip of his beer. He looked at Lydia in a reassuring way. Apparently, it was just as difficult to offend Hans as it was to motivate him. "Okay," he said, "so what's this really about?"

Lydia sighed. "Thisbee is here in, what, two days? And we're still doing what amounts to an hour-long trust fall in our meetings. And the saddest part? I keep trying, as if Gil might see the effort I'm putting forward and think, 'You know what? I was wrong about her.' Which is ridiculous, of course. Like, last meeting, we were drawing maps of the Dig Site, but with everything drawn to a scale based not on size but on the importance of workflow."

Hans scratched his temple with the ridge of his beer can. "What does that even mean?"

"I don't know. But did I try my best? Yes. And I finished early. When I tried to slide my paper across the table to him, though, he ducked. He's like a land mine."

"Land mine makes him sound hotheaded," Hans said.

"A land mine of worry," Lydia said. "A land mine of anxiety."

Hans nodded. "Better."

Terrance emerged from the crowd, a glass of red wine in his hand. "You talking about land mines?" he said.

Hans shook his head. "Gil," Lydia told him, and Terrance looked genuinely disappointed.

"Big land mine fan, Terry?" Hans asked.

"Defense technology in general, really," Terrance said. "I'm a collector."

"That's pretty strange," Lydia said. She reached into her glass for another ice cube but found nothing.

Terrance held up his hands in protest. "No, no! Don't mean I'm stockpiling for the revolution or anything like that. I just think, mechanically speaking, it's interesting stuff. Not that I don't like shooting every once in a while. One of the reasons I came out here, actually. The desert. Good for skeet shooting. We could go sometime, you know? Ride out a little past CamperTown. It'd be great. I can give lessons if you're nervous about doing it wrong."

"Maybe," Hans said. Lydia let his answer, and moreover its undertone of apathy, be hers as well. Really, she wished Terrance would give them a break. He clearly had trouble meeting people, but his continued presence served only to re-inforce the overwhelming sense of stagnation that had fallen over things recently. Hans took no pictures, Terrance made no friends, Lydia made no progress. Orville's moodiness had metastasized into something quieter and grimmer, but they hadn't reconciled (or even talked about) whatever was off be-tween them.

Lydia could count one notable development in the past few weeks: the Displaced Travelers had started to come into CamperTown more frequently. Apparently, they'd been going en masse each night to the casino to ride the elevators up and down in a state of meditative bliss that unnerved the few other guests there. But they were banned only when some-one found two of them engaging in lewd acts in a hatchback that had been left unlocked in the parking lot. Since then, they'd been seen at the café and The Bars more often. They offered payment to have each enclosed and air-conditioned, but both Nina and the proprietor of the café refused. Rumor had it the plans didn't call for windows. Lydia scanned the crowd for them now, as if they were a four-leaf clover she could wish upon for action, but found only the same people as usual. When she turned back to Hans and Terrance, she saw Orville approaching.

As had been his custom lately, he showed up to The Bars about an hour later than them and didn't get a beer, didn't even go up to the bar. He walked right up to their corner and ducked under the fence to get in.

"Orville!" Hans called out, as if his arrival were worthy of a celebration. Whether his attitude was because of Orville's recent sourness or in spite of it, Lydia couldn't tell. Terrance appeared to interpret it as sincerity. "Good evening, sir!" he called out.

Orville looked at Terrance like a bush that has rustled, then turned to Lydia. "How's the meeting?"

It might've seemed like a nice gesture, but he spoke as if small talk pained him. Lydia didn't care to give her response much thought. "Like stepping on a land mine that hates feet. Everybody loses."

"Where would a land mine like that get made, Terrance?" Hans said. "Somewhere Nordic, maybe?"

Even in the dying light, Terrance's face seemed to tan under their gaze. Humor, the three of them had realized, affected him like poison ivy. Hans got a kick out of it, but it mostly just made Lydia sad. "It's a joke," she said.

"Oh," Terrance said. "Ha! Right, yeah. I don't know where you'd find a land mine like that." He looked around, desperate for something he could use to reinstate the seriousness he preferred. His eyes fell on Orville. "But what I do know, sir, is that after a long day of digging, when my arms are begging me to just hang up my shovel and move on, and when some of my Dig partners are . . ." Terrance trailed off here for a moment, before regaining a shaky footing. "I guess what I'm trying to say is, hearing you and Bernard talk each afternoon really reminds me of why I'm here."

Another point to illustrate stagnation, Lydia noted: Terrance's attempts to impress Orville with his concern. Lydia had thought to pull him aside and tell him to cut it out, but then again, Orville hadn't reacted with anything other than vague annoyance. Until tonight. He stared at Terrance for a long moment, his eyes sharpening, before he spoke. "You feel good about listening in on my personal business?"

This, Lydia had not heard before, and she felt, despite herself, small pockets of excitement mixed among the tension. Maybe she wanted things to get a little nastier, just so they'd be different.

"I mean, I just thought—you know, a lot of people listen," Terrance sputtered.

"Yeah, but they're not here confessing it to me as if it's virtuous, are they?"

"C'mon, Orville," Hans said. "Give him a break." He reached out and put his hand on Orville's shoulder. Orville shook it off. He wouldn't look at Hans, only at Terrance.

"What? Do you think I wouldn't talk to him off air if I could? Do you think I want everyone hearing what we have to talk about?"

"I'm sorry, sir," Terrance said. He held his wine tightly in both hands, like it was a sacred protective object.

"Stop with the 'sir' shit," Orville said, his voice raised. "I asked you a question: Why do you feel that it's your right to intrude on a private conversation I'm having with my brother?"

"I didn't think it was an intrusion," Terrance sputtered.

"You're right about that. You didn't think. And it was an intrusion."

Orville was just about shouting now, and other people at The Bars were starting to look at them. "Sounds like the brother," Lydia heard someone say. This attention, not what seemed to be playing out in front of her, returned her from spectator to participant. If she let this get out of hand, it could do permanent damage to her reputation. She took Orville by the shoulders. He squirmed, but she dug her fingers in. "Go get a beer," she said.

"I'm not drinking," Orville said.

"Then just walk to the bar, stand there for a minute, and come back."

Her tone seemed to get through to him, and he stalked off, pushing through the crowd and disappearing.

"Should I . . . ?" Hans asked. Lydia shook her head.

"Really, I didn't mean anything," Terrance said.

"He's fine," Lydia said, then corrected herself: "He'll be fine."

♪

BY THE time he got to the bar, Orville was still mad, but he could feel his energy draining, his willpower receding. The Bars, his longstanding reset button, still worked, but now disastrously so. He'd end the day of digging feeling exhausted and anxious; he'd listen to the call in which a man pretending to be him spoke to his brother; he'd vow to take action; but it was always here, at The Bars, that he realized he had no idea what he might do. Each afternoon, he felt primed and ready for drastic measures—ideally, to lay out a plan for his revenge, but if not that, then to at least perform some basic prep work for later action—and yet, even when he tuned his mind to the most desperate wavelength, nothing presented itself.

In the time since he'd stopped drinking, Nina had built a sort of halfhearted tiki hut over the bar, probably to give herself some shade as the days got longer and the sun refused to go down well into the drinking hours. It was the mid-evening lull—not the first rush of the night, not last call—so nobody lingered there except for the Displaced Travelers. They stood huddled at the far end where the thatched awning hung just barely over the simple wooden counter, and chatted excitedly with one another, paying him no attention.

Orville stood there, staring at the wood of the bar and trying to regain the fiery anger from a moment earlier with Terrance. It had felt nice to have a target, someone or something he could address face-to-face. All he could muster now was exhaustion.

"Haven't seen you in a while."

When Orville looked up, Nina was in front of him. "I've been here," he said.

"I mean at the bar," Nina said. "What can I get you?"

"I'm not drinking," Orville told her.

"Ah," Nina said. Then, in the sullen deep voice of an old man, so strikingly unlike her own, "Takin' a little break, huh?" When Nina did her impressions, it was like ventriloquism, like someone else entirely spoke. Orville blinked, his mind racing. As if she knew what he was thinking, she said, "Hey, you never told me about your visitor a couple weeks ago. You said it was someone from the entertainment industry. Wanted to buy your story or something?"

"Nothing like that, no," Orville said.

"Everything okay?" Nina asked.

"No." The word felt involuntary. It escaped Orville like a grunt he might make opening a jar. Nina, picking up glasses along the bar, stopped.

"Do you want to talk about it?" she said.

Orville did, he wanted to talk about it more than anything. He fought to control himself by asking a question. "Hey, what about my voice? Do you think you could do my voice?"

Nina made a face that Orville couldn't read. She looked like she might be about to laugh or spit. "What does that have to do with anything?"

"You did voice work, right?"

It felt like a betrayal bringing it up so directly. Nina stiffened and didn't speak, only looked at him—not with the unfeeling glare she reserved for inquisitive newbs, but with suspicion.

"You don't have to tell me anything," Orville said. "But I just wanted to know, did you ever do any weird jobs?"

"What do you mean by 'weird'?"

Orville couldn't tell if nerves or embarrassment drove him to lower his voice. "Like, not for TV or radio or anything, but in real life. Like a prank. But not a prank, really."

Nina leaned on the bar and looked him in the eye, taking a deep breath through her nose.

"Like a prank," she repeated, "but not a prank, really?"

Orville allowed himself the slightest nod.

Nina considered this for a moment, then reached under the

bar and held up a stack of dirty glasses, adding the ones she'd just gathered to the top. "I need to bring these to the sink." She motioned for him to follow. "I feel like maybe we should have this chat in private."

He followed, looking over his shoulder as they made their way around the back to where Nina had a shed for washing dishes and storing liquor. He didn't know if he wanted to be seen leaving or not to be seen leaving. The light at The Bars was mild, really—a few torches, a few lights clamped along the fence—but Orville's eyes felt fuzzy as soon as he stepped out of it. Hal Cornish's warning rang in his ears.

Nina turned on a small lamp in the shed, the kind that took time to achieve full illumination. She put the glasses in the big plastic tub she'd converted into a sink, with a garden hose in the corner, and started running the water while Orville watched the room come to light. "So, uh, I don't know exactly where to begin." He turned now to face Nina, but the sink stood unoccupied. Watching the water run out of the hose, wasteful and likely expensive, a thought flashed through Orville's head: Had he miscalculated something?

As if to answer, an arm took him by the neck and put him into a punishing chokehold. Orville tried to free himself but could not. There was something sinister to the hold his attacker had on him. It didn't just slow his breathing. It seemed to signal surrender throughout him. His arms went numb. His legs locked, capable only of keeping him upright. After a moment, he gave up struggling and puzzled over how someone could've snuck in behind them until his thoughts turned to syrup from lack of air.

He felt himself drifting to the ground. Just before he lost consciousness, the arm released him, leaving him there on his stomach. His arms were forced together. Something tightened around his ankles and then wrists. Then, he was rolled over. Nina, only Nina, knelt over him.

"I'm sorry, Orville," she said. She sounded underwater. "I want to believe you but I can't be too careful. I need to go back out now. Then we can finish talking."

She had a roll of duct tape in her hand. After she sealed his mouth, she rolled his head to one side, then the other, folding back each ear. Orville didn't know what she might be looking for. Whatever it was, she didn't seem satisfied.

23

ALL THE WAY TO THE BANK

WITH HIS arms and legs in zip ties, Orville had snaked his way across the floor of the shed to the door, but Nina had locked it. He pressed his face to the small opening between the doors and the ground and tried to scream, but achieved no significant volume through the duct tape. His throat grew sore and he eventually gave up.

Nina came back some hours later, closing time. When she opened the door, Orville tried to wriggle out. Nina sighed and pulled him back in by his legs. She sat him up against the far wall and then retrieved something from a cupboard in the corner. She knelt down to show him what she had: a pair of pliers.

"I don't know what I'm going to use these for," she said. "I hope I don't have to use them at all. But trust me when I say this: there are things I can do with these that go beyond your wildest nightmares. So when I take off the tape, you're going to calmly answer my questions. No screaming, no spitting. I just need some information. Okay?"

Orville leaned away from her as she reached and tore the duct tape off.

"Shit!" Orville said.

Nina tapped her pliers against her empty palm. "That was close to a scream."

"It hurt," Orville said. "What the fuck, Nina?"

"It hurts less that way," Nina said.

"No, I mean what the fuck is going on here? What did I do? Who are you?"

Nina gave him a frustrated look. "Orville, you're raising your voice."

"Sorry," Orville whispered, and immediately felt ashamed for both his obedience and feeling the need to apologize.

"Anyway, like I said, we're going to start with you. Let's get it all out, okay? I want to know everything. You mentioned a visitor?" Nina pointed the pliers at him, indicating it was Orville's turn to speak.

"A guy named Hal Cornish," Orville whispered. He refused to meet Nina's eyes. They were too calm. "He's some radio asshole. For Bernard's station. He came to my camper because he wanted me to read ads on the air. I told him no, and they brought a damn imposter to take my place."

Nina stiffened now. "How come you didn't just call?"

"They shut the phone bank down," Orville said.

"Who did? The radio station?"

"Yeah," Orville said. "I mean, I guess. They sent a company. I talked to the guy as he was doing it. He didn't mention the radio station, but as soon as it's shut down, there's a guy talking as me on the radio."

"What was the company called? That shut down the phone bank?"

Orville looked at her now, confused. "Uh, Starlight, I think."

"And how do you know that?"

"It's in the logs, and on the sign."

"There's a sign?" Nina said, her eyes widening. This was not the piece of information Orville expected would excite her.

"Yeah," he said, "on the fence around the phone bank."

Nina reached out with the pliers and took hold of the zip tie around Orville's ankles. With a quick twist, she snapped it. Orville struggled to his feet as Nina replaced the pliers in the cupboard, exchanging them for a small pistol. She held it at her side.

"What about my wrists?" Orville said.

Nina shook her head. "First, let's go take a look."

❧

RIDING HIS bike to the phone bank after a day of work, Orville felt as though he could blink and be there. Now, on foot, in the middle of the night, his hands still zip-tied behind his back while Nina, with a pistol in hand, trailed him fifty-some-odd feet behind—"To be safe" was all she said by way of explanation, though Orville suspected his own safety had nothing to do with it—it felt as though days had passed by the time the phone was in their sights.

When they finally arrived, Nina pointed her flashlight to a place on the ground. "Lie down," she said, "on your back."

"I don't know what you think I'm up to here," Orville began to say.

"Orville, just do it." She sounded, as she had in the shed, calm. If anything, her voice lilted with mild exasperation, like she was speaking to an unruly patron rather than a hostage.

Orville got to the ground, which, without the use of his hands, basically meant falling over. From there, he watched Nina walk to the fence and inspect the sign. Her flashlight tracked across the letters, but came to a stop at the *i*. This seemed to be all she needed to see. In an instant, she was at his side, rolling him over onto his stomach.

"Nina, please," Orville said, but then he felt his hands come free. He quickly rolled over, sat up, and massaged his wrists.

Nina stood over him and flipped her pocketknife closed. She'd tucked the pistol into the back of her pants. "I imagine if I just told you to forget about this without any explanation, you wouldn't like that?"

"Not exactly," Orville said. "But there's a lot I haven't liked about tonight, to be honest, and you're the one with the gun."

"I needed to know," she said. The sky was just beginning

to lighten. Nina motioned for Orville to follow her, then began to make her way back to the fence. "Let me show you something." It surprised Orville that, after all that had happened tonight, she would turn her back on him with apparently zero fear he might rush her from behind. It was almost insulting, but Orville's curiosity outflanked his pride.

Nina pointed her flashlight at the sign on the fence, again settling on the *i*. "Do you see that? How it's slanted, just slightly?" With her free hand, she traced the *i*'s stem. Orville hadn't noticed it before, or didn't think it was anything worth noticing. "All the other letters are straight up and down, but not the *i*."

"I don't get it," Orville said. "You brought me out here to talk italics?"

"It's not in italics. It's a tiny microphone," Nina said. "Like this one." Now she turned the flashlight to the side of her face. With her free hand, she pulled her ear forward. The light illuminated a small tattoo on the lobe, an identical *i* to the one on the sign.

"What does it mean?" Orville asked.

"It's bravado," Nina said. "They love this sort of stuff. Hiding in plain sight. It's not that they want to get caught, exactly. It's more like they want something obvious to point to if they do; something to say, 'You should've known.' Theatrics. They get no credit for what they do. Their egos need to find some release."

"No credit?" Orville pointed to the sign. "Then what's that?"

Nina shook her head. "It's not them. It's a dummy company. A big job might require four or five just like this one. But it's always there, their little symbol. You said you met the guy who shut down the phones, right? Did he talk funny in any way?"

"Yeah, actually," Orville said. He looked past the sign, to the phone the man had been working on. "His voice was real monotonous. Wouldn't stop saying what he did and didn't have to do, how he went above and beyond."

"That's another sign," Nina said. "When they set up these companies, they do it for two reasons. First, because sometimes they need to do something beyond voice work for a job. In this case, they needed to shut down the phones. It would be too dangerous to do that themselves, so they make a fake company that seems real enough and they contract out work to people who think everything is good and aboveboard."

"So he thinks this is all legitimate," Orville said. He leaned up against the fence, willing the man to reappear so he could hear all of this, know he'd been duped.

"For now," Nina replied. "They might let him behind the curtain, if they have some other use for him. For now, he thinks he's just a phone guy. But he's more than that, really. That's the second reason they set up these companies: for inspiration. His gear, his work vehicle—they're listening always, then imitating, in case the way he talks comes in handy. They might need one of his vocal tics for a client someday. That's something they always say: 'You never know when a voice will come in handy.'"

Had Orville nodded off briefly? Had he fallen asleep standing up and missed the most crucial piece of information? "Who the hell are we talking about?" he said.

Nina took a deep breath. "They have no official name beyond the symbol, but those who know about them call them the Vocalist Cartel."

"And they're impersonators?"

"They're voice actors without morals. They're willing to do anything for a price."

"Even imitate a man trying to call his brother who's trapped some indeterminate distance under the rubble of the Heap, just for a cut of some radio station's ad revenue?"

Nina nodded. "Yes, and much more than that too."

"And you've got their symbol on your ear."

"I used to be one of them," Nina said. "I left. I made a

mistake, one they couldn't forgive, and I fled. I've been wondering if they would find me and open my throat. But if that's what this was about, they wouldn't flaunt it, not like this. Still, it's enough to warrant some caution." She tapped her pistol, as if it stood for all they'd been through that night.

Orville took a moment to consider the oddness of the phrase: "Open my throat." It sounded almost poetic, and yet Nina had spoken with no flourish.

Eventually, he asked the only question that remained: "So what do I do?"

"You go to Hal Cornish and you accept his deal. It's the only way out of this."

"No." Orville tried to control himself, but his voice cracked with frustration. "That's not an option. I won't comply with these people. It's not right what they're doing to me. Getting some guy to be me, some guy who could be halfway across the world for all I know."

The sun was beginning to rise, and in the low light Orville could see Nina clench her eyes shut for a moment, as if he was giving her a headache. "You don't understand. This man they've got imitating you? He can't just be anywhere. They care deeply about their craft. They want to get things right: the right climate, the right level of physical activity. They believe the vocal cords register it all. He'll be close, and he'll be doing exactly what you're doing. You have to be careful. You want to end this as quickly as possible. For you. And for me. That's why I'm telling you this. Because if they find me, they'll kill me." She waited for this to sink in. "You'll do the right thing, Orville? Promise me you'll do the right thing."

"Yeah, of course," Orville said. But his mind was suddenly elsewhere: miles down the road, heading back toward the casino.

24

SOME TIME TO THINK

LYDIA WAITED outside Orville's camper, resolute to finally call him out on his mopey bullshit. Or not exactly. She would approach the subject with more delicacy than that. She had her whole speech planned—how she respected what he was doing here, how she could never understand what it was like to dig when you wondered if each shovel-load might uncover your long-buried brother, and how because of that, maybe, just maybe, he should consider taking a few days off. She would appeal to his ego, tell him he worked harder than most other Dig Hands, especially if one factored in the energy it took for him to balance the personal baggage—no, better word there: personal *connection*—with the strenuous physical labor of rubble-moving, a labor best performed with a clear mind, which Orville, reasonably, could not have.

She'd begun to put it together the night before, after her anger subsided. "Is this real?" she'd said to Hans as the crowd at The Bars began to thin out, Orville nowhere to be seen. "It's going to be like this now? Is this really all it takes to set him off?" Hans appeared to almost cower at her words, mumbling, "Maybe he went to sleep." It had gotten to Hans, Lydia could tell. And that was it: that was the sign that however one wanted to diagnose Orville's mood lately, it had gone from benign to malignant and would need to be treated using more than an eye roll.

She made her plan under the pretext that Orville's outlook

could be salvaged, that he might, at some point, be as lively
and warm with them, his friends, as he apparently was when
he spoke to Bernard. She didn't want to think about moving
forward in a different direction if Orville remained moored in
his sourpussery—for example, a Reorganization of Dig Group
Request (Lydia knew all the processes)—so instead, she'd
played out this encounter in her head close to fifty times last
night before she fell asleep, and another ten times this morning on her walk over. Not one of those times did she consider
that Orville might approach from any direction other than out
of his camper, and yet when Lydia paused outside his door at
seven in the morning and glanced around, she spotted him
ambling up from the path around the Heap. He saw her and
waved happily, and in spite of herself, she waved back in much
the same way. Lydia felt her resolve weakening suddenly. As
he approached, all her convictions were overridden one by one
by the all-consuming force of a single question: *Where did you
just come from, Orville?*

"Morning," Orville said when he reached her. "I'm glad
you're here. I was going to come find you." His voice, like
his wave, seemed almost cheerful. Sure, he could be faking
it, but faking it would entail a knowledge of there being a
need to fake it—that even if he felt just as glum as before, he
understood the impact of that glumness on others enough to
fabricate its opposite.

"We were worried about you last night," Lydia said.

Orville nodded. "I'm sorry. I needed to go for a walk."

"Have you been walking all this time?" Lydia said. "An
eight-hour walk?"

"More or less." Orville cleared his throat. "Look, Lydia,
I'm sure you've noticed that I've been dealing with some stuff.
I know I've been tough to be around lately. But please, believe
me when I say I'm finally getting a hold of myself. Things are
getting, well, not better, necessarily, but clearer."

"That's . . . good," Lydia stammered.

"It is," Orville said. "But even so, I think I need some time, a few days away from the Dig. Some time to think, you know? Will you and Hans be okay without me?"

Lydia blinked and half expected, when she opened her eyes, to be back in her camper, having just had one of those annoying good dreams where your day gets off to such a perfect start that waking up feels like a setback. She didn't exactly know how to process this. On the one hand, he had not only expressed cognizance of his recent insufferableness but also appeared to be taking steps to curtail it, steps which, on the other hand, she had planned to pitch to him in an arduous and emotionally distraught negotiation process that she'd imagined would take the better part of the morning. His seemingly psychic compliance, along with his rehearsed tone—a tone she had worried she herself would have—left her feeling an amalgam of relief and suspicion.

"That sounds like a good idea," Lydia said.

"Just one thing: I'd like to use the apartment in the Heap, if that's okay." He pointed over her shoulder at his camper. "Could get pretty hot, being stuck in there all day. Would you mind, you know, keeping out?"

"Of course," Lydia said. "I'll talk to Hans. And boss and the doctor too." She could hear her own eagerness. She had come here to take action, and now she snatched up this chance at it. "We want what's best for you."

Orville nodded. There was a distance to his manners. "How about you?" he said. "I feel like it's been a while since we really talked."

"The Committee's awful," Lydia said. "Gil's in over his head with the Thisbee visit but doesn't seem to realize it. I can't get through to him." Once again, Lydia's frustrations could not resist invitation into the world. "Sorry. I know I'm just retreading the same old stuff."

"And the tour is?"

"Tomorrow," Lydia said. She braced herself for some

acknowledgment of the conversation that seemed to have started all this, maybe even an apology.

Orville only nodded. "I was thinking, on my walk back—"

"Back from where?"

"Just around," Orville said, absently rubbing his wrists. "Anyway, I was thinking about when I moved out here. Packing. Did you own a house?"

"I rented," Lydia said. She didn't understand what the question had to do with anything.

"Me too. Had to pack everything up, put it in a storage locker. Moving is basically cleaning, isn't it? And yet, every step of the way, stuff seems to get messier. Your furniture gets pushed out of the way to make way for your other furniture. You uncover fields of dust you never knew existed. It's only when you take that last box out that the place actually looks clean."

"Are you saying you're moving?" Lydia asked.

"I'm saying the process doesn't always makes sense. If I said, 'There are pots and pans all over the floor,' you wouldn't think, 'Oh, that sounds like a clean house.' But that's just what it takes sometimes. You have to make things messy to really clean them up. You have to do things that seem wrong, but they're the right things in the end."

Camper doors opened around them, people getting up and getting ready for the day. Lydia stepped closer to Orville, to speak lower. "Is this about what you need to do or what I need to do?"

Orville looked at her for a long moment. "I already told you," he said at last. "I just need some time to think. But I could use a nap before I get to that. Thanks for stopping by, Lydia. Good luck with the Dig and the Committee."

"The Committee is taking a week-long break after the tour," Lydia said. "I'll see you before the next meeting, right?"

But Orville had already walked up the couple of stairs to his camper and shut the door behind him.

25

LARGE COVETED OBJECT

MOVING RENTALS

THE LARGE Coveted Object Moving Rentals building was one of the nicer ones in all of CamperTown: a prefab structure that looked like a car dealership at the far end of the Ass, allowing them to store their vehicles in a "lot" that was really just a section of flat desert. And they needed the room too, because they always had their full fleet. As far as Orville knew, nobody'd ever found a large enough, intact enough, and coveted enough object to justify renting one. Clearly they hoped for more. The benches of the waiting area to Orville's left, arranged like a living room around a coffee station, suggested that whatever entrepreneur had established the place had imagined there would come a time when large coveted objects ran so thick that people would be forced to take a number.

Orville left his shovel propped next to the door and made his way to the counter. He'd dug up a clump of sand in front of his camper before coming and rubbed it across his clothes. He needed to look like he'd been working to rent an object mover, and also for his walk through CamperTown. He didn't want to evoke any suspicion. But he'd seen nobody, save for a few Displaced Travelers who couldn't see him. They'd been sitting in the open-air communal living room—an empty lot among the campers housing a congregation of furniture pulled from the Heap, intact but too torn to get any money in the Sale—and they'd moved from couch to couch, pairs of them gathering together under blankets with a flashlight. Orville thought perhaps they were engaging in something profane, but when he listened all he heard was casual conversation.

At the Large Coveted Object Moving Rentals building, the radio was on. "There's really no room," Bernard said.

"I'm just saying," a woman said, "you really should try to stand up. To make sure your knees still work."

An old man sat on a stool a few feet back from the counter reading a magazine. Behind him, a sign advertised three free tie-down ropes in each truck, "For a limited time only." Orville stood waiting to be noticed, forcing himself to appear patient. He felt invigorated. The nap he'd taken had been short but satisfying, as deep as it was brief. Anticipation, usually a sleep deterrent, had not hampered his rest.

But the old man did not look up from his magazine, even when Orville cleared his throat. It angered him, but he suppressed the feeling. No use winding himself up now and getting tired out again. He would need his anger later.

A younger man emerged from a back room with a clipboard. He looked first at Orville, then at the old man, then back at Orville, and sighed. "Welcome to Large Coveted Object Moving Rentals, for all the big things in life," the young man said, putting his clipboard down on the counter.

"You sound like an answering machine," the old man mumbled.

The young man turned to him. "You know, Ed, that's an astute observation, because I feel like an answering machine, coming out here to pick up the calls you missed."

"Don't raise your voice at me," the old man said. "It's my birthday today, I'll have you know."

"If you don't want to work on your birthday, then take it the fuck off," the young man said. He turned back to Orville.

"I apologize, sir, for my coworker's behavior. Now, what can I help you with today?"

"I just need a vehicle," Orville said. "To move a large object. A large coveted object."

The young man smiled. "Well, you've come to the right place. Would you mind describing the object?"

Orville felt a rush of panic. He scratched at the straps of his backpack. It shifted easily on his back, its only contents a bottle of water, a long tube sock, and a business card. "What do you mean, 'describe'?"

"We have to ask for measurements," the young man said, "to ensure our movers are big enough for the job."

"Oh, right," Orville stuttered. "It's about six feet long lying down, and about this wide." He indicated the width of his shoulders.

The old man looked up. "Wait, is it a person?"

"You'll need to call the doctor if it's a dead," the young man said.

"It's not a dead," Orville said.

"Is he alive?" the old man asked.

"That's Survivor Services. They need to sound the siren." The young man tried to sound administrative, but Orville heard the excitement in his voice.

"It's not a person."

The old man was incredulous. "What's the size and shape of a person but not a person?"

"Could be a sarcophagus," the other said.

The old man scoffed. "A sarcophagus?"

"Tons of rich people lived in the Vert," the young man said. "Rich people have all sorts of fucked-up shit." He glanced at Orville. "Sorry, sir."

"Does it look like Cairo out there to you?" said the old man.

"Well, let's see: a city in the desert, in the shadow of a massive ruin. Yeah, you know what, it actually does look a little like Cairo around here."

The old man extended his index finger, trying to find a retort. The young man, drained of all cordiality, didn't wait. He turned to Orville. "So, what is it? What are you moving?"

"You're exactly right," Orville said. "It's a sarcophagus." He pointed to the poster on the wall. "Tell me about these tie-downs."

26

MAKING MESSES

LYDIA COULD imagine no one less likely or qualified to give a pep talk than Orville. And it really wasn't a pep talk. It was some stoic yet rambling monologue about "fields of dust" and "pots and pans" and about how things get messier just before they get clean. It really sounded like a metaphor for his own situation, a rundown of the murky emotional work into which he would be wading while holed up by himself in the buried apartment.

To Lydia, it was a puzzle, and she couldn't keep her mind off of it: not on her bike ride to boss's trailer or to the hospital to see the doctor (they each had approved Orville's time-off request as well as his demand to use the apartment, citing concern for his mental well-being, though Lydia knew it had more to do with the place's booze reserves being depleted), and not during the morning dig with Hans.

By the time they broke for lunch she was convinced Orville had meant the little speech for her, whether he realized it or not. It all aligned perfectly. Her previous offer to drag away the old camper was an offer to tidy things up. But Gil didn't think things needed tidying up. Or maybe he did, somewhere deep down, but an honest assessment of the facts and the voicing thereof was too much for someone so allergic to any potential conflict. Gil couldn't accept her help because to do so would be to admit his negligence, to stare in the face his inability to clean up even the most minor of messes. So he chose to pretend there was no mess.

Therefore, what Lydia needed to do was what Orville intimated: make it so the mess could not be overlooked. She didn't need to drag the camper farther out into the desert. She needed to drag it closer. Then, with it impossible to ignore (due to both proximity and timing, there being only an afternoon and a night separating them from Thisbee's visit), she would offer her help once again and receive her reward. It would be obvious, of course, that she was the one behind its encroachment, but that just made it better: it would prove to Gil how far she was willing to go to make her point, and thus how dangerous it would be to ignore her.

"Lydia?" Hans said.

"Huh?" Lydia held the balled-up tin foil from her sandwich. Lost in thought, she'd squeezed it into a compact shining nugget. Hans gently opened her hand and took it from her, then pitched it, with his, over his shoulder. The concept of littering didn't really exist on the Heap.

"I asked you how Orville was this morning," Hans said.

"Oh, great, really great," Lydia mumbled. "I mean, as great as you can imagine, given the circumstances, you know."

Hans gave her a suspicious look. "Are you okay?"

"Of course," Lydia said. "Or, you know, I'm fine. I'm doing fine. But I was just thinking, since you brought it up, since you brought up if I'm okay or not, how a little bit of private time with my thoughts—how if we *all* took a little private time with our thoughts—like Orville is taking, I think that would be helpful. Know what I mean?"

"Sort of," Hans said.

Lydia couldn't stand it. Thisbee would be here in less than twenty-four hours. If she wanted onto the tour, it was now or never.

"I'm taking the rest of the day off, Hans," she said. "That's what I'm saying. To gather my thoughts."

27

FROM THE LATER YEARS:

DISPUTES

Surprisingly, our proximity to one another did not drive us into endless disputes or arguments. Or, to look at it differently, perhaps it was an acute awareness of our proximity to each other that kept us from endless disputes and arguments. We so feared the simple-argument-gone-nuclear that we policed our neighbors with a relentlessness bordering on obsession.

This was clearest in how we treated the businesses local to our individual floors. Those on the lower levels experienced an ever-growing number of commercial spaces as the base expanded, which should have inspired a healthy sense of competition. But even the widest floors occupied far less space than a traditional city's smallest neighborhood. Within such confines, we reasoned, no amount of competition could be "healthy." Two coffee shops operating within the same thousand square feet might spark a coffee war that could tear the local community apart, with each resident choosing sides and interpreting the choices of others as something indicative of more than just roast preference.

As a solution to this, we favored whichever business of a certain type was there first. This was often to our own detriment, and to the benefit of the business owners, as maintaining a customer base required simply being "the original" rather than creating a superior product. The business owners

themselves pushed this further by lobbying for the Order Or-
dinance, a rule within the Vert that required each business to
post, on its entrance, its place in the floor's chronology. So, the
initial coffee shop would be labeled #1 and each subsequently
founded coffee shop would be labeled #2, #3, etc. New busi-
nesses tried to circumvent this ordinance with clever label-
ing. Rather than a coffee shop or a bakery, they might call
themselves a "confectionery" with "hot beverages to comple-
ment the product." And if they had better baked goods than
the bakery, or better coffee than the coffee shop, we would, as
residents of the floor, pretend to order these items as an af-
terthought so as not to appear lacking in loyalty. The cashier
might say, "Would you like a cup of coffee with that?" And
we might, after looking over our shoulder, respond as if this
had just occurred to us: "Yes, actually. You better add one on.
Because I don't have time for another stop this morning."

What we feared even more than ill will ignited by pref-
erence for one shop or restaurant over another were interper-
sonal conflicts. Two inner-unit neighbors in different time zones
might disagree about appropriate dinner party volume, or an
outer-unit resident might take issue with a species of flower-
ing vine climbing from another deck onto his. But before three
heated words could be exchanged, the surrounding community
members would fall upon them with aggressive reasoning and
mediation. These interventions were often successful, though
not in the way the interveners might hope. If anything, they
would draw the parties involved in the initial dispute closer
together. "It was a simple argument," they would say to each
other. "There was no need for everyone to butt in like that." And
just like that, their once-mild animosity might become a strong
alliance against the others around them.

28

A BETTER SHOVEL

IT HAD been some time since Orville had piloted a vehicle bigger than a bicycle. Despite spending his days scaling a towering mound of rubble, he felt as though he sat impossibly high up behind the wheel of the object mover. Then there was the issue of the power steering. The men had warned him not to take corners too hard, which was fine—Orville was going slow, giving himself time to closely survey the landscape so his destination wouldn't sneak up on him—but he really did have to crank the wheel whenever he rounded even the mildest bend in the road.

In the passenger seat: his backpack and his shovel. He drove widely around CamperTown in the desert to avoid the gate, only merging onto Access Avenue two miles out. Orville's mind raced, but he rerouted all his energy to his eyes. Soon enough, he saw the moguls. Then, finally, he saw the fan.

Orville at first mistook him for a cactus. Only as he passed did he see the outline of a head, arms, and a torso, visible from the waist up in his hole. He was too far out in the desert for Orville to see clearly. He knew from his trip to the casino that traffic tended to be light, but not so altogether absent that the mover would garner the man's attention. Between the deliveries, the rubble removal trucks, and the shuttle, he'd likely grown accustomed to the Heap's comings and goings.

When the blur of the morning's wavy hot air at last erased the man from his rearview, Orville pulled the object mover onto the side of the road and killed the engine. He put on his backpack, got his shovel, hopped out, and started to walk. This was difficult, and not because of the heat. Orville knew the heat by now. The hard part was to keep himself from taking off in a sprint. He stood on the precipice of revenge. He needed to be measured.

Once the man came back into sight as a speck on the horizon, Orville adjusted the angle of his approach so that he might be hidden behind the mound of cast-off dirt. It was risky. If the man had seen him, he could potentially hide and wait for Orville to arrive. About fifty feet away, though, when Orville stopped, he heard what he wanted to hear: the man's heavy breath, the crunch of his shovel making contact with sand, and the soft rain-like patter as the load was pitched over his shoulder onto the pile. He hadn't stopped digging.

Next to the hole lay a bike. For some reason, this made Orville tighten his grip on his own shovel. He knew, had known all morning, that he was about to meet the man who'd assumed his identity. And yet, this detail—that he rode a bike to his false dig site—made the perversity of it all suddenly real. This was not a man digging in the desert for no reason. This was a man digging in the desert so that he could better deprive Orville of his most important role: that of Bernard's brother.

Rage bloomed in him, but he channeled it into slow, calculated footsteps. He crouched just a bit more with each step forward so that the pile would obscure him. When at last he reached it, he got down on his haunches, closed his eyes, and counted to three. Then, he sprang to his feet and walked boldly out.

"Afternoon," he said loudly.

The man turned and squinted up at him. He was strange looking, his face wide, his eyes close together. He wore overalls, just like Orville did. He pulled his headphones off and reached into a pocket to pause his tape player. Orville thought that maybe he heard the tinny miniature of his own voice in the split second before the sound cut out.

"Good day," the man said. "Can I help you with something?"

When he spoke, his voice came out so high-pitched and nasal that it threw Orville off for a moment. He felt pulled in two directions, insulted that his own voice could be on the same register as this one, so dweeby and unbecoming, and suddenly concerned that maybe he'd been wrong. He'd expected a confrontation as soon as he spoke, but the man seemed only pleasantly surprised to have company.

Orville took a step forward. "I thought I could help you with something, actually."

"Oh, thank you," the man said, "but I don't need any help."

"At least let me give you my shovel," Orville said.

The man patted the handle of his own shovel. "This one suits me fine."

Orville felt his resolve fading. "But this is a true ConductionSens. And beyond that, it's mine. Doesn't that make it better?"

The man, still smiling, cocked his head, confused. "Pardon?"

"Because you want to be me. Because you are me. On the radio."

He couldn't keep the embarrassment from his voice, resolved to be wrong about this whole thing before he even finished what he had to say. So when the man threw down his shovel and reached into his overalls, Orville half wondered if he'd been bitten by something. Then he saw the sun glint off a silver handle. Without thinking, Orville leaped into the hole, bringing his shovel down onto the man's head just as he loosed the revolver. It flew from his hand and landed next to him as he face-planted in the sand. Orville scurried to grab it.

The impersonator groaned as Orville rolled him over, but he didn't resist. He was too disoriented from the blow. Orville put the barrel to the man's head as a safety precaution, in case he was faking it, but didn't pull the trigger. He wasn't going to kill him, not here. He needed to move him. But first, he had to be sure. Orville pulled back the man's ear. No flashlight required. The high noon sun illuminated the tattoo without any trouble.

THE BIBLE PEOPLE

THE MOST obvious course of action was to rent an object mover under an assumed name and use it to haul the burned-out trailer closer to CamperTown, but when Lydia got to the rental building she found that, despite their having ten movers, only one of them was operational.

"I'll take that one, then," Lydia said.

"Sorry," said the young man behind the counter. "It's taken."

Lydia suspected they might be lying to get out of work and asked what anyone could possibly have found that would warrant a mover.

An old man appeared from a back room. "You all talking about the coffin?"

"Sarcophagus," said the young man.

"It's a coffin," the old man said. "That's what a sarcophagus is."

There followed an extended conversation about Egyptology, under which ran such a genuine current of giddiness that Lydia concluded that if this was an act, it was a very good one. When they started out-and-out screaming at each other, she decided to leave.

In the Assistance Sector, she went to the café and sat down at the counter. She didn't need coffee, not in this sun, but the seats were for customers only and the young man working there would not budge on the rules. The café was a good vantage point. From here, she could survey the whole sector.

Across the street was the shuttle station. The shuttle was locked up in a makeshift garage a quarter mile down the road. Breaking, entering, and carjacking seemed a bit too showy, though. She wanted to make a mess for Gil and Gil alone.

Farther down the path was the hospital. The doctor had a station wagon to use as an ambulance in the case that someone needed medical attention that he couldn't attend to himself. But one day he'd made a drunken show of taking the keys and throwing them into the Heap, proof, he seemed to think, that there were no procedures he could not handle himself. So that was a nonstarter.

She turned, looking for something else that might inspire her, and her eyes met Terrance's. The path was mostly empty aside from him, but when he froze, as if Lydia had caught him doing something terrible, two assistance workers walking a few steps behind nearly ran into him.

He made his way to the café and sat down next to Lydia. "Oh, hey."

His voice was thick with strange guilt. Maybe it had something to do with the night before, Lydia thought, but it seemed to run deeper than that. He appeared uncomfortable to even be sitting there with her and looked around the café suspiciously. He ordered a coffee and they sat quietly. Lydia couldn't tell why exactly he'd even sat down. It wasn't like she'd beckoned him over. Talking to Terrance was never something she really wanted to do, but especially not now, while she had things to figure out.

Still, it would be rude to just get up and walk away, so without ceasing to search her surroundings for a vehicle she might be able to use, she said, "You're off early."

Terrance went rigid. "No!" he said. "I mean, yes, I'm off the Heap early, but I completed my work. I mean, I was going to go back to my camper, but only for a moment. Then, I was going to ride out to . . . well, I guess, with what happened last night, I just thought I should, maybe, I don't know. It doesn't matter. Anyway, my dig partners . . ." He trailed off.

"Say no more," Lydia said. She meant it literally, not that she understood what he was trying to say, only that she wanted him to stop talking. But Terrance wasn't done.

"Do you ever get the feeling around this place," he said, "that nobody wants to be here?"

Lydia turned to him now. "Does this have anything to do with Orville?"

Terrance's eyes went wide. He looked down at the mug as if it were something he'd been caught stealing. "No! Not at all! If anything, it's everyone else."

"It's not exactly glamorous, what we do, Terrance. We were brought here by a tragedy."

"That's not what I mean. I probably said it wrong. It's as if a lot of these people here, they don't care? Like, it's not just that they don't want to work. It's something deeper, like they—" He glanced over at the barista. Though the young man clearly wasn't paying any attention to them, Terrance spoke lower. "Like they have no impulse to do almost anything. They act like they're working, they talk like they're working, but that's all that they do."

Lydia didn't want to admit it, but she immediately thought of Hans. "Motivation can be hard for some people," she said, taking a contemplative sip of coffee.

Terrance nodded. "Or maybe I'm just on the wrong dig team." He was unsatisfied, Lydia could tell, but he didn't say more. It was true what he said. When Lydia'd first arrived, people had seemed a lot more motivated. The Bars had buzzed with a contagious hope. Dig Hands left CamperTown each morning in a mass exodus on their bikes, shouting affirmations as members broke free of the group at their respective dig spots, which were chosen with care based on what needed most attention. And it wasn't uncommon on sort days for a whole other dig team to show up at your station, ready to pitch in and help because they'd already finished with theirs. But when the task proved so grueling and slow—and the rewards too fleeting—many of them gave up and moved on to other causes with more immediate results. That left a small number of hypermotivated selfless workers, but most of them were the opposite. They were comfortable. They had their campers and their stipends. It wasn't a great life, but it was easier than leaving and finding something else to do.

"You just went through orientation," Lydia said to Terrance, "so you probably know some of the logistics of this place better than I do. If I needed something that could do some towing, where would I go? Large Coveted Object Moving Rentals is off the table."

It seemed to relieve Terrance to have something else to think about. He stared straight ahead with intense focus for some time. "That's tough, without the movers. Maybe wait for when the rubble removal trucks come and ask for their help? Aside from that, it's not really from orientation, but maybe I'd ask the Bible people? Although, with those folks, I don't know if it's worth it."

"The Bible people?"

"I mean, they're some kind of religious, right?" he said. "You know the ones. They're real strange. I found a doorknob the other day. It looked kind of cool, like glass or crystal or something, so I took it with me. Well, one of these people was out for a walk. She sees it in my basket from about fifty feet away somehow, flags me down, and talks to me for near forty minutes about doorways, and the way the doors to her condo used to open. They live on those RVs, right? Those things can tow, I think."

A bolt shot through Lydia. The Displaced Travelers. Her coffee had cooled and she gulped it down as quickly as she could. "Terrance, thank you," she said. Before he could ask her why she was so excited, Lydia was on her bike and halfway across CamperTown.

30

THE PLAN PROCEEDS

THE NEXT steps of Orville's plan proceeded with haste. He loaded his impersonator into the object mover and drove to the casino. In the parking lot, he checked the man's pockets and found the keycard to his room. It was still in the paper sleeve with the room number on it. Orville went there and put in a call to Hal Cornish.

His assistant answered. "Office of Hal Cornish, how may I help you?"

"Tell Hal I'm taking back my rightful place," Orville said. "If he doesn't want any more dead air, he knows where to find me."

With phone access and no competition, he considered waiting until the end of the workday so he could give Bernard a call, but he didn't trust himself. He might break down, tell Bernard what was going on, and who knows what Sundial Media would do then. Best to drive back to the Heap and be ready for when they showed up. Returning to the object mover, he found the impersonator was just regaining consciousness. He looked sweaty from being shut inside with the windows closed. Orville didn't feel much pity.

To his credit, the man didn't squirm or make any noise on the drive. He seemed ready for this, which didn't exactly set Orville at ease, but at least made for a quiet ride. On the radio, Bernard's breath was only audible over the roar of the engine with the volume turned all the way up. "You missed your call," Orville said. The impersonator stared out the windshield but didn't appear to be taking in the scenery.

Back at the Heap, the Dig Hands had already signed off for the day, so Orville had no problem loading him into the apartment unnoticed. The man was still remarkably patient and compliant, even as Orville used the additional tie-down ropes to tie him to a wooden chair from the kitchen table that he'd dragged into the bathroom.

Orville didn't have any questions planned. This wasn't an interrogation. It was a kidnapping. Still, he felt weird not asking anything, so he untied the tube sock he'd used as a gag. "What do you have to say for yourself?"

"Not much, to be honest," the man said in Orville's voice. "You know me. I'm not the talkative type."

Orville laughed. As if that would get to him. "Nobody can hear you down here. You don't need to talk like that anymore."

The man sighed. "That's good to hear, because I much prefer talking like this." He spoke in Bernard's voice now, and Orville didn't find that funny at all. It wasn't even a perfect impression: a little too nasal, a little too thin, the voice he'd spoken with in the desert—*his* voice, Orville imagined— creeping in around the edges. On the other hand, Orville was the closest thing to an expert on Bernard's voice there was, and it still managed to bug him. Without saying another word, he retied the gag. The man didn't protest.

Orville climbed out onto the Heap and found a large sheet of what appeared to be Plexiglas. It took some effort to yank out from where it was lodged, but he got it eventually and maneuvered it over the entrance. It could still be seen, but it would be harder for anyone to get in, and even harder to leave.

He drew some ire from the Large Coveted Object Moving Rentals guys, especially when he told them that the large coveted object he'd found turned out not to be a sarcophagus.

"What was it?" the older man asked.

"Just some rocks, actually," Orville said.

They looked at him oddly. "How'd you confuse a bunch of rocks for a sarcophagus?" the young man asked.

"Too tired, I guess," Orville said.

"Well, that's just great," said the old man. "I stay well after my shift on my goddamn birthday, and it turns out the guy can't see."

"I'm sorry," Orville mumbled, but the two of them were already turning the lights off and shutting the place down.

In his camper, Orville stashed Hal Cornish's card back in the love seat, really buried it down in the clothes. He took the mirror he had hung next to his bed and propped it up next to the window so that, lying on the floor, he could see when someone approached the door. Then there was nothing to do but wait. Orville got down on the ground. He rested the impersonator's revolver on his chest.

The carpeting beneath him was not plush, but it immediately seemed to soak up his energy. The adrenaline that had been fueling him through the day ran out. Orville fought to keep his eyes open, but he'd done so much, and slept so little.

31

DIFFERENT WALKS

THE DISPLACED Travelers' camp was quiet. None of the RVs were running, not even "the office." Lydia hadn't expected this. She stopped just inside the little courtyard. In the silence, it felt almost haunted and she jumped when she saw something move. It was just the man with the glasses and the mustache. He shifted in his seat at a table in the far corner.

"They're not here," he said. "They've been walking more recently."

Lydia didn't want to come back later. There would be unforeseeable obstacles that would certainly cost her time, and she wanted to get started sooner rather than later. But this man wasn't the man she wanted to deal with. She knew almost nothing about the others individually, but she understood them as a unit from reading *The Later Years*. This guy? He was barely one of them. He was the most mysterious member of the mysterious group. Yet he was here, so he was who she got.

Lydia took a seat at the table next to him. "You don't go with them?"

The man shook his head. "They only walk around the Heap. I've seen it already. I had a different relationship to home than the rest. I miss it, but not like they do. For me, the Vert was neither a building nor the people it contained. It was a feeling. So, I don't write with them, and I take my own walks."

"Why do you stay here, then?" Lydia asked.

The man shrugged. "I've been trying to figure that out myself." He gestured to the office. "The pages are in there. You can take them if you want. You're the only one who reads them."

"I'm actually here for something else," she said. "A favor. A pretty big one, actually."

The man didn't look at her. He cracked his knuckles slowly, one finger at a time with his thumbs.

"I'd like to borrow an RV," Lydia said, placing her arms at the end of the table and leaning forward in a position she hoped read as "poised to do business."

"Yes," the man said.

"Yes, I can?"

The man finished cracking his knuckles and removed a pack of cigarettes from his breast pocket. He shook one loose and lit it. "Yes, it is a big favor to ask."

Lydia focused deeply to suppress a rising wave of humility. "It's for some important business."

"On the Dig?"

"No."

It was dangerous, what she hoped to do. She'd felt comfortable enough lying to the Large Coveted Object Moving Rentals people—they were nobodies—but the Displaced Travelers were different. The more they integrated into the CamperTown community, the more she would need their support, if she ever did find herself in the position of power she sought. Because of this, she didn't want to turn them against her. She would not lie, but instead hoped to speak vaguely enough that they couldn't know what she had planned. All she needed were the right questions.

The man nodded. "So it's for the Committee, then?"

Lydia's humility transformed instantly to fear, as if spurred by some chemical reaction. "How do you know I'm on the Committee?"

"Like I said, I take my own walks." The man grinned

slightly to himself as he exhaled smoke. "I imagine you need an RV to do something for Peter Thisbee's visit. He'll be here tomorrow, right?"

"Yes," Lydia said. "I mean, yes, he'll be here tomorrow. Not that it's what I need the RV for. Although it is. Sort of."

"Will you be showing Peter around?"

"No."

The man's use of Thisbee's first name, as if the two of them were chummy, threw Lydia off her game, and so she allowed, against her will, the single word to betray her frustrations.

The man said, "You'd like to, though, and that's why you need an RV?"

"It's complicated," Lydia tried.

"No, I get it. You must really want to meet Peter," the man said. "Why?"

This was it, the moment Lydia had waited for, an opportunity to test her tag lines, but they twisted in her mind into nonsense. "I guess I've just never met someone like that," she sputtered. "Someone capable of the things he's capable of. A leader."

The man puffed smoke out of his nose, either snorting with ire or breathing a gunshot-quick sigh of satisfaction. Lydia couldn't tell which. She had the distinct feeling it was both at the same time.

"I can't lend you an RV." The man looked her in the eyes for the first time. "It wouldn't do you much good. Whatever you're doing, it seems to require delicacy, and an RV is anything but delicate."

Lydia only then relinquished her grip on the table. She must've looked just as crazy as she felt. She attempted to replicate the man's snort-sigh, but it came out all wrong.

"Do you need a tissue?" the man said, lowering his cigarette. "I can get you one from inside."

"No, I was just laughing," Lydia said. "At you. Telling me

what these things require when you don't even know what I'm planning to do."

"No, you're right, I don't know why you want an RV," the man said. "But I imagine it has something to do with subverting the power dynamic of the Committee for Better Life in CamperTown, in a bid for a place on the Thisbee tour. Am I close?"

Lydia's mouth opened but she couldn't speak.

"So I am." The man rested his elbows on the table and made his hands into a hammock for his chin. The lit end of the cigarette, which he held between his pinkie and his ring finger, nearly touched his nose. "Well, I can think of quite a few ways to achieve that, no RV required."

Lydia leaned forward again. Her voice came out in a desperate whisper, but she had no more time for playing it cool: "Like what?"

"I won't waste your time running through all the possibilities." He quickly untangled his hands, put out his cigarette directly onto the table, and stood. "Besides, I have some work of my own to attend to. I'm sure you'll figure out something. Good luck out there."

He straightened out his shirt and walked from the camp, leaving Lydia alone and confused.

FROM *THE LATER* YEARS:

VISITORS

There had been more visitors very early on, before the time change: tourists interested in seeing our way of life. Ironically, they saw very little. They asked about nearby hiking trails, about day trips, and we stared back at them blankly, or recommended a particularly clean section of stairwell. They left disappointed, confused about their decision to go on a vacation inside what amounted to a condominium joined with a shopping mall. Had they visited some years in, they would've experienced something truly unique. But they didn't. And they didn't return.

    Those tourists that did come later could be described, universally, as "the wrong kind of person." Mostly men, they'd heard of Los Verticalés as a place where it was always both day and night; therefore the bars never closed and certain activities that would seem obscene in the daylight happened at all hours. Perhaps they'd even heard of the sexual freedom of our parking garage. They came expecting a distinct kind of unhealthy experience. They stayed in hotels, but only a few of them ever admitted this. Most pretended to be one of us. We knew they were not, of course. There were tells. They expected the elevator door to be held for them, for example, and they in turn held the elevator door for others. We never did this, except for friends following closely behind us. The elevator banks were too crowded with those getting on, getting off, or just passing through. The successful boarding of an elevator was your responsibility and yours alone.

Beyond the giveaways there was just a sense. It was as if we could smell it, or see some aura of wonder and discomfort around them. This is why these tourists, too, often left disappointed, though in a way they could not articulate. They achieved what they came to achieve: they remained in a mostly sleepless state of inebriation for days at a time, perhaps pressed P with a part-ner whose name they would not remember, if they even knew it in the first place. But in the end, they had not infiltrated us, and they certainly had not become one of us. They wanted to experience a sort of freedom—from time, from sobriety, from monogamy—yet they had not anticipated our distance, had not expected to be kept inside a protective sleeve. They were not ready for us to ignore their attempts at conversation even when they stood inches from us in a hallway, the way in which we grimaced at their jokes, as if they spoke a poisonous language.

Still, these visitors, despite their questionable motives, at least understood how the Vert functioned. Far worse were the people from our past: our uncles, our cousins, our former friends. They had not seen us in so long and wanted to know how life was going in "the tower." They wanted to come spend some time with us, but we were always so busy with things: work, social functions, etc. It was never a good time. There eventually came the news that they'd bought tickets to the nearest airport. They couldn't wait. We told them to make sure they locked their rental car when they parked it in the garage, and, if possible, that they should opt for the extra insurance that covers dam-age done to the interior. Dangerous? they wanted to know. Not exactly dangerous, no, we told them.

In the outer units, visitors had an easy enough time, but in the inner units, they had to reckon with the time change. The visitors claimed they could handle it, that they had trav-eled before, but they underestimated how hard it is to take a trip within the country and then conform to a clock set perhaps twelve hours forward or backward.

Hence, the invention of the Los Verticalés flu.

Every explanation of it differed slightly: something about the recycled air, the UV screens, the building material—it all combined so that those new to our atmosphere essentially passed out within a few hours of arrival. We had all experienced it ourselves, we claimed. This was a lie. The Los Verticalés flu was a crushed-up sleeping pill sprinkled over dinner or into a cocktail. We'd sneak it to them at our assigned nighttime. They'd wake up the next "morning" groggy but on the correct schedule.

The regret, this time, was ours. We realized after every visitor that we would have preferred them to be disoriented and tired, asleep when we were awake and vice versa. Then maybe they wouldn't have talked to us about mowing, about highways, about weather, all the things we sought to escape.

33

ACTING ALONE

ORVILLE AWOKE on the floor with a start. A creaking noise had stirred him. He looked to the door, but it remained shut. He heard it again, from outside, and looked at the mirror he'd set up. Hal Cornish, in the same white linen suit, shifted awkwardly in one of the Adirondack chairs. Orville slowly got to his feet and, tucking the gun into the front pocket of his work overalls from the day before, made his way outside.

"Good morning, Mr. Anders," said Hal Cornish. He didn't even look up. He sipped from a paper coffee cup. His hands quaked. He was nervous.

"You get my message?" Orville asked.

"Why else would I be here?" Hal Cornish said.

Orville sat in the chair opposite his. Over Orville's camper, the sun was rising.

"Would you like to hear my demands?" Orville said.

"All in good time," Hal Cornish replied. "But this is very serious business, Mr. Anders, and we really do care about doing things the right way. Therefore, before we proceed, I just need some clarification. On the message you left, you said something about how you 'took your rightful job back.' Could you clarify?"

The question bugged Orville, but he reminded himself that he had the power here. "I mean I took your guy."

"Our guy," Hal Cornish repeated.

"The guy, the other me. I found him digging a hole out in the desert and I took him. And I've got him now. I'll give him back, but only if my demands are met."

"Yes, yes, of course," Hal Cornish said. He seemed to be sitting forward with his chest pushed out. If it was meant to be intimidating it wasn't working. "But just so I'm clear: you found the man impersonating you, and you took him hostage, correct?"

"That's right," Orville said.

"And you acted on your own," Hal Cornish said.

"That's right," Orville said. He scooted to the end of his chair. "What the hell aren't you understanding here, man?"

"And you didn't work with me or any other employee of Sundial Media."

Now Orville was confused. "Why would I work with you people?"

Hal Cornish stood. "Well, this has been an enlightening conversation, Mr. Anders. We've got a team working on this. I'll take this information back to them and see what they can do. We will be in touch as soon as possible."

Orville stood too. "What are you talking about? You haven't even heard what I want."

"I understand, but there is an order to these things."

Orville didn't care about procedure. He stepped up to Hal Cornish now and tried to grab a handful of the man's shirt, but his hand found something hard underneath.

"Mr. Anders, please!" Hal Cornish struggled to get out of Orville's grip for a moment, but went still when the revolver came out. "He's got a gun," he said, angling his chin down as if to speak to his stomach.

Orville opened a button on the man's shirt and drew it down, revealing the edge of a black box.

"What is this?"

"It's too late to destroy it," Hal Cornish said. "They're listening and they've already heard everything."

Orville felt fear intruding upon his confusion. "You bring the cops out here?"

Hal Cornish laughed a little. "No, not the cops. Definitely not the cops. You still don't get it, do you?"

Orville cocked the hammer back and pushed the barrel right into the man's temple. "It's them, isn't it? It's the Cartel. You think I'm afraid of them? After I took one of their guys? I'm not afraid of shit." Orville leaned in toward the box. "I'm not afraid of shit, you hear me?"

Hal Cornish closed his eyes. "We always wanted you, you know," he whispered. "We hoped this would push you to reach out, make a deal. It'd be better for all of us that way. You could talk to Bernard, and we wouldn't have to keep paying them for their services. We're hemorrhaging money. The cash that comes in? It's not enough. This was never supposed to be sustainable."

A voice over his shoulder called out: "Let him go, Orville." It was husky and deep, so of course, when Orville swung around, letting go of Hal Cornish to get a better grip on the gun, he found Nina standing next to her bicycle. Hal Cornish dashed off among the campers.

"Put it away," Nina said, nodding at his gun.

"What the hell?" Orville said. He kept the gun raised. "You trying to distract me, talking like that? I thought you were . . ." But Orville didn't know who he thought she was. The situation seemed to be boiling over with unknowns.

"He was wearing a wire," Nina said. "I didn't want the Cartel to know it was me."

"I don't get it," Orville said.

"I noticed," Nina said. "Otherwise you would've listened to me and made the deal with Sundial. Now, I thought I told you to put that away."

Orville tucked the revolver into his overalls.

"You said you've got this guy somewhere?" Nina said. Orville nodded. "Good. We're going to go get him."

"For what?"

"To give him back," Nina said. "Then you'll leave here, and you'll make the deal with Sundial. The Cartel will watch you forever, but you'll be safe as long as you keep quiet."

"But I was just getting somewhere with all of this," Orville said. "I was close."

Nina sighed. "The only thing you're close to right now is death, Orville."

34

THE DOER

LYDIA DID not so much wake up as decide to stop feigning sleep. If she'd slept, it had been in fitful bursts. Most of the night, she'd lain awake, listening to the noises of CamperTown—the thrum of activity at The Bars, the stragglers making their way home when it closed, what sounded like the shuttle to the casino starting up and driving away, and eventually the total silence of the desert. But she would not let lack of sleep stop her. She would get up and take action. She would seize the day by the scruff of its neck like a misbehaving cat. She would subdue the day, neutralize the day's claws. But she herself would not be subdued. She herself would not be neutralized. She would make this day her own somehow, but not in the way that cats make something their own. She would not rub herself all over the day or mark the day. She was not the cat. The day was the cat. She was Lydia, doer of things, taker of action, seizer of cats (days).

It rang hollow, contaminated on all edges by a strange sense of crippling malaise that Lydia could combat only through a steadfast refusal to acknowledge it. She made instant coffee, stirring it with great force, afraid that even the minute it took to brew would be enough time for reality to catch up to her: that she had done nothing and today her failure would be complete.

What frustrated Lydia was that she'd given up so easily. After leaving the Displaced Travelers' camp in a stupor, she never came to her senses. The conversation with the man with the glasses and the mustache left her disoriented. The idea of untapped possible courses of action had stun-gunned her progress. She kept trying to unlock just one of them, but her mind found no purchase. When she'd gotten to The Bars that night, the official end of "actionable time," part of her had felt happy to be done. This idea of someone else seeing things so clearly while she herself remained in an endless loop of brainstorming was all she needed to cede control of the situation.

She'd hoped The Bars could provide her with some distraction, but the energy had been all off. First, Terrance and Hans had both treated her with an infuriating delicacy, each having experienced a quick exit earlier in the day, and each afraid, it seemed, to trigger another. When they spoke, they discussed Orville's absence. "I guess he's not coming here either," Terrance had mumbled.

Lydia wasn't sure if Hans had told him about Orville's off-time or if he was referring to the call-in. Apparently Orville had missed his talk with Bernard that afternoon. From what Lydia had gleaned, Bernard at first refused to take any further calls for the rest of the afternoon, sitting in silence for some time, then piping in what sounded like hold music. It was all anyone could talk about, which meant there was no escaping the air of wrongness among the three of them.

The trip to the bar was what finally did the night in. Terrance covered their first two rounds, an attempt to buy his way out of responsibility for awkwardness. Hans didn't appear concerned with this. He ordered a shot and a beer each time, combatting the awkwardness with drunkenness. Lydia didn't like it, though. Letting Terrance pick up a third round felt mean, so when they needed another refill, she volunteered to get it. At the bar, Nina had looked tense. She didn't budge when Lydia placed her order.

"Where's Orville?" she demanded. "I heard what happened this afternoon. Is everything okay?"

Lydia hadn't realized Nina and Orville were so close. She tried to sound reassuring. "Trust me, he's fine," she said. When Nina made no move to get her drinks, Lydia added, "He's just collecting himself. Life here is harder for him than most. He's taking a few days off from the Dig. Maybe he just got lost in his thoughts."

This had not had the calming effect she'd hoped for.

"Taking a few days off?" Nina said. "You mean he wasn't with you today? Where was he?"

Lydia thought of the apartment. "He has a nice place to relax."

"Where?" Nina didn't so much ask as demand.

"It's really up to him if he wants people to know where he is," Lydia said.

"But you've seen him there? Relaxing?"

"I don't think it would be very relaxing if I was there watching him." Lydia laughed to lighten the mood. Nina did not laugh with her. She walked off and returned with Lydia's drinks, placing them on the bar without a word.

By then, Lydia was spent. She downed hers right there and brought the other two back to Hans and Terrance, staying only as long as it took to hand them each a glass and mutter a good night. Another quick exit, sure, but it was time to go home. Everything, it seemed, was coming apart, and she wanted nothing to do with it. Lydia knew this illustrated a fault on her part. She should have stood up to Nina and told her to mind her own business. She should have told Terrance and Hans they were flattering themselves if they thought her mood had anything to do with them. But really, she should have done neither of these things. She should not have been at The Bars. She should've left the Displaced Travelers' camp and gone home, schemed, worked, spent the night concocting a new plan, something ingenious and revelatory. And when she finished it she would see: it had not been procrastination as much as patiently waiting for all the pieces to fit together, and now she finally had a fool-proof course of action.

That was what a real doer would do. But Lydia was not a real doer. She was the inflatable model of a doer. She'd sat on her hands for weeks, hoping for an opening, and as soon as she'd had a viable idea to set things in motion, she'd just as quickly abandoned it based on only a few words about "deli-cacy" from a man whose name she didn't even know. She didn't have it in her to get things done. It made sense that she would realize this today, the day that she'd circled on her calendar weeks ago, the day of Peter Thisbee's visit.

She stepped outside with her cup of instant coffee, hop-ing to find something in the fresh air that might kill these thoughts. She instead found Benjy slowly making his way to her camper door. When he saw her emerge, he changed his course slightly and took a seat in the camp chair she had out-side, out of breath and annoyed.

"People at the gate want to talk to you. Wouldn't come here themselves," he said.

"Who?"

"Who's it we've been talking about at our meetings?" Benjy said.

"Peter Thisbee?"

Benjy nodded. "But I've only seen his assistants so far. They sent me over here. They're waiting for you."

"What are you talking about?" she said. "What about Gil?"

"That's what I said. According to them, he stepped down on the sudden just last night," Benjy said. "Named you his replacement." Though he made no move to get up himself, and though he had hardly been rushing to get over here, he motioned the way he came. "Better get going. They seem like the type to time a person."

At that moment, a man sprinted by in a white linen suit.

He paid them no heed and appeared to be unbuttoning his
shirt as he went. Lydia didn't recognize him.

"Was that one of his people?" Lydia asked.

Benjy shook his head.

"Then who was he? He's not from here."

Benjy shrugged. "You'll have to check the logs."

35

FURTHER COMPLICATIONS

ORVILLE PEDALED furiously, Nina riding beside him on her own bike. They easily skirted a group of Displaced Travelers talking excitedly about custodial work, from the sounds of it. But just a minute later, rounding a sharp bend, they both had to clamp down on their brakes, and went skidding in opposite directions to avoid hitting boss and the doctor in the medicart. Though it was only just the beginning of the workday (if that) there was a six-pack between them. Boss leaped out and ran to Orville's side, where he lay on the ground, a small scrape on his knee beading with blood. The doctor grabbed a can and followed. Neither paid Nina any attention.

"Christ, Orville, thank God!" the doctor said.

"We were coming to find you," boss said, helping Orville to his feet. "To see if you were okay."

"We thought for sure you were buried," said the doctor.

"Buried?" Orville said, shrugging off boss and righting his bike. "I just needed time to think. Didn't Lydia tell you?"

"She said you were at the apartment," boss said. "Said you were going through some stuff. We thought, hell, maybe some company would help."

"That's not what I want," Orville said. "Company's the opposite of what I want."

"Really?" The doctor nodded to Nina, who'd stepped up beside him and stood clutching her bike's handles, ready to keep moving.

Orville felt himself losing it. He tried to control his voice. "Lydia was supposed to tell you to stay away from the apartment."

"Orville, we're just coming from the apartment, and we've got some bad news," boss said.

"You went there?"

"It was Hans's idea," said the doctor.

Orville looked around. "Where the hell is he, then? Did Lydia say this was all right?"

"We didn't talk to Lydia about it," boss said. "Hans is still back at the apartment. Or where the apartment was."

"What do you mean, where the apartment was?" Orville turned to Nina as he said this. He wasn't hoping for an explanation from her. She knew less about the apartment than anyone. He just had a feeling they were about to get some bad news. The look she returned conveyed a blankness that terrified Orville.

"There was a Heap shift," boss explained. "The apartment's gone."

"No," Orville said.

The doctor waved behind him. "Go check for yourself. Hans is back there digging."

Orville felt himself shaking all over. "What for?"

"You," boss said. "We didn't know if you were spending the night in there or what."

Orville got back onto his bike. Nina did the same. "Tell him I'm okay. Tell him to stop."

"Honestly, a little sweat wouldn't hurt him," boss said. "He's still pretty drunk from last night."

"Guy might have a problem," said the doctor, popping the top on his beer.

"I said tell him to stop," Orville said.

"Fine," boss said.

"Right away," Orville said.

"Sure, sure, right away," boss said. He looked to the doctor, who halfheartedly nodded while taking a long drink, some beer dribbling onto his chin.

Orville didn't have time to make sure they followed through. He got on his bike and he and Nina took off back toward CamperTown.

36

THISBEE AND COMPANY

LYDIA MANAGED, through some miracle, to channel her jitters into a power walk. She couldn't jog, which would only increase the risk of sweat, nor could she bike, which felt podunk and unrefined, though Lydia couldn't say exactly why.

As she made her way into the Assistance Sector, the crowds of workers on their way to clock in obstructed her path. They lingered, chatted, laughed, and sighed. Lydia managed to duck and dodge her way through them without slowing down. The gate was still a little ways out the other end of the Assistance Sector, and she relished the quiet this stretch of path gave her. She refused to consider the confluence of events that had brought her to this moment, afraid careful consideration would collapse her hopes into dust.

She had envisioned a cavalcade awaiting her, a swarm of agents like a private secret service. She found only three people, one with a shaved head, wearing athletic shorts and a gray hoodie, his hands in the front pouch—security, Lydia imagined—standing off from two men in crisp suits. One of these would be Thisbee. Lydia could not say which one, not even as she got closer. All the articles she'd read used the same photo, a nondescript straight-on shot that appeared to be at least ten years old. Lydia had glanced at it many times but never actually studied it beyond taking in the shape of his hair, an oversight she now saw: it was the most malleable of all features.

She made her way up to them and cleared her throat, and only as they turned to her did she realize she had no introduction planned. Doubt quickly took up residence in her, not only in her skills, but in her desires too. She'd finally gotten what she wanted, but she experienced none of the joy she had anticipated. It was just timing, she told herself. Lydia wasn't given enough time to process the end of Gil's reign before stepping in and fulfilling his most crucial duty. Yet she wondered if it was more than that. She wondered if maybe, somewhere along the way, she'd lost the ability to properly assess her own criteria for satisfaction. Which would make it possible that this moment that she had dreamed of—when the figurative keys to CamperTown had been entrusted to her, when she would be the voice for its people—was not actually a moment that she had dreamed of, and what she had really dreamed of was the negative of this moment, this moment's outline, made only to feel like this moment by how crisply and definitively it was not.

She stood not speaking for what felt like ten minutes but was really about twenty seconds. One of the men, the younger one, pointed at her. "Lydia, right?" he said.

Lydia nodded, and the two men in turn nodded at each other.

"Coffee?" said the young man.

Lydia had carried her mug of instant with her from her camper. She held it up and finally managed to speak. "I have my own, but thank you."

The man blinked in a way that registered to Lydia as a sigh. "No," he said, "where is the coffee?"

"Oh, sorry, of course." Lydia gave him directions to the café. The man sprinted off without a word of thanks or even acknowledgment, leaving her alone with the older of the two. He smiled at her kindly and she smiled back.

"It's an honor to meet you," Lydia said.

"Thank you," the man replied.

First impressions seal in minutes, after which point they're impossible to break. Lydia knew she had to say her piece now, or else forever be seen as a gaping, inarticulate moron. She counted to three in her head and then forced the words out of herself.

"As the new chairperson of the Committee for Better Life in CamperTown, I understand we'll be working together in the future. And so I wanted you to know, the Committee isn't simply something I do here. It's the *reason* I'm here. My interest in politics is, in a lot of ways, not an interest in politics at all. Really my interest is in engineering. In the societal sense, I mean. What I'm talking about is taking the support structures that keep this community unique and reinforcing them, while also streamlining the various operational mechanisms. If that makes sense."

Lydia let a deep breath out through her nose as slowly as she could. She'd flubbed her lines but had gotten the gist right.

"That's great to hear," the man said. "Really, it is. Anyway, few quick things. We mailed this all to what's-his-name who was supposed to do this, but obviously, given the constraints on time, I'll just have to give you a quick rundown in person." He looked over his shoulder, then leaned in and spoke quietly. "While showing Peter around, we ask that you refrain from discussing the collapse, unless Peter himself brings it up, in which case, you may discuss the collapse, but we ask that you do your best not to prolong the discussion of the collapse in any way, for example with follow-up questions concerning the collapse. This is not meant as a denial of the collapse's occurrence or its tragic implications. It is merely Peter's belief that the Dig Effort's success relies on a positive, future-facing outlook. Do you follow so far?"

Lydia—who had been shocked to hear Peter Thisbee refer to himself in the third person before realizing (with

no small amount of embarrassment) that this man was not
Peter Thisbee, at which point she'd begun to search, out of the
corner of her eye, for where they might be keeping him, and
had thus heard almost nothing of the man's speech—said,
"Of course."

"Good." The man put his hands together for a single
soft clap before continuing. "Additionally, Peter requests
that you refrain from asking about the technology behind
the ConductionSens shovels, the workings of the Sale, the
prospective future monument, or any other such information concerning one of Peter's innovations or business ven-
tures that are ancillary to the Dig Effort. If Peter himself
discusses any such information, you are prohibited, once
again, from posing follow-up questions to prolong the conversation. Furthermore, we ask that you share none of said
information with any media sources, or make investments
based upon it. Understand?"

"Yes," Lydia said.

"Good." He turned now, and spoke louder. "Mr. Thisbee,
the chairwoman of the CamperTown Betterment Committee
is ready to provide you with a tour."

"Committee for Better Life in CamperTown," Lydia tried
to say, but the assistant wasn't listening. He was motioning to
the bald man Lydia had assumed was security.

"Thank you, Thomas," he said when he arrived. He
gave just a slight nod and the assistant stepped away quickly,
remaining at a distance of about thirty feet. "You must be
Lydia," said the bald man. "I'm Peter."

He held his hand out to shake, and Lydia took it. Peter
Thisbee shook without much force. He smiled. He appeared
affable, friendly. He was not particularly tall, not particularly old, not particularly young. The pattern of stubble atop
his head betrayed that he shaved it out of necessity rather
than for style. She saw a white sheen on it and smelled suntan

lotion. She tried to reignite the nervousness she'd felt just a few moments ago, to remind herself of her own respect, but her mind was still all haywire from the misunderstanding.

She'd just found the words, the same words that she'd used on the assistant—"It's an honor to meet you"—when the other rushed up and handed Thisbee a coffee.

"Unfortunately," the younger man said breathlessly, "their options in the dairy-alternative department were lacking, to say the least."

Thisbee took the cup, popped the top off. His previously warm expression turned stern. "It's dark. What kind of tea is this?"

The young assistant feigned a look of good humor, but Lydia could see him turning red. "It's coffee."

"When I travel," Thisbee said, "I drink tea. For gastrointestinal reasons I'd prefer not to get into in front of our new friend."

"I'm sorry," the young assistant said. "I just thought you might be tired, with last night's lackluster accommodations . . ."

"I slept fine," Thisbee said. "If you'd prefer the comforts of home, I'd be happy to leave you in the city next time I travel."

"No!" the young man cried. "I mean, that won't be necessary." He took the cup from Thisbee. "This situation will be rectified, immediately."

He sprinted off again, back into the Assistance Sector, now emptier, the workers having found their way to their various posts. Lydia watched him go. The other assistant, still standing at a distance, stifled laughter.

When Lydia turned back to Peter Thisbee, his face wore the warm expression of before. "Now, where do we start?"

"We're supposed to look at a cubicle building, the hospital, some bodegas," Lydia said.

"I'm pretty well aware of how all those things work," Thisbee said. "After all, I set this place up."

"Of course," she said.

Thisbee grinned. "More to the point, what do you mean 'supposed to'? You're in charge here, Lydia. Where do you want to go?"

37

THEY'RE COMING

ORVILLE SAT at the dinette of Nina's camper. The ride back to CamperTown after running into boss and the doctor left him wheezing, and he had to catch his breath before explaining the apartment, the abduction, and everything to her. "And now, apparently, it's all underground because of a Heap shift."

Nina nodded, her face still unnervingly blank. She stepped into the kitchen and emerged with two shot glasses of tequila. She put one down on the table for Orville, kept the other for herself.

"I don't think it's a good idea to drink . . ." Orville said.

"You've chosen a strange moment to show some discretion," Nina said. "Besides, maybe it'll calm you down."

It was true: No matter how hard Orville tried, he couldn't keep himself from shaking. It was like shivering but he didn't feel cold. "So, what do we do now?"

Nina sat down across from him. "I'll leave."

"Why?" Orville said.

"Are you still not getting it?" Nina said.

"No, I mean, why now?" Orville said. "Why didn't you leave as soon as you saw their symbol in the sign?"

"Because it thrilled me, to know they might be close." Orville must've made a face because Nina shook her head as if he'd said something. "It's not that I wasn't scared. I was terrified. But remember what I said at the phone bank, about how they like to leave clues? About how they love to hide in plain sight?"

"Yeah," Orville said.

"This was like that for me," Nina said. "It was exciting. That probably sounds crazy to you, but you don't understand how addicting the near misses can be, the rush of barely making it through a job. Because you're not one of them."

"You're not one of them either," Orville said.

"I don't work for them anymore," Nina said. "But I'll always be one of them. That's something I need to admit to myself. I got out, but the Cartel will always be part of me."

"If you love near misses so much," Orville said, "why don't you just stay?"

"This isn't a near miss, Orville. It's a head-on collision waiting to happen."

Nina pushed Orville's tequila closer to him. He took hold of it but didn't raise it to his lips. "Where will you go?" he asked.

Nina let out a bitter laugh. "The less you know the better. These people, they can make you talk."

"The one I took didn't seem so tough," Orville said.

"There's a spectrum. Some are more actor than soldier, some the other way. Then there are the goons, who aren't actors at all."

"Should I leave too?" Orville asked.

Nina downed her tequila. "You can't follow me, if that's what you're asking."

"I mean on my own."

Nina shook her head. "That'll only draw things out. Orville, one of their guys is probably dead because of you. They'll follow you, and you'll only be able to stay ahead for a little while. I know this sounds terrible, but don't prolong it. They're coming for you, probably as we speak. Let them, and it'll all be over quickly."

Orville understood that she was advocating for him to wait and die, but it didn't seem real. "I'm sorry," he finally said, "about all this."

"That doesn't mean much, in light of everything," Nina said.

"I didn't realize," Orville said. He didn't finish the sentence. There were many things he had not realized just forty-eight hours ago.

"That's why I told you what I did. So you'd realize," Nina said. "It obviously didn't work. Now drink up and go. I have to pack." Orville finished his tequila and stood to leave. At the door, Nina called after him, "Wait. Do you have a gun?"

Orville patted the revolver in his overalls.

"I mean a real gun," Nina said. "That's for close combat. And if they're close, it's too late. You need something that can cover distance."

She got up from the dinette and went into the bedroom area, reemerging with what looked an oversize briefcase. She laid it down on the dinette table and opened the latches. Orville stepped up next to her. Inside, nested in plush, were the pieces of a complicated rifle.

"It makes almost no noise," Nina said. "Set it up in your window, and keep watch. They'll look suspicious. They're actors. They're dramatic. They like to play things up for effect. You'll know them when you see them, and if you see them, pull the trigger before they do. You're still at a disadvantage, but this gives you a chance."

"I don't know how to use one of those," Orville said. "I don't even know how to put it together."

Nina shut the case and handed it to Orville. It felt remarkably light. "There's no time for lessons. They're coming. Now go."

With that, Orville found himself outside her camper. The warmth of the tequila in his chest and the warmth of the late-morning sun combined into a scratchy sensation that he didn't like, but if what Nina said was true, there was no time to stand around feeling crummy. Orville ran back to his camper, the briefcase thumping against his leg as he went.

38

FROM *THE LATER* YEARS:

EDUCATION

*Initially, school was a problem for the children of Los Verti-
calés. An elite private school moved into the twenty-first floor,
but only the wealthiest outer families could afford it. The rest
were loaded into several school buses, specially chartered for
them, and driven to nearby schools, "nearby" being a relative
term. The closest school was just about an hour away. The rest,
nearly two.*

    *The distance proved divisive among parents. Some hated
it. They complained that they felt more like hosts than mothers
and fathers, seeing their children for a brief time at night and
in the morning. Others enjoyed it. It allowed them a freedom
not usually afforded to parents: time to themselves (or time out,
given that the bus ride home occupied the same part of the day
as most happy hours).*

    *Still, we were proud of our children. Each of the schools
made special lists of only those Los Verticalés students on the
honor roll. These were sent home, copied, and posted in promi-
nent places throughout our hallways. In the beginning, there
were dozens of pages, thick with names. Then, seemingly overnight, the lists thinned dramatically. For several months this
continued. Was there a mistake? The schools, when called, assured the parents there was not. So who were these students who
had so suddenly lost their high academic standing?*

The children of the inner units.

The families of the outer units, as usual, delighted in feeling sorry for those stuck inside. It was—they would say to one another, struggling to hide their glee—an issue of vitamin D deficiency, surely. It had been wrong to subject children to such a life, they claimed. They were responsible parents. They gave their children what they needed to succeed: true natural light. Never mind the price difference; a good parent didn't use finances as an excuse.

The true explanation was far more problematic than exposure to the sun. The month in which the grades dipped was the month in which the new time zones had been instated. The children who lived in the inner units had not given up. They were being woken up in the middle of the "night" to get on the bus. They were tired, sure, but moreover they were disoriented. That any of them had remained on the honor roll—and some had—showed an amazing work ethic and intelligence.

The inner units demanded a change, and just as with the issue of hallway traffic, Mitner obliged—just not how any of us expected. He discontinued the contract with the buses, increased the condo dues, and introduced the Los Verticalés Residency for Outstanding Scholars. The condo board invited researchers in a variety of fields to live with us, offering them a generous stipend and lodging in which to conduct their work. In exchange, they agreed to run workshops and instructional sessions "as the community deems necessary."

Only when they arrived did it become clear they were simply schoolteachers, running classes out of their living rooms at odd intervals throughout the day and night to account for the varying time zones. Their own time zone was amorphous. The condo board set their UV screens to show day during times when class was in session, and night all other hours. It proved terrible for their own work, and worse for their teaching. Often, a scholar might return home to his or her condo from a bar, drunk and ready for bed, only for the doorbell to ring, and a class of boisterous third graders to come in. But being upstart academics, they cherished having any modicum of stability, and few of them sought other opportunities.

The children, for their part, loved it. They could wake up later and join the bustling hallways, going from one scholar's condo to another until the end of the day, when they could return home in a matter of minutes rather than hours. And despite there being no weather to speak of, they still received an allotment of snow days. Each day in December and January, they waited by their radios, hoping to hear school was canceled for their time zone. When it was, they'd rush to the designated stairwell, which had, through use of an inflatable surface, been transformed into a luge track for indoor sledding.

As students progressed, the program shifted to more of a professional training curriculum, allowing them to transition smoothly into a career in Los Verticalés. Some chose to follow this path, while others applied to college. Perhaps surprisingly, their scores on the entrance exams were strong, but this is often where their luck ended. The children of Los Verticalés, especially those without a deck or windows, struggled in the outside world. They'd forgotten all about their long trips to school, and now they called home constantly, claiming they'd been blinded by a mild breeze. When they sought directions to some campus building or another, they asked, "Which elevator do I take?" And those who forgot to reset their watches might arrive at their assigned lecture hall and find that their class ended six hours earlier.

We would see the college students when they came home for summer vacation or a holiday break. Even if we didn't know them personally, we could recognize them. They were the ones standing in the middle of the hallway as traffic struggled to get around them, sometimes with their eyes closed, just smiling and greedily breathing in the stale air.

39

SIMPLICITY

TWICE WHILE showing Peter Thisbee through Camper-Town, Lydia swore she saw people weaving among campers, just in flashes. But these were merely tricks her eyes were playing on her, the only evidence of her rough night of sleep. Otherwise, she felt invigorated.

She took Thisbee through the "arts district," where residents set up easels outside their campers to paint or built elaborate sand castles. She explained why, while most campers were arranged lengthwise in neat lines, occasionally you'd see two campers arranged to face each other, creating a courtyard: these were couples.

"There's a certain amount of social clout," Lydia said, standing in front of one such set of campers. "Because they have a whole camper for entertaining. Otherwise, it can feel intrusive going into someone's camper when you know they sleep 'right over there.'"

"And if there's a breakup?" Thisbee asked.

"Very awkward," Lydia said.

Thisbee stepped between the two campers and stood for a moment, as if trying to imagine what it would be like to live there. "How do they arrange it so they're right next to each other? Do they haul one camper to the other?"

"No," Lydia said. "They have to trade campers with their partner's neighbor. It can be difficult, though. There's no rule that says the neighbor has to trade with them, especially if the camper they'd be trading for is on a less ideal street or is an outdated model. Not that anyone complains about the campers . . ."

"I'm not offended, Lydia," Thisbee said.

Lydia blushed. "Right. Anyway, there's a higher success rate for couples that trade onto bad streets or into two bad side-by-side campers."

Thisbee took a sip of his tea, finishing it. He held out his cup and one of his assistants, following them from a distance, sprinted up to take it from him and then away to find a trash bin. "But what if the relationship doesn't work? You're just stuck on a bad street or in a bad camper or both. Seems risky."

"It is," Lydia said. "That's why most people try to date on their own street."

"Interesting," Thisbee said, and Lydia could tell: He meant it. He actually found these things interesting. She thought back to all the days the Committee had spent "planning" for this tour, how wrong they were, and how right she'd been all along. What was interesting about the Los Verticalés Dig Site was not the Assistance Sector, not the Heap itself. It was CamperTown.

She took him through almost all of it, consciously avoiding any area with a view of the camper in the desert. She took him to the open-air communal living room and explained that they hosted book clubs and knitting groups here, a quiet alternative to The Bars, which she also showed him, though obviously it was closed. They followed the extension cords running from the main grids to a series of six or seven shabby armoires pulled from the Heap, or "the saunas," as they were known. Each had an electric kettle to make steam and a timer. You entered, turned on the kettle, set the timer for fifteen minutes; when the buzzer went off, you ceded the sauna to the next in line.

"Do people ever try to take extra time?" Thisbee asked.

"Not really," Lydia said. "You're too vulnerable in there. To tipping, I mean."

Peter Thisbee laughed. It emboldened Lydia, seeing how open he seemed to be. On the walk to the library, where the reception was to take place, she said: "It's a lot like Los Verticalés, don't you think?"

Thisbee stopped abruptly. His face took on a look of intense contemplation. "How so?"

Lydia glanced over her shoulder. The assistants had stopped too. They stared at her with wide eyes. One of them, the older one, whispered something to the younger one. Was this something she wasn't allowed to say? Could they even hear her?

"I just mean, it's not like any other place," Lydia said. "It's a community uniquely defined by its layout."

For an interminable moment in which Thisbee considered this, Lydia wished she could disperse like the steam that billowed from the doors of the saunas when they opened. But eventually, his features eased. "I'm sorry. It's just hard for me to think of them as parallel," Thisbee said. "Los Verticalés involved so much technical ingenuity. Sway control, for example. Or base expansion. It only occasionally registered on the conscious level for the people who lived there."

"Like if you got innerized," Lydia said.

Thisbee looked at her, impressed and curious. "Exactly. Like if you got innerized. But even if it didn't affect you directly, living inside such a complicated thing as Los Verticalés, you still felt it subconsciously. There was an energy that ran under everything. Really, though, it's a difference in focus. Here, it's singular. The Dig makes it so that every job is connected. Everyone is working toward one goal. Everyone is doing their part to help clean up and, in the process, to find Bernard. Honestly, I'm impressed with what you've all managed here, but at the end of the day this is a relief effort. You could never sum up Los Verticalés so easily."

"But I thought it was the city that grew up rather than

out." Lydia spoke tentatively. She didn't want to accuse him of anything. She wanted a conversation.

Thisbee began walking again, slower than before, and Lydia matched his pace, her hands behind her back, trying to look like the best listener she could be. "Yes, we did say that. But honestly it was more marketing than anything," Thisbee said. "My investors were uncomfortable, and I needed something to sell them. Hell, I needed something to sell myself, a way to dumb it down, convince myself this wasn't crazy. Over time, I came to realize my mistake. It was crazy, and that's what made it itself. Having one goal would've killed it."

"So you had many goals?"

"In a way."

"What were they?" Lydia lowered her voice, sure now that she was asking questions Thisbee's assistants would frown upon.

Thisbee shrugged. "Not sure."

"What?" The word came out sounding almost disgusted. Lydia tried desperately to backtrack. "Sorry, what I mean is—"

"Relax, Lydia," Thisbee said. "That's the correct response. But I mean it. I'm not sure. You seem to have done your homework, so you probably know that some people think this was all an experiment. Well, that's exactly what it would've been, if I'd had a neat little list of goals. I'd be asking, 'What can we achieve here?' Or 'What does this prove about urban planning?' But I wanted Los Verticalés to feel organic rather than academic. I fought the urge to set any specific goal, or goals plural. Because that would simply make it a means to an end. Not enough people can see the benefit of the loose grip. But that's how you create something truly intricate. Not through meticulous planning. It's the opposite, really. It's by letting things go a bit wild."

This candidness spoke to something that excited Lydia: a level of success where nonchalant self-reflection was the ultimate way to flex one's figurative muscles; a place beyond the ruthlessness or brazen ambition she'd always imagined. She wondered what it took to get there.

"So now you can see why I struggle with the comparison," Thisbee said. "Life here isn't very wild. There's a common goal, and plenty of space. You don't need any ingenuity to grow. You just add more campers. Jobs are guaranteed, and so is housing. It's a simple place, really."

Lydia had to focus to keep from cringing. "So then what would you do to make CamperTown buzz like Los Verticalés did?" she said. "How do you let things get a little wild without losing sight of the ultimate goal of the Dig?"

Thisbee stopped walking again now, this time to look at the rows of campers around them. "I guess I'm not sure I'd see any reason to do that. I apologize. I've been rambling. I've spent so much time thinking about the magic of Los Verticalés that I sometimes forget to make clear a crucial point: that buzz I mentioned, the chaos that some found so intoxicating—you can't say it alone caused the collapse, but it probably didn't help."

"So when you say CamperTown is simple, that's not a bad thing," Lydia said.

Thisbee smiled. "Not at all."

40

A KNOCK AT THE DOOR

ORVILLE HAD put together chairs before, had hung hammocks, had even constructed a shed once, years ago, from a kit bought out of a catalog. None of it had prepared him for the rifle, or more specifically, none of it prepared him for the psychological weight of assembling the rifle. Previously, had his forays into assembly gone wrong, the result would be a collapse or a mess. But what happened if you fired a misassembled rifle? Did you get burned? Could it explode in your hand? Would the result to you, the holder, be equivalent of what a properly put-together rifle did to its target?

Which is all to say, he didn't simply fail to put the rifle together. He failed to even touch it, failed to get any further than opening the briefcase and staring at its parts, letting his hand hover briefly over the scope—the only part he could surely identify in its long slot in the plush—before snatching it away, closing the case, and clicking the latches shut. He then opened the love seat trunk, found two ugly Christmas sweaters—why, he wondered, had he brought these along?—wrapped the case in them, and shoved it down into the rest of his excess clothes, before pulling it back out, along with the rest, so he could fold everything neatly to reduce potential suspicion.

Did he really expect anyone to look there? The tequila had calmed his nerves a bit, but it also scrambled his logic. After he'd reburied the rifle, Orville stood staring at the closed love seat for some minutes, as if the briefcase might leap out.

He heard someone knock on his camper door.

He looked back and forth from the love seat to the door—unsure of whether he worried whoever it was would sense what hid inside, or if he half expected to find the briefcase on his front step.

"Orville, are you there?"

At hearing Lydia's voice, he felt relief and anger in quick succession. All he'd asked her to do was keep the others from the apartment, and boy had she done a bang-up job. Although, was this really her fault? No. Nor was it boss's or the doctor's or Hans's fault. Had Orville just swallowed his anger and struck a deal with Hal Cornish like Nina said out by the decommissioned phone bank, none of this would've happened. The Heap shift would've crushed an unoccupied apartment and Orville would not currently be in a situation that required a complicated rifle that he didn't know how to assemble. He really had only himself to blame. But the morning's excess adrenaline turned this much introspection into nausea.

Orville made his way to the door and swung it open with a little too much force. "Well, look who it is," he tried to say, but he made it only as far as "look" before the butt of the pistol came down on his forehead. The irony was, had Orville followed his own advice and actually looked at who it was, he would have seen not Lydia waiting for him on the other side of the door, but three strangers—two men and a woman—and he might've had a chance to slam the door in their faces. But not anymore.

Orville stumbled back and the three strangers crowded into his camper, shutting the door behind them. One of the men pushed Orville onto the love seat and held him by the shoulder. The other, with the gun, peeked behind the curtains to see if anyone had seen them. It was nearly eleven in the morning. CamperTown was deserted. The woman sat on Orville's bed and crossed her legs. She picked up the revolver he'd left there and handed it to the man standing guard at the window. He examined it and issued a nod.

They all wore black suits and pressed white shirts. The man at the window was tall and narrow, slouched in the camper. The woman was exceptionally pale, as if the whites of her eyes had leaked, diluting the whole of her face.

Orville laughed, made brazen by his helplessness and his throbbing head injury. "Bet you're glad to be out of the sun." The hand on his shoulder squeezed and now Orville looked up to study the other man more carefully. "Wait, you?"

Standing over him, one hand on Orville, the other holding a duffel bag, was the man who had decommissioned the phone bank. Orville had so often fantasized about seeing him again, of going back in time, stepping under that caution tape, and giving him the kind of bruises that come with true structural damage. Now, here he was, and not only did it irk Orville that their positions were reversed—him being on the receiving end of some punishment—but the strength of the man's grip implied that he might've miscalculated his own physical advantage, even without the shooting pains bouncing off the walls of his skull.

"I have taken on a new position from that which I held previously," the man said.

"That's right," the woman said. "You've met Charlie before. Not Stefan, though." She turned to the tall man. "This is your first time to the desert, isn't it, Stefan?"

Stefan, again, nodded. His mouth remained closed so tightly it looked almost ornamental, like a board that poses as a drawer.

"And you?" Orville said.

"You can call me Joan. You won't have many opportunities. And it really doesn't matter who I am. What's important is you know who *we* are. And you do, don't you?"

"I do," Orville said.

"We know about you as well," she said. "And we know

what you've done. All of it." She fished something out of
her suit jacket's inside pocket and held it up: the wire. "You
don't have Hal here somewhere, do you? We found this on
the outskirts of your"—she struggled to think of a word—
"community."

Orville shook his head. Even such a simple motion hurt.
Things felt loose inside.

"That's too bad. And unnecessary, really. He didn't have to
run away. We really were going to let him go. That's why we
didn't rig him up with anything more than the wire. But no
bother. We're really not concerned about him. He's weak, you
know. The suit, the knowing smile, it's all a facade. Wherever
he's running, it won't be far, and he won't do much damage. He
won't"—the woman leaned forward for emphasis here—"steal
one of our operatives."

"I can take you to him," Orville sputtered. "Your opera-
tive, I can show you where he is." He had no plan. He only
wanted to get them outside, where he might find some upper
hand.

The woman looked at him, unmoved. "I'm sorry. You'll
have to excuse me. I act mostly with my voice. My prop work
has faded since I was a student at conservatory." She shook
the wire. "You might think the extent of our knowledge ends
at what we heard on the other end. This is not the case. When
I say we know 'all' of what you've done, I mean literally that:
We know about the apartment, about the collapse. We know
about everything."

Orville looked to Stefan, then to Charlie standing over
him. Both stared back at him blankly. He turned back to the
woman. "I meant, I can take you to where he's buried."

"No, you didn't," the woman said. "But it's no matter. We're
not here for him. We're here for you, Orville. You wanted to
stop us from impersonating you, but I have bad news: you, the
role, will outlive you, the person."

Charlie released his grip on Orville and unzipped his

duffel bag, pulling out a tightly folded tarp, which he held out to Stefan, who had moved from the window. The woman stood so that he could lay out the tarp on Orville's bed. Whatever they planned to do, it would be messy.

"But it's not worth it," Orville said. "Hal Cornish said so. You heard it yourself. They can't afford to keep paying you to be me."

"There are things that mean more to us than money," Joan said.

Orville scoffed. "Could've fooled me."

"We did fool you, Orville," Joan said. She motioned to the door. "When you let us in, remember?"

Orville opened his mouth to form a comeback. Nothing came.

"No," Joan continued, "money shouldn't be an issue. We'd be willing to do this one pro bono from here on out. It would be bad for business if we don't. Imagine what our clients would think if they found out one of our operatives compromised himself on a mission, and our response was to simply walk away without making amends. Besides, it's just an hour each day. And for a good cause too. You don't want people to lose interest in Bernard when you're gone, do you?"

Stefan laughed out of his nose. It sounded involuntary.

Joan glared at him for a moment before returning her attention to Orville. "Besides, who will know? You might not realize it, but to most people, out there, in the rest of the world, you already are just a voice. They don't care where you're calling from. Around here will be trickier. But we can handle it. We'll spread the news of your 'travels,' about how, as much as you wanted to find Bernard, you could no longer stomach the emotional toil of being here, so close and yet so far away all at once." She smirked. "You'd almost believe it yourself, wouldn't you?"

Charlie took hold of him again. Was his grip tightening, or did it just feel that way because, having spent his brief unfettered moment listening, Orville was now attempting to squirm free? One last thought managed to surface through the pulsing head pain: "Nina! Nina will know! And she'll bust this whole thing wide open." Stefan stopped preparing the tarp. He exchanged a look with Joan, who exchanged a similar look with Charlie. "You didn't think about her, did you?" Orville shouted. "You didn't even know she was here! And now she'll—"

A hand was clamped over his mouth.

Joan shook her head. "How do you think we know everything? How do you think we found your camper or had any idea what your friend Lydia's voice sounds like? Did you imagine we'd gone door-to-door gathering information?"

Orville stopped squirming now. He couldn't speak with the hand over his mouth, but his eyes must have conveyed the terror.

"You're right. We didn't know Nina was here. Until we ran into her on our way in. She seemed to be going somewhere, fast. Very poor timing for her, but lucky for us. It's telling, though, that you'd be so quick to sell her out. I'd say you should feel bad about that, but you don't have time." The woman motioned to the man holding Orville down. "Bring him to the bed." Then to Orville: "He's going to take his hand off your mouth now. If you raise your voice again, what's about to happen will be twice as painful."

The man lifted Orville to his feet, escorted him to the bed, and forced him to lie down. Resting his head on something soft brought about some involuntary relief. The tarp had been tucked in around the edges of the mattress. It crinkled beneath him. The tall man stood and opened his coat. Inside, a series of what looked like razor blades or scalpels. Orville only glanced at them before turning to the woman. "Where's Nina?" he whispered.

"Please," she said. "Don't ask questions when you don't want to know the answers."

41

ALL ALONG THE HEAP, II

NINA LEFT a trail across the desert, but it didn't concern her. The wind would pick up and the sand would cover it. She was losing a lot of blood, but didn't feel any lighter. If anything, her body felt impossibly heavy. Her legs wobbled more with each step. Behind her, she could just barely see CamperTown through the heat's haze.

She probably could have made it back. Maybe she could have even stumbled all the way to the hospital and gotten stitched up. The idea was tempting, but she didn't trust it. It seemed like exactly what the Cartel would do—wound her with such precision that she felt she could survive, only to collapse, finally, at the gate, steps from salvation: a perfect tragic moment. In any case, it didn't matter. Nina had chosen not to risk it, not to play into their hands. She walked the other way, into the desert, away from CamperTown.

After she'd given Orville the rifle and sent him on his way, there'd been a decision to make: strike out across the sand on foot or ride her bicycle right out the main gate. She chose the latter, which would afford her more speed. Plus, it had been some time since their encounter with the man wearing the wire. The Cartel were probably already in CamperTown somewhere, Nina imagined.

She was wrong. Almost as soon as she'd gotten around the gate onto Access Avenue, she saw the minivan parked out in the desert. Three figures approached from it. Nina pulled her bike over to the side of the road, but by the time she'd drawn her pistol, theirs were already trained on her. This all could've easily been witnessed by the old man in the gatehouse, had he simply looked up, but he didn't. And Nina wouldn't shout to draw his attention. There was no use.

Joan was surprised and delighted to see her. "What a treat," she said. They took her back to the van, where the two henchmen held her down in the middle seat. It wasn't necessary. Nina knew better than to try to escape. Joan knelt in front of her and asked her some questions before outlining the details of a potential deal: if Nina gave her a voice, one that Orville would trust, they would still kill her, but they wouldn't take her cords. Nina complied. After a few minutes, when Joan was sure she had the voice down, she'd driven the knife into Nina's stomach, slid open the door, and pushed her out. They left her there, making their way widely around the gate into CamperTown. Nina watched them for a time before turning in the other direction, away from her old home, away from the Heap, toward the horizon. She began walking and she kept walking now.

It was true what she'd told Orville, that she was still one of them, whether they wanted to pay her or to kill her. And now, at the grand finale, she'd made the only viable compromise. The thought of being picked clean by vultures, perhaps, or reduced over time to a mysterious skeleton half buried in the sand satiated her desire for a dramatic death. But she would not be found. No body meant no murder to solve, and no murder to solve meant Strom wouldn't have to take measures to keep it unsolved. In this way, she would live out her last moments as one of the Cartel, while making sure the part of her that always belonged to them would never hurt anyone again.

Nina pushed herself forward. Or tried to. Her legs felt suddenly even heavier, the air thick. She looked down and found she'd fallen to her knees. She tried to stand but could not. There followed desperation, then anger, and finally, relief.

❧

HANS DUG. He didn't know how long he'd been digging. He'd given up calling out Orville's name. Even if Orville called back, he wouldn't hear it. The sound of his own blood pumping filled his ears. He thought momentarily: *Why do things like this happen to me?* Followed by: *Things like this don't happen to me, or they didn't until now.* Followed by: *Nothing happens to me.* Followed by: *I do nothing to make things happen to me.* Followed by: nothing. Thinking didn't help. He sweated heartily. Boss and the doctor had gone to check Orville's camper, but Hans had commandeered a shovel from a passerby. How long had they been gone? He couldn't tell. Drunkenness had a way of skewing time. But was he still drunk? Or was he hungover? He'd had enough to drink the night before to warrant either possibility. When Lydia had left, it broke the tension. He walked around. He talked to people he didn't usually talk to. People bought him drinks. He didn't sleep. Now his head throbbed. His shirt was drenched. His sweatpants too. He hadn't dressed for work. He pitched his shovel with clumsy abandon. He began coughing and kept coughing. His hands shook and he dropped his shovel. He doubled over. His coughs grew thick. It took him a moment to realize he'd thrown up. His body felt a kind of reprieve. His head still ached, his blood still pumped, but not as loudly. Through it, he heard another noise. Someone speaking. It sounded distant and alarmed. "Hello?" it called. "Orville?" Hans called back. It wasn't Orville, but it sounded familiar. A voice he'd heard, every day. Hans ran or Hans fell. Or Hans slid. Down, down, down the side of the Heap. It wasn't made of mud. There were jagged edges there. He would hurt from this later. His throat too would hurt, from shouting. "I found him!" he

called out as loud as he could. "I found him!" That was all.
But Hans's tone left little doubt about who he meant.

✎

EACH MORNING, Douglas went over his mustache with eyeliner, making the thin, feeble hair look full and luminous.
His glasses had no prescription. He wanted control of his ap-
pearance, or, moreover, he wanted control. This morning, he
neither applied the eyeliner nor put on his glasses. He wore
an undershirt, sweatpants, sandals, a baseball cap. There was
no need for artificial control. He smoked a cigarette quickly
in the RV courtyard, then left to find the tour. Once he had
eyes on them, he hung back, weaving between the campers,
following after Peter's assistants. He fell behind briefly, hiding when he saw a trio of figures—one pale woman and two
men, all in black suits—sneaking through CamperTown. He
assumed they were security, but they went in an entirely different direction than Peter. Douglas reassumed his trail, kept
his distance. He couldn't hear what they said, but he didn't
want to risk getting closer. Lydia might recognize him.
Peter would not. In all his time working for the man—if
you could even call it that; there was no official paper trail—
they'd never met. His job required a degree of separation,
anonymity. Even the members of the condo board didn't
know him. He pulled strings. He made things happen. He
created controversy when it helped, snuffed it out where it
hindered. At the time of the collapse, he'd been visiting with
his therapist. He made these visits twice each year. He didn't
want to risk working with a therapist in the Vert. He wanted
someone to whom he might confess when he finished a particularly immoral project, not someone to talk to while he
was knee-deep in the actual work. It required a surrender
of self, followed by long periods of guilt. When he'd found
his home had collapsed, he'd joined the Displaced Travelers,
not because he couldn't handle the real world, but because,

if anything, his skills were even more valuable there. He
didn't want to do those things anymore. He didn't want to do
anything, for that matter. He wanted a place where nothing
would be asked of him. Then, last night, talking to Lydia, he
thought: Maybe one more time, he could make things happen, click things into place. And maybe this time, he could
do something helpful rather than simply profitable. Gil had
been difficult to reason with but easy to intimidate. Douglas himself had delivered the resignation, complete with
instructions for replacement, to the casino. He'd taken the
shuttle driver's keys and driven there late at night, slipping
it under the door of Peter's assistant's room. He'd even managed to send the other Displaced Travelers to the far end of
the Heap for the day, claiming someone had found a fully
intact janitor's closet with mops and all, so they wouldn't get
in the way. Watching Lydia talk to Peter, he looked for some
evidence that she understood what he hoped she would understand, some sign of disgust or betrayal, however minor.
Instead, she nodded often. She seemed genuinely interested
in what Peter had to say. Douglas had miscalculated things.
He'd hoped to throw Peter off his game by giving him a tour
guide eager for his knowledge, rather than one like Gil, who
would submit to his whims without question. But Peter did so
well at shaping nothing into something that seemed significant. That was why he was who he was.

§

AS THEY made their way to the library for the cheese reception, Lydia's body seemed to realize the tour was coming to an
end. Her energy plummeted and her vision softened. It wasn't
a bad thing. She felt accomplished. Everyone outside in the
Assistance Sector went about their business, but she still felt
quick glances in their direction, whispers that were all some
version of: "Is that *him*?" At the beginning of the tour this

might've bothered her, but now, in a state of victorious fatigue, their attention felt almost blanketlike.

The siren evaporated this sense in an instant. Lydia froze steps from the library, and for a moment felt embarrassment, thinking it was some sort of alarm. Suddenly no one even glanced at them. Everyone stood still and looked toward the Heap. A second later, they erupted into movement. A few had been clear-headed enough to grab their bikes, but most ran. The doors of the library burst open. The members of the Committee for Better Life in CamperTown put in charge of the reception rushed out to join the masses. Lydia turned to Peter Thisbee. He stared off at the Heap, listening to the sound. His face creased with deep thought.

Lydia's mind was capable of no such thing. "That's the . . ." she started to say. Thisbee's attention snapped to her.

"Yes," he said. "You should go."

She nodded, stammered some slurred mix of "thank you" and "okay," and took off after the rest of them. Everything was happening at once and Lydia quickly felt overwhelmed by the crowd. She veered off, cutting back through Camper-Town. It was farther, but less crowded, and she had an important stop to make on her way to the Heap.

Orville had asked for privacy, and when Lydia arrived at his camper, his shades were drawn, but his bike was out front. She wouldn't forgive herself if she let him miss this.

BERNARD

THE WOMAN, Joan, had just touched the blade to Orville's throat when the siren sounded. She flinched, nicking him just above the jugular.

"What is that?" she asked. She seemed to be addressing her henchmen, but neither offered as much as a shrug.

"It's the survivor siren," Orville said at last. The weight of those words only occurred to him as he spoke them. The survivor siren. Someone had found a survivor. All four of them listened to it.

Outside there came no shouts, no hysterics, only the sound of footsteps, a voiceless stampede as the backing track to the siren's wail.

When it died down, the world felt different. It felt new and—even with the scalpel inches from Orville's throat, waiting to take his vocal cords and his life—hopeful.

"They'll miss me out there," he whispered, mostly to himself, but Joan looked at him. She seemed to be considering the point.

Orville saw his opportunity. "They'll come here. Right to this camper. They'll break down the door. If it's him."

"That," Joan said, her face contorting into a smirk, "would be something."

There was a knock on the door, followed, just like last time, by Lydia's voice.

"Orville?" she called. "Orville, I know you said to leave you alone, but if you're in there, come on! Did you hear it?"

The two henchmen reached into their jackets, drew out pistols, and aimed them at the door. Joan raised her hand, informing them to hold. She mouthed: *We'll wait it out.*

Orville whispered: "She'll go to the Heap next. When she finds out from Hans what happened to the apartment, she'll be back."

Joan registered her displeasure with only a crinkle of the nose.

The knocking continued. "Orville? Seriously, if you're in there, open up!" Lydia called.

Joan cleared her throat. "Sorry," she called, in Orville's voice. Could every one of these people do an impression of him? "Was just getting a nap in. Will be right out." The knocking stopped, and they heard Lydia walk back down the steps to wait for him. Joan leaned down and whispered into Orville's ear: "You won't see us, but we'll be watching. We'll be reading your lips." She slowly undid his overalls and pulled up his shirt to expose his chest. Orville was confused, but did not squirm. He would not push his luck.

Stefan, the tall one, handed her a device—one end a tiny plastic box, the other a small hypodermic needle—and a roll of medical tape.

"What are you going to give me?" Orville asked.

"Nothing, if you don't cause any trouble," Joan said. "It's a prototype for a product that was never released: a remote-controlled syringe, designed to administer treatments from afar to violent inmates in correctional facilities. Insulin shots, for example. But we find it's more useful when loaded with something more potent."

She pricked the needle just barely into the skin under Orville's left nipple, then taped it into place. "The needle is spring-loaded. I have the remote. If we see even a twitch of the mouth that suggests you're going to tell someone about us, we press the button. You ostensibly have a heart attack. We can make a scene just as easily as we can keep quiet. One of us diverts attention, another sneaks in and removes the needle without anyone noticing. You'll seem to have died of excitement. Understand?"

Orville nodded. It seemed like it would be difficult for them to pull off, but then again, here they were, in his camper, holding him down and speaking in his voice. The woman pulled his shirt down and redid his overalls. Looking down, Orville could barely make out the bump.

❧

ORVILLE EMERGED and closed the door tightly behind him. His face was stern. Lydia didn't know what she expected. Eagerness, maybe? But of course not—not from him. This was a moment he'd been waiting for—or at least for now, it *could* be—so it made sense that he'd be tense. Still, she'd hoped he'd at least seem refreshed after a day off. No such luck. He looked like he'd neither showered nor shaved. His eyes were somehow both wide and empty. There was dirt all over his shirt and he absently touched a small cut on his neck. Apparently it took more than twenty-four hours to get out of the dishes-on-the-floor phase of cleaning himself up.

"Let's go." That's all he said. Then they jogged to catch the rest of them. Orville's stride seemed short. He held his shoulders high. His chest tight. Lydia glanced at him, but he didn't glance back.

They rounded a corner of the Heap. They were getting close to the apartment when they saw the crowd gathered. They stopped running and Lydia felt a rush of exhaustion. Her steps went wobbly. She reached out and squeezed Orville's arm, but he yanked it away and looked at her, terrified.

"Deep breaths," Lydia said to him. Orville did not appear to take her suggestion. They were at the back of the crowd now, at the center of which, Lydia gathered, was the survivor.

She wished she could get a better look, but she couldn't just muscle her way to the front.

She coughed, out of breath, and a man in front of her turned around and looked at her, then at Orville. His eyes went wide and he punched his neighbor in the shoulder. "What's your problem?" his neighbor said, but the other man whispered something to him—"That's him, I think," Lydia heard, "that's the brother"—and the two of them got out of their way. There followed a hushed chain reaction, a parting of the assistance workers giving way to a core of Dig Hands, who themselves stepped back, revealing a small opening in the middle. The mumbles died away. An absolute silence fell over the crowd. Everyone watched them, even the Displaced Travelers. Lydia had never seen them so lucid, so in step with the world around them. In the center of it all were three men. One was boss. One was Hans, looking rough. The other Lydia couldn't make out. He faced away from them.

Orville didn't move until she took his arm—gently this time—and walked him down the path carved through the entire population of CamperTown.

§

ORVILLE LET Lydia pull him along. They would see if he resisted, right? They said they'd be reading his lips, but what about his feet, his shoulders? Where were they watching from, anyway? Maybe they weren't watching. Maybe it was all a bluff. But could he risk it?

He stared down at his feet. He had a bad feeling. If it was Bernard, Orville had basically sealed his fate. He'd be emerging from his dark hole directly into the hands of the Vocalist Cartel, and it was all Orville's fault. He should've doubled over with tears, thinking about how he'd delivered his brother from one form of captivity to another, if they were lucky enough to live, but he maintained some faint sense of composure. And it wasn't just because of the needle under his shirt. This idea, of being finally reunited with Bernard? It was too optimistic. Everything felt too wrong for that to happen. Finding a survivor so soon after the Heap shift, and here of all places, close to where the apartment had been.

Lydia stopped, so Orville did too. They were in the center of everyone now. He looked up at the three of them—boss, Hans, and the man. He wore only his underwear. His body was cut up pretty badly from the shift, but he stood on his own two feet. Didn't anyone see the red around his wrists left by the tie-downs? He'd fashioned his white T-shirt into a bandage, which he'd wrapped tightly around his apparently mangled face, but Orville recognized the eyes, so close together on his wide face.

Boss came up and clapped Orville on the back. He felt the needle shift under his skin, but the tape held it on. "Can you believe it? We forgot to tell Hans to stop, and look what he finds!" Orville looked at Hans, who smiled at him woozily. "You were right all those weeks ago, when we first found the place," boss whispered. "He was just underneath us the whole time."

Orville nodded but tried not to look at the man. The crowd remained silent behind him.

"Well, go ahead," boss said, with a laugh. "He looks a little worse for wear, but we found him."

Now it seemed unavoidable to meet the man's eyes. He smiled under the makeshift bandages. "Hello, brother!" he said. It was Bernard's voice.

Lydia released his arm, and boss pushed him forward. Then the man was in front of him, wrapping his arms around him. He seemed to feel the needle through the overalls, and Orville sensed a thrill travel up the man's body.

Orville didn't lift his arms to return the embrace until the man whispered, in Orville's voice this time, "Hug me back if you want to live." He might as well have spoken it aloud, screamed it even. Nobody would've heard. The hoots and cheers from the crowd were deafening.

III

THE

PRESS

TOUR

43

FROM THE LATER YEARS:

RUMORS

Our close proximity to one another sometimes clouded our sense of size. There were times when Los Verticalés felt more like a small community on steroids than a city confined. We lived, quite literally, on top of each other, allowing rumors to spread and mutate with as much speed and thoroughness as in a gossipy hamlet, only with more reach. As such, certain events, and the people involved, took on a folkloric quality. Take, for example, the case of Gary and Juliet.

The story went like this: Gary Henson had caught his wife riding the elevator to the parking garage with a man other than himself. He was distraught but willing to work it out. Unfortunately, she was not. Being caught in the act actually came as a huge relief. She'd long ago stopped loving Gary, and now she no longer needed to deny it. She left him, giving up their beautiful ninety-first-floor outer unit for a lower-level inner studio, close to the parking garage. Gary, unable to see a way forward, walked out onto his deck one day and leaped off. This, he thought, would be the end, but he didn't account for one thing: wind. A strong gust sent Gary crashing through a window several floors below. Due to some combination of velocity, airflow, and the fact that he landed on a bed, he managed to survive, breaking only one of his legs.

The unit he landed in belonged to Juliet Vonderwich. Juliet lived an isolated life, even by the standards of the Vert. She earned a comfortable living making designer bow ties and only ever left her home for purposes of shipping and receiving, the post office being just four doors down the hall. When Gary crashed through her window, she called the hospital thirty stories up and asked them to dispatch a stretcher. The hospital was allowed its own cargo elevator and made it to her unit in just five minutes, but as it turned out, five minutes was all it took for the two of them to hit it off. Juliet demanded Gary's leg be treated right there on the bed and refused to let them take him away. She would nurse him back to health over the coming months, and the two of them would, of course, fall in love.

Nobody knew who first told the story. It wasn't in the wedding announcement. The incident actually received just one line: "What could have been tragedy turned out to be romance." Still, we all accepted it, even with its disastrous consequences. In the month of their engagement alone, on particularly windy days, three men and two women jumped from their outer-unit windows and fell to their deaths. They were later described by their neighbors as "lonely" and "heartsick."

Whether these descriptions were accurate or a fairy tale spin on true suicidal depression did not matter. Word got back to Peter Thisbee and he announced he'd install netting on every other floor. President Mitner, in a rare moment of dissent, objected on grounds that it would require an outrageous hike in condo dues to cover. (Truly, we all knew it was because for Mitner, and the rest of the outer-unit residents, the nets would be an eyesore.) They would police themselves, Mitner declared. Outer residents would keep tabs on one another and report bad breakups and cases of unrequited love to security. Security officers would, in turn, make regular visits to their condos, to check in, and to the decks of the condos below them, to keep watch.

This was actually far more intrusive than the nets would've been, and with the increased security hours needed to carry it *out, it wasn't exactly cheap either. Even as a symbolic victory for Mitner over Thisbee, it seemed suspect. The conspiracy theorists among us believed the rift between Mitner and Thisbee to be staged, that the two had agreed on a course of action long before, and that Thisbee had engineered the whole ordeal to keep closer tabs on us. The motives were irrelevant, though. The important thing was that it worked. In the two years following the uptick in security, we experienced only one recorded incident of a "lover's leap."*

Then again, perhaps security was only part of the solution. Perhaps it had more to do with the extensive exposé run by a newsletter seven months after the incident, which shed light on some of its skewed or outright false details. Some of it was fraught with typical inner class-related anxiety. For example, did it need to be discussed that Juliet Vonderwich was independently wealthy and did not subsist merely on her bow tie sales? Other sections bordered on character assassination, especially the discussion of Gary Henson's gambling addiction, which, per the essayist, "gave his wife no other option than to leave him."

Still, the true account of the incident itself—recounted by a neighbor and later confirmed by others—shocked us: Gary had not leaped at all. When he found out about his wife's elevator ride, he'd gotten dangerously drunk, walked out onto his deck late at night, and shouted loudly and angrily at nothing in particular. For reasons even Gary likely didn't understand, he'd desired an elevated stage, so he tried to step up onto his deck's railing. In doing so, he slipped, fell over, but managed to grab hold of his deck's edge. Juliet, who lived not several floors down but directly below him, had come out onto her own deck when she'd heard the commotion. She guided him down as best as she could—he did slip and sprain his ankle—and then helped him sober up. He limped back upstairs to his own condo that very night and returned the next day to apologize. Thus, the two became friends, then lovers, then engaged.

Outer residents pretended not to be bothered by the story. They'd never believed it anyway, they claimed. It had always been meant as a fun little tale. They largely ignored the deaths and initial panic it had inspired. If you asked one of them who lived nearby whether they'd heard Gary yelling that night, they wouldn't answer. They'd chuckle and shake their heads, as if confused why anyone would be interested in such a silly thing.

For the inner units, the exposé was a miraculous victory. They outwardly claimed it didn't matter that it painted such a villainous picture of those with windows to the outside world; they cared only about the truth. This was all for show. They'd actually been brooding since the story first emerged. After all, they had no decks to jump from, so what was the story of Gary and Juliet other than proof that outer privilege extended to every corner of life, even attempts to end it?

44

A PERFECTLY GOOD CAMPER

LYDIA WALKED among the cars in the early morning, some dinged and dusty, but all remarkably well preserved. Two Displaced Travelers held hands and looked at a gray sedan a row over, their expressions forlorn. Aside from them, Lydia was alone out here in the "lot," though really, like that of Large Coveted Object Moving Rentals, it was just a patch of desert.

They'd done it. They'd tunneled into the parking garage and excavated the cars. There'd been a number of deads down there, more than anyone anticipated, and the doctor had to work overtime to update the Victims Log. Still, just the fact that they could take on such a project spoke to the Dig's considerable growth in the four months since Bernard's rescue put them back in the news. That Peter Thisbee planned to sell the cars in the Sale suggested a new age of prosperity in CamperTown's future. And to think, Lydia would be here for it all, at the helm: the chairperson of the present and the future.

She talked to herself in this self-aggrandizing way to transmute her disappointment into something more productive. While Lydia may have had the title she'd always desired, the actual power Thisbee allotted to her was more akin to that of a high-ranking officer of a middle school student council than a member of a municipal government. She was relegated to plucky go-getter initiatives, projects that she herself could organize and oversee. She had found some success in this regard. For example, she'd introduced the Work-for-Wheels program, allowing Heap workers capable of automotive repair the chance to use, until sold, any car from the lot they could restore to order. But when it came to CamperTown's big picture concerns, the kinds of things that would require Thisbee's backing to carry out, she got nowhere. He was always unavailable, couldn't find time to come by or meet at the casino, couldn't talk on the phone or even send an assistant. He was too busy sorting out supply issues that came along with the influx of new workers.

She told herself she had to be patient. Her time would come. Otherwise, Thisbee wouldn't have increased her stipend and made the chairperson position full-time, relieving her of her digging responsibilities. Her time spent as a Dig Hand, and her ties to Hans, Orville, and thus (indirectly) Bernard, gave her enough clout for most people in CamperTown to be unbothered by the move. To appease the few who were put out by it, she set up shop in the conference trailer all day every day, leaving the door open so she could be both visible and accessible. It was all performance. She didn't have enough work to actually fill a day and instead spent most of her time fantasizing about the future, making plans for projects that she knew might never see the light of day. She stopped going to The Bars at night. This, too, was for appearances—she was a serious politician now; she had to control how people saw her—though really she feared she might just have one too many drinks and let spill her dissatisfaction.

So here she was, wandering through the parking lot until she came to the truck—the one nobody could get running, making it an ideal meeting room. She got in and sat in the driver's seat. Soon enough, Terrance emerged. He had a rifle over his shoulder, which had alarmed Lydia the first time he'd come to meet her, but since then, she'd grown used to it. "I like to walk way out so it's not too loud and shoot a little," he'd said. "Clears my head before a long day of digging." It was weird, sure, but Lydia pretended it made sense because she needed him.

They'd been conducting these little rendezvous for the last couple of months. Being so far removed from the average CamperTown resident, Lydia was forced to use Terrance as a way of keeping an ear to the ground. He gave her a view into the mood within CamperTown she might otherwise get by going out each night. Meeting with him also staved off the loneliness of her new position, though Lydia was loath to admit this.

Today, as he got in, shifting his rifle between his legs, the Displaced Travelers observed the two of them and exchanged a knowing smile before walking away. Lydia wanted to yell after them that it wasn't what they thought, but they were harmless. Though more integrated in the CamperTown community than ever, they still spoke in what seemed to most people like some kind of code. She watched the two of them disappear behind a sedan before turning to Terrance.

"What's the word?" Lydia asked.

"Fire pits," he said. "Someone found some old recording of Orville and Bernard talking about them and now folks just want to sit out by the fire. Makes sense. Getting colder and all."

"What's stopping them? Do they need supplies or something?"

He shrugged and tried to make it seem casual, but he wouldn't make eye contact. "I don't know. That's just what people are talking about these days. Fire pits."

It was Terrance, so Lydia expected a degree of awkwardness. This was different. "There's something you're not telling me, isn't there?"

Terrance turned from the windshield to look out the passenger-side window. "I don't want to upset you."

"C'mon, Terrance. Just tell me."

"It's just . . . well . . ." Terrance paused and took a deep breath. "And this is what people are saying, but there's folks in tents sleeping on pool floaties waiting for the next wave of campers to come in."

"Thisbee's people are working on it," Lydia said. "Until they find more campers, there's nothing I can do."

"Yeah, but there's a perfectly good camper that's unoccupied!" He seemed to have snapped for a moment, but collected himself. "Again, this is just what I'm hearing."

Lydia rested her hands on the steering wheel and considered this. "The old shell of one, out in the desert? I don't think it's livable."

Terrance sighed. "That's not the one."

Of course it wasn't. Lydia could kick herself for not thinking of it sooner. "You mean Orville's camper."

"Yes, ma'am," said Terrance to the window.

Lydia had, in her new position as chairperson, taken the reins on several less-than-glamorous organizational duties that Gil had always left up to Thisbee's people. These were her only duties that really meant anything, and one of them was to assign incoming Dig Hands to vacant campers. Problem was, she felt a connection to the place Thisbee's people didn't, so when Orville left the same day they found Bernard, without officially signing his Intention to Leave papers, she used it as an excuse not to reassign his camper. She knew she should—Orville's sudden and silent disappearance didn't indicate he'd be returning to the Dig anytime soon—but to do so would be to acknowledge that their present reality was not some mere test drive, and that she could not go back to a happier time when her goals were out of reach.

It was unfair to Orville. He was with Bernard on some sort of speaking tour; of course *he* wouldn't want to go back. More importantly, though, it wasn't fair to CamperTown. She'd let her emotions get the best of her, and now people were talking. It wasn't a huge deal—they needed way more than just one camper—but she didn't want there to be any lingering doubts about her leadership ability once things started to pick up speed.

"I'll fix it," she told Terrance. "I'll go over and clean up his camper this afternoon. It'll be ready for a new resident by next week."

"Just make sure everything's disconnected." Terrance turned to her now and gave her a wink.

"What?"

"You know," Terrance said. "The phone line. It's underground, right? I always wondered."

Lydia stared at him. "Orville told you about this?"

Terrance shook his head. "I just assumed." His face lit with revelation. "You're messing with me. Because I'm not allowed to know. That's it, isn't it?"

He spoke with such breathless excitement that Lydia looked out the windshield to make sure the Displaced Travelers weren't within earshot. "Not allowed to know what?" she said.

"How he made the calls," Terrance said, "when the phone bank was closed."

45

A DISCONNECT

HANS NEVER mentioned the day they found Bernard, but Lydia could tell that it had left a mark on him. They didn't see each other that much anymore, and Hans didn't like to discuss it, so Lydia knew only the vague details: going a night without sleep, then digging all day for Orville only to find Bernard. Nobody would've blamed him if he'd said he just needed a break from digging, but Hans wouldn't do that. Instead, he claimed it to be injuries that forced him off the Dig. And he had suffered more than he'd first realized when he slid down the Heap that morning. No broken arm, no severed fingers or anything like that, but a litany of bruises and scrapes and sprains and tweaks that still ailed him. Lydia, boss, and the doctor pushed for him to stay on as a full-time orientation leader, and the powers that be allowed it. It worked well for everyone. Hans finally got time to take pictures of the Heap in action (and he actually did take pictures now), fielding questions everywhere he went, and the Dig retained a valuable symbol: the man who dug up Bernard. It said to the new recruits, *Do your work and you'll be taken care of, even if you can barely hold a shovel anymore, even if you walk with a limp.*

And Hans did walk with a limp. It slowed him down on their way to Orville's camper, but at least it gave Lydia time to run through what Terrance had just relayed to her.

"You remember the big spat?" she said. "The whole, 'Grrr, who dares trespass on brother time?'"

"How could I forget?" Hans said.

"So, Terrance felt real bad about it and wanted to apologize."

"We sure raised that boy right, you know."

"But he didn't want to do it at The Bars," Lydia said. "He wanted to get Orville alone, to really lay it out. And he thought it wouldn't be a good idea to go to Orville's camper, because it needed to be on neutral ground. So he went when Orville usually called Bernard and he waited along the path to the phone bank."

"Hold on," Hans said. "He wanted to apologize for intruding on his call with Bernard, so he decided to talk to him right after his next call to Bernard?"

"It wasn't the perfect plan," Lydia admitted. "But anyway, so he waited. And he waited, and he waited. But Orville never came. Finally, Terrance decided he'd go all the way to the phone bank and see what was taking so long."

"Christ, Terrance!" Hans shook his head in disbelief. "Orville must've been pissed."

"He wasn't," Lydia said. "Because he wasn't there. Terrance found the whole phone bank totally shut down."

"This was the day before we found Bernard," Hans said. "So that would explain the radio silence."

"You'd think," Lydia said. "But Terrance, ever-persistent, can't-leave-anything-alone Terrance, he found a sign on the fence—some telecom company—and he decided to check the logs at the gate to see when they came in."

"Why?"

"Because Orville had called in the day before, so he figured they must've just put it up. Maybe they were still there. It looked dusty, but everything looks dusty here, so he figured he'd check."

"I'm still not getting you," Hans said.

"I think he thought there'd been some misunderstanding," Lydia said. "So if someone from the company was still there, he could explain how necessary it was to at least leave one phone open. And then maybe Orville, who Terrance imagined would be distraught to find it shut down, might forgive him."

Hans laughed. "It's like, that's Terrance in a nutshell. Sweet and stupid all at once. Had they left yet?"

"Yeah," Lydia said. "Three weeks before."

They could see Orville's camper just a little ways down the road, but Hans stopped. He squinted at it for a moment, then turned to Lydia. "What?"

"Exactly," Lydia said. "And I checked too. I went straight from the car lot to the gate and told Benjy to give me the logs. Sure enough, there it is: three weeks and change before Bernard was found, it says, 'Starlight Telecom.' They only turned it back on recently, with all the new recruits coming in. Apparently, some newb complained and boss had to get a company to fix it. It was the first he'd heard it'd been shut down."

"Benjy didn't think to say anything?"

Lydia shook her head. "Benjy keeps the logs, but Benjy doesn't read the logs."

"What about that trip Orville took to the casino?" Hans said.

"That's what I thought too," Lydia said. "But he only went once. Anyway, so Terrance thinks Orville had an underground phone line."

"That seems like a stretch," Hans said.

"We'll see."

"And if we do find one, what are we going to do? Disconnect it?"

"It could be dangerous to move otherwise," Lydia said. "Live wires, you know."

"Does that happen with phone stuff?" Hans said. "I thought it was just a thing with downed power lines."

"You can never be too careful," Lydia said. She didn't explain why they would need to move it at all. Truthfully, she didn't know herself. She just wanted to poke around a little bit, see if she could find something interesting.

It looked like she would be disappointed. Orville's camper appeared immaculate. There was nothing on the floor or the kitchenette table save for a thin layer of dust. Even the windows looked wiped clean. They checked the closet and the cabinets. No phone. No anything. It was empty.

"Where would it be?" Hans asked.

Lydia shrugged. "Maybe he disconnected it when he left? I didn't realize Orville was so clean. But he had been talking about moving."

Hans looked at her. "Even before we found Bernard?"

"It was more of a metaphor," Lydia said. "I just don't get why he wouldn't tell us about this stuff. He should've known that we wouldn't rat him out."

Hans didn't answer. He was sitting on the love seat, sort of bouncing. "Regina, in her camper, the love seat doubles as a sort of storage space. She didn't even know about it for a while."

"Regina?" Lydia said.

Hans felt around the edge of the cushion. "New bartender at The Bars since what's-her-name just left without telling anyone. You're not there to keep me from making friends anymore. Anyway, they make them hard to open on purpose. You can keep stuff there, safe and out of sight. That's where he'd keep a phone, I know it."

Lydia was about to say something about how it was laughable to think she, so valued as a member of the community, would be the one holding him back—not to mention, they were both adults; they didn't have to use phrases like "making friends"—when Hans stopped moving and stood up. The cushion opened and Lydia stepped forward to look in.

"Clothes," Hans said.

Lydia couldn't hide her displeasure. The idea of Orville keeping a secret from them had excited her. Maybe it would be more than a hidden phone, but even just a hidden phone would be reinvigorating enough. Since taking her new position, she'd grown jaded. The idea of something, anything going unseen and undiscussed gave her at least a different level of the community to consider, an underbelly to expose.

Hans, sensing her mood, tried to appease her. "You're probably right. He took care of it before he left."

"Or there's some other, more reasonable explanation," Lydia said. She couldn't think of one, but she was bound to later. Maybe Orville had worked out some agreement with Starlight Telecom. Maybe he'd been warned about the phone bank shutting down and was given special accommodations, a nice little room all his own somewhere in the Assistance Sector. He probably wouldn't want to mention this, for fear of it seeming like favoritism. At any rate, a little extra comfort might explain the chattiness during those weeks. "We'd better get rid of this stuff. Don't want the next resident to have to deal with it."

They began to pull everything out, piling it on the floor. They'd donate it, Lydia thought. Before today, she might've considered keeping it someplace safe, in case Orville came back for it. But Orville was gone, and maybe they'd never really been that close to begin with. It didn't seem right. The three of them had shared plenty, but maybe they'd only ever been friendly coworkers rather than actual friends. He didn't even tell her about the phone bank shutting down. Keeping quiet about such a mundane detail didn't speak to some hidden agenda. It meant he didn't think she would understand. Maybe, Lydia thought, his dourness was not some change in him, just in him giving up on the facade of their friendship.

Halfway through the trunk, they came upon two Christmas sweaters, side by side. Hans laughed. Lydia didn't. She reached in, grabbed a sweater in each hand, and yanked them out. Something shifted underneath. They both stared at a large briefcase.

Hans seemed to be overstating his enjoyment of the task to counterbalance Lydia's frustrations. "And what could this be?" he said, taking it out and clicking the latches open. Lydia moved to grab more clothes, but when she turned to chide Hans on getting back to work, she saw him frozen, staring at the contents of the case: a massive gun, in pieces, all nested in plush. Her breath caught.

"Lydia," Hans said. "What the hell is this?"

"I don't know," Lydia said. "I really have no idea."

They were both jittery with excitement now, but worked with greater caution. None of the other clothing yielded weapons, but at the bottom, Lydia found a business card. It showed a picture of someone with an immaculately white smile. The face looked familiar, but Lydia couldn't place it.

"Hal Cornish," Lydia read, "Director of Advertising— Sundial Media." She handed it to Hans. He stared at it in disbelief.

Lydia stood, feeling suddenly alive, and paced. "I know, I know. This guy might have nothing to do with this. But we need to know what's going on here, and it's worth trying everything. So I say we go to the phone bank right now and we call that number. We'll have to make up some story."

"No," Hans said.

Lydia stopped. "What do you mean, 'no'? Of course we will. If he senses there's something weird going on, he'll hang right up. And let's be honest"—she pointed to the briefcase, still open—"there's definitely something weird going on."

"He won't answer." Hans struggled to his feet and handed the business card back to Lydia. "Because he won't be there.

He's here. He was in an orientation session a couple weeks ago. He was always quick to raise his hand whenever I asked a question, a real go-getter type. And he wouldn't stop smiling, just like that."

Now it was Lydia's turn to stare at the card in disbelief. "This guy? 'Hal Cornish'? He's here in CamperTown?"

Hans nodded. "I'm sure it's him. But he doesn't go by that name."

46

FROM *THE LATER* YEARS:

FLOORS

The layout of each floor differed slightly. A floor that housed an amphitheater might have higher ceilings and smaller units. A "park" might occupy an expanse of what would otherwise be valuable outer real estate, meaning an even more dispropor-tionate spread of inner- to outer-dwelling residents. Still, the actual hallways themselves looked more or less the same. Per-haps one floor would be painted in a light blue, another in a burnt orange or a turquoise. But many of the features—such as the font of the signage, the pile of the carpet, the quality of light—remained consistent in all public spaces.

More than any of the mechanisms that kept Los Verti-calés upright for so long, this, we reasoned, was perhaps Peter Thisbee's most ingenious move. Had each floor possessed its own visual aesthetic, those who lived there might be content to let it speak for itself. Lacking any notable surface-level differ-ences encouraged us to build an identity that superseded mere appearances.

To be fair, these too often existed mostly on the surface. A floor with two or three fitness buffs might be deemed "sporty" or "health-conscious" by those who lived on it, and "meat-headed" by those who lived above or below. One painter was all it took for an entire floor to be considered "artsy." And the presence of visiting scholars—despite having been relegated, without any say, to some of the most cramped and uncomfortable living quarters—might cause their neighbors to boast about living in "a hotbed of intellectual curiosity."

Regardless of whether we ourselves possessed any affinity for the identity of our given floor, we clung to it, and paid homage to the residents who—by way of profession, personality, or hobby—defined us. This homage was never spoken, but there was a nod we reserved for whenever we saw one of them in their sweat-drenched athletic wear, or in their paint-speckled overalls, or carrying their notebooks. It was slight, barely more than a twitch, yet weighted with reverence. Because these individuals gave us more than just an identity. They allowed us to move.

With the supposed differences between one floor and another, those among us who felt restless always had an excuse to pack up and find a new unit. "I'm more of a creative type," one might claim, and thus he could be free to leave without additional justification. Those who remained behind never questioned these decisions, nor pointed out incongruities in the reasoning. They helped him load boxes into the freight elevator (which we were allowed to use for moves with the purchase of a short-term permit) and wished him well, even if he'd never expressed any inclination toward the arts.

Likewise, if he saw his departed neighbors at a party, they would not ask snidely what new creative projects he was working on, or observe aloud any apparent personality changes. Doing so would only invite conflict, which, like all disputes, would be quickly snuffed out without any satisfactory conclusion. And besides, even if the argument were allowed to play out, they knew the uncomfortable truth: that it was just as likely their former neighbor had always been like this, and it had been his proximity to them that kept it below the surface so long.

47

KYLE AND HAL

LYDIA WENT to the camper at dusk and found the man sitting there in an Adirondack chair, looking so comfortable that for a moment she wondered if she had the wrong address. But when he looked at her and smiled she could tell Hans had been right. It was him. Hal Cornish. Again, Lydia felt a rush of involuntary familiarity, and not just because she'd stared at his card for the better part of two hours while she waited for the workday to end.

"Evening, Kyle," Lydia said as he stood to greet her. He apparently went by Kyle Eckles since arriving at the Heap, a name that required patient enunciation to keep it from sounding like a noise chickens make.

Hal stood and shook her hand. "The chairperson! In my own front yard, speaking my first name like an old friend. To what do I owe the honor?"

"I'd like to say I take walks sometimes and introduce myself to the residents of CamperTown who might not know me," Lydia said.

Hal kept smiling but raised an eyebrow. "You'd like to say it? But you won't?"

Lydia looked at her feet for a moment. She wanted to appear pensive, but didn't want to overdo it. There was something polished about him that made her think she'd have to do things just right. "Truth is, Kyle, this is a business call. We could use someone like you on the Committee for Better Life in CamperTown."

Hal Cornish laughed. "I don't know how much use I'd be. I haven't been here too long. But I'd be happy to chat about it if you'd like."

He motioned for her to take a seat, but Lydia remained standing. "It's not a position that requires a lot of prior knowledge," she said. "We're dealing with an issue of messaging. We do a lot for the community, but we rely too heavily on word of mouth to get it out to the masses. It used to work when CamperTown was much smaller, but as our numbers grow we need to be more strategic. That's where you'd come in. We'd need someone with experience"—she leaned forward here, and whispered—"in advertising."

Hal Cornish's smile straightened a bit. "Interesting," he said. "And you've sought me out because?"

"Because you used to work in advertising," Lydia said. "For a radio station. Isn't that right, Hal?"

Now he stopped smiling altogether but said nothing.

Lydia motioned to his camper. "If you'd prefer, we can continue this conversation in private."

Hal obliged. She hoped from here things would be easier, but the few steps from the Adirondack chairs into his camper seemed to be enough for him to regroup. When they'd passed through the door he was smiling again and offering Lydia a glass of wine. She accepted and sat down at the dinette while he went rooting around in a drawer for a corkscrew.

"So, you've found me out," he said, opening a cupboard. "I knew it would come to the surface soon enough, that I'd run away from my past life. But you've been out here so long, you've probably forgotten what it's like back in the 'real world.' Wrangling sponsors, dealing with the higher-ups, the on-air talent, it can get to feel so self-serving. I wanted to get my hands dirty, you know?"

"So you're working out on the Heap?" Lydia looked around. The few new campers Thisbee's people had managed to wrangle were often spare and cheap. This one was a small open room. Hal kept it as immaculate as his teeth, but there were imperfections even he couldn't hide. His closet had no door, showing his shirts and pants hanging crisp and neat. Something at the far end caught Lydia's eye—something white and long. Lydia sat forward and stared at it until a glass of rosé obstructed her view.

"That's right," Hal said.

Lydia took the glass and turned to him. "Sorry, what's right?"

"I'm on the Heap, a Dig Hand." Hal sat across from her. "It's rewarding work, after so many years behind a desk. I could do without the smell, but I'm told you get used to that."

"Oh, right, sorry. Yes, on the Heap. And you will," Lydia said. She held her wine but did not take a drink. Adrenaline pulsed through her. "But you know what smell you never get used to?"

Hal cocked his head theatrically. He seemed to think Lydia was flirting with him. "Tell me," he said, raising his glass of wine to take a drink.

"Bullshit. Like all the bullshit you're feeding me right now." Lydia had to focus to keep herself from grinning.

The glass of wine froze inches from Hal Cornish's lips. His smile, once again, disappeared. He opened his mouth to speak, but Lydia beat him to it.

"I knew I'd seen you before, but I couldn't place it. Now I remember." She pointed to the closet, the white linen suit. "The whole, 'I ran away from the high-pressure corporate life to work with my hands' shtick is a classic. But generally, it doesn't involve any literal running through the streets of your future community at the fuckcrack of dawn. Point being, you're here to escape more than a desk and you know it. So here's a promise: if you don't tell me everything—and I mean *everything*, but especially why I found your business card in my friend Orville Anders's old camper—I'll go to the phone bank, I'll put a call in to Sundial Media, and I will ask them why one of their former employees is hiding out here with a new job and a new name. Does that sound fair?"

Hal Cornish nodded.

"Good." Lydia took a sip of her wine. "Let's start with the big stuff: Who exactly are you and why are you here?"

"I'm Hal Cornish," said Hal Cornish, "former director of advertising for Sundial Media, which owned, among other properties, 103.1, the radio station of Los Verticalés. And I'm here for penance."

"Oh, come on," Lydia said. "You're hiding out."

Hal Cornish slammed his wineglass down on the table. It was cheap plastic and made only a small sound, which seemed to disappoint him. "Yes, of course I'm hiding out! But you think this is the only place I could've gone? You saw me that morning, but that was months ago and I've only worked here for two weeks. You think I was just biding my time? That I was just dying to return to this place? No, I was taking stock of what I'd done and what I could do next. To come here was my only option. I could never make up for what happened to Mr. Anders, but I could at least do some good."

"You're going to have to explain what you mean by 'what happened to' Orville. According to the newbs, he's a celebrity. Half of them only came here because they saw him and his brother give one of their talks somewhere."

"But that's just it," Hal said. "That man is not his brother."

"I thought I told you that I didn't want any more bullshit," Lydia said.

"I'm being serious," Hal said. "He's an impersonator, I'm certain. We hired him. Of course, I never met him. I arranged for his services over the phone. But I snuck into one of their speaking engagements. I've seen the people they travel with in the audience. They're the ones who brought me here that morning."

"You hired someone to impersonate Orville's brother?"

"No. We hired him to impersonate Orville."

The conversation had, until that moment, been going as if affixed to a track, her questions following each other neatly like train stops, but now Lydia found herself in a depot. In each direction a new track she could take, a new series of questions she could ask. The choices overwhelmed her and when she opened her mouth, she could think of nothing to say.

Luckily, simply revisiting the past seemed to send Hal Cornish into a sort of disgusted reverie. "You hear about these people, but you don't remember how or when. That's the truth, I swear. I don't know how I heard of them. This is designed, I'm sure. They want to be discussed in hushed, embarrassed tones only."

" 'Them'?" Lydia said. "It's a group?"

"Yes." Hal drank from his wineglass now. "A collective of vocal impersonators."

"And they work primarily for radio stations," Lydia said.

Hal Cornish nearly spit up his wine laughing at this. "No! Absolutely not! They work mostly with bigger clients than Sundial. Politicians, lobbyist groups, that sort of thing. That's all rumors, though. There's no official list of their jobs." He looked out the window, his eyes distant, as if reliving some long-ago trauma.

Lydia wanted none of it. She stood and helped herself to another glass of wine. "I have to be honest, Hal. I have no idea what the hell you're talking about. Why don't we keep things a bit closer to home." She sat down again. "What were your dealings with these people?"

Hal let out a defeated sigh, as if resigning himself to the idea of clarity. "We had sponsors lined up. We wanted

Orville to read promotions. We approached him about this, offering compensation, and he refused. So we brought in these people, as a way to intimidate him. It was only supposed to be temporary."

"Then they found Orville," Lydia said, "and hired him."

This suggestion seemed to horrify Hal Cornish. "No, he found them. Or, he found *him*. And they didn't hire Orville. Lydia, your friend is a prisoner."

48

FISSURES

THEY DROVE, they gave speeches, they spent their nights in motels. This was Orville's life now.

ᨘ

THERE WERE the same four others that had been there that day on the Heap: Joan, the two henchmen, and Orville's impersonator, a man named Harvey. Orville was not allowed to call him this. He was to refer to him only as Bernard.

ᨘ

THE SPEECHES were scripted. They stuck to smaller cities, maintained a tour route that would look from above like indeterminate scribbling. This was by design, to keep people from following them, to drum up wider appeal by appearing to be everywhere. They did not make the tour route. Strom did. Strom was the leader of the Vocalist Cartel. This much Orville had gathered. Each night, they booked two adjoining motel rooms. Joan would step into the other room to talk to him on the phone. Then Harvey. Then Orville. But Orville never spoke to Strom. He spoke to the real Bernard.

ᨘ

THEY'D TAKEN Bernard off the air, killed the frequency. It amazed Orville how easy this had been for them to achieve. It sure helped that Bernard had been playing hold music at the time of his apparent rescue. But it wasn't just luck. It seemed as if they'd preemptively put some measures in place to take the whole station down, so it was easy as flipping a switch. Orville imagined that perhaps these measures had been installed when the impersonator had taken over for him, but he couldn't be sure about that, nor about why they'd even thought something so drastic might be necessary in the first place. He wasn't sure of much these days. They told him almost nothing. One thing he could intuit was that they'd turned off Bernard's signal without Sundial Media knowing. Harvey delighted in bringing up Sundial's cluelessness throughout the process. He winked at Orville every time radio personalities from other Sundial stations came to their talks to shake his hand and introduce themselves as "colleagues."

≀

IF ORVILLE did a good job—said his lines, gave the right emphases, etc.—he could speak to his brother. He didn't need to dial Bernard's old station number. Strom would patch him through. They'd established a secure connection when they shut down the frequency. It meant that only they could call Bernard, no one else. Orville asked how this was possible, but Joan only warned him against asking too many questions. These conversations with Bernard were Orville's reward, but most of the time they didn't feel like one. The first night they talked, it hadn't been so bad. Orville needed to make sure it was him. He asked about the other stations Bernard had worked at. He asked their mother's name. It embarrassed him that he was relegated to such basic information for proof of identity. But he couldn't ask about their conversations. They'd all been public. Finally, Orville had an idea. "What have you been thinking about, Bernard?" he asked. And Bernard asked "How much time do you have?" before launching into a theory about how minutes had a different shape when there was no one to talk to. It was him. Orville could tell.

Just listening to Bernard returned Orville to a time before the impersonator, back to when his routine involved digging and calling and little else. But since that initial conversation, Bernard had grown more and more despondent. He spent all day alone, talking to no one. He was losing it.

ONE NIGHT, when they talked, Bernard said, "Maybe you should stop calling. You might start believing that guy's actually me. You could be happy, Orville. You deserve to be happy." Orville didn't know what to say because there was nothing to say. This was a situation that required action, but he could take none. It was like those nights at The Bars, when he stewed about his replacement but could do nothing, a sensation with no release. He wanted to free his brother, to put him back on air at the very least. It was what was best for the both of them, and he was starting to feel overwhelmed by the responsibility of being Bernard's sole conversation partner. It reminded him of just how little they really had to say to each other. But how do you help the trapped when you're trapped yourself?

A MAN approached them once, early on during the tour, with a shovel to sign, and Orville tried to convey some sense of desperation through a series of blinks for nearly a half minute before anyone caught on. The henchmen managed to send the man away before he could understand what was going wrong with Orville's eyes. Afterward, Joan told him that not only would he be missing out on his call to Bernard that night, but if he ever tried to signal anyone like that again, the Cartel would have no choice but to make that person disappear. "And it'll be all your fault," she had said.

❧

DURING THE performances, Orville wore the syringe. When people arrived at the venue, Joan and the henchmen disappeared into the crowd. Joan held the trigger inside her jacket. Orville looked for her among the crowds each night. When he saw her hand tucked into her coat, he felt the skin around the tip of the needle tingle.

❧

DESPITE THE sellout crowds, Orville could not understand how this could be profitable enough to warrant such a large operation, especially considering the high-level work Nina had implied the Vocalist Cartel did. But the tour kept going, so it must've been good for something.

❧

OUTSIDE OF venues and motels, they stopped only occasionally at convenience stores. During these stops, either Joan or Harvey would use a pay phone to check in with Strom. Orville observed these calls from the van. They were not conversations, nothing more than intermittent responses of "yessir, of course, sir," sometimes accompanied by an involuntary head nod. They didn't discuss things with Strom. They listened and received orders.

❧

PERHAPS STROM'S cleverest move was for them to spread the conspiracy theories themselves. They called in to talk radio shows. They pointed out the strangeness that nobody had heard Bernard so close to the surface, the fact that in none of the accounts did anyone, even Hans, mention hearing the ConductionSens shovel whistle to indicate he'd struck power. Surfacing these concerns cleansed them. Their voicing made them seem suddenly ridiculous, despite their truth.

❦

WHAT STROM couldn't oversee was the group's dynamic. Fissures were growing. Orville could see them. Harvey, the star, grew arrogant. Joan, relegated to a more managerial role, grew envious of him. Charlie talked too much. Stefan never spoke.

❦

ONE PERFORMANCE, Harvey blew past his closing line. He was supposed to say: "And I definitely would've given up if I didn't know my brother was up there every day, digging to find me." But when the audience did not applaud as much as they usually did, he added, "Not that I wasn't sweating your arrival." The theater fell into an awkward silence. Harvey looked to Orville with concern. Orville would be blamed for this somehow, if he didn't find something to say. What he said was: "You think you were sweating? Try working a shovel in the desert sun all day every day! Down in that hole must've felt like air-conditioning compared to what I was dealing with!" This got a big laugh. Orville felt a thrill of joy in spite of himself. They were able to get offstage. After the show, Harvey said, "Air-conditioning? That was fucking perfect!" But rather than give Orville the credit, he spent the rest of the night trying to figure out how he could be the one to say the line next time.

❦

THERE HAD been an issue with tape. When the roll of medical tape used to affix the syringe ran out, Joan bought what she thought was an equivalent tape at an office supply store. Charlie, whose job it was to remove the syringe each night, expressed regret over her tape choice. He argued in much the same way he'd argued with Orville at the phone bank that day. Joan grew frustrated. As a solution, she reassigned duties:

Stefan would now be in charge of removing the syringe because Stefan didn't complain.

HARVEY AND Joan had their biggest fight yet. Joan, punchy from not doing enough acting herself, used the long van rides to work on voices for a character. Sometimes, she used them to speak with the venue owners when acting as their manager, and sometimes she asked questions at a given event's Q&A. They grew more elaborate as her frustration mounted. The current profile: a New Zealand expat who'd spent a decade in France. Harvey, never one to withhold his thoughts, asked about the "saliva static" with which Joan punctuated her speech. Joan, in the voice of someone who had a palate expander, explained that this character had a palate expander. Harvey, frustrated, asked if she really had to keep talking in the voice while they workshopped it. "Oh, that's rich," Joan said. "*You* asking *me* to drop a voice." Harvey claimed it was part of his technique that he speak as Bernard always. Things got personal. Harvey called Joan jealous, which Joan countered with an accusation: "You know what I think? I think when everything collapsed around you, you were down there, in the dark, thinking that if you didn't die, then certainly Strom would kill you when you got out. You allowed yourself to get captured. You think he would've just let you right back into the fold?" Harvey's mouth hung open but he could find no reply. Joan continued: "Strom managed to make something of the mess you put us in. He managed to make a lot of it, in fact. But trust me, when this whole thing fades— when the world begins to forget about Bernard Anders, the Voice of the Vert—let's just say you might want to brush up on your bartending." The van went silent after that. Guilt shot through Orville at the mention of Nina. It mixed with the satisfaction of watching them argue. And yet, the hope he felt—that they might ever grow so dysfunctional as to allow for his escape——was thin, tenuous.

❧

OVER THE course of several hours, Orville watched the landscape grow sparse and turn to desert.

49

SWEATERS

"I'M SERIOUS," Hans said. "I know you have a lot on your mind; if you want me to drive . . ."

Lydia's hands tensed on the wheel, jerking the car just slightly onto the shoulder. They'd only been on the road for about an hour, and it was the second time Hans had offered.

What she wanted to say was that just because he was a man did not mean he was more adept at driving under the weight of distressing knowledge. Lydia had told him everything Hal Cornish had told her—about the impersonator, the abduction, all of it—so it was not as though his head were free and clear.

What she said instead was, "I'm fine."

"I'm just saying," he said, "if you'd be more comfortable—"

"It might be hard for you," Lydia said, "with your leg, the pedals, you know. I don't want you to get us into an accident. You'd feel terrible."

This quieted Hans for a moment. "The thing I keep thinking," Hans said, "is that these voice actors show up around the same time the bartender who does voices disappears. Isn't that kind of eerie?"

Lydia, who had considered the strange timing of Nina's departure, kept her eyes on the road. "I don't think we need to go any deeper than the troubling stuff we do know at this point."

Hans fell silent and pretended to consult the map. "You

don't think anyone will notice this car is missing, will they?"

What was funny was this all started because Lydia hoped to correct something that might be perceived as an abuse of power, i.e., her refusal to reassign Orville's camper. Now, she was no closer to reassigning it. Instead, she'd spent two whole days running around conducting investigative work that served her own interests. That she had canceled the week's Committee meeting to commandeer a repaired hatchback for her and Hans from the lot—a violation of the user guidelines she herself had put in place—didn't necessarily send a message of responsibility. She hoped she'd built up enough goodwill for this to be regarded, when all was said and done, as a minor pimple on a smooth and luminous career in local politics. But given that, after all the time she'd devoted to this little project, she found herself only at the outset of a rudimentary plan brimming with potential for failure, it wasn't looking good. Or, in sticking with the pimple analogy, it was like if the skin had been inflamed and taut for days and had yet to even form a whitehead. Which was really just a gross way to think about it, and besides, Lydia hadn't driven a car since before she arrived at the Heap, so her focus needed to be on that, not pimple-related metaphor construction.

Lydia had outlined an idea for saving Orville (or at least getting him back to CamperTown), then gone to Hal Cornish and shaken him down for some industry contacts who might be able to get her some details on the touring schedule. "I hope this helps settle my debt to you," Hal had said with a dramatic tortured sigh, a balls-out dumb thing to say, as Lydia informed him, because, um, no. When your actions set in motion a series of events that lead someone to be taken and held captive against their will and in plain sight, a few phone numbers does not an even-Stevens make.

"We'll see how this thing turns out, and I'll let you know where you stand," she'd said before she left for the phone bank to put in a few calls.

The hope had been to find a date when the tour would be close by and use that as a deadline to refine her plan. She wanted a month—just long enough to think it through thoroughly, not long enough to overdo it. She got three days: that was when Orville and the man parading as his brother would be closest. Hence, her and Hans's current road trip to a theater for *A Night with the Anders Brothers.*

It was strange driving into the town. Since joining the Dig Effort, Lydia had gone to the casino once or twice, but otherwise, the farthest she'd traveled had been from her camper to the Heap, and she barely went even that far anymore. She'd forgotten what true civilization looked like. There came gas stations at the far outskirts, a few scattered homes, followed by strip malls and new developments, before narrowing to a denser, older downtown. CamperTown felt so large recently, especially considering how much it had grown in the last three months. Yet it seemed as though the entire Assistance Sector could fit into two municipal lots like the one they parked in. It might've been daunting, an illustration of just how far they had to go, if Lydia didn't think of what Thisbee said during the tour about simplicity, and the danger of the metropolitan buzz that had encapsulated life in Los Verticalés. *It's all just so unnecessarily complicated,* she thought now.

They arrived early. Lydia thought they'd get into the theater and wait—maybe Orville and "Bernard" would be there, setting up—but the line for will call wrapped around the block and the ticket booth was unoccupied. A sign in the window informed them the show was sold out.

"Shit," Lydia said. She almost threw down her canvas bag on the sidewalk, but thought better of it.

Hans nudged her and motioned up the street. A minivan approached, making a turn into some special lot behind the theater. "That's them," he whispered. "The guy, Bernard, or not Bernard, you know what I mean. I saw him. Or I think it was him. Last time, with the bandages, hard to tell. Hey, wait!"

But Lydia didn't have time to waste matching Hans's limp-slow pace. She was already around the corner, running up to the van before it came to a stop.

AS SOON as they parked, Charlie called back from the driver's seat, "Please, all, remain in the van. There is some-one approaching, likely someone seeking to speak to either of the Anders brothers. I will give the appropriate verbal warning and attempt to remove her from the premises of this parking lot. If you see me returning to the van, please do not take this as an indication that the parking lot is clear. I will inform you of such upon my return, but only if I am—"

"Just go and deal with it," Joan said, and Charlie got out.

Orville remained slumped in his seat, his head turned away. He had learned during other encounters with rogue fans that the less they saw of him and Harvey, the quicker and easier their removal would be.

"I don't know why we have to treat them like they're animals," Harvey said. "They probably just want an auto-graph or something."

Joan sighed and cleared her throat, ready to make a re-buttal, but decided against it, instead turning her attention to the encounter in the parking lot. "Oh, Christ," she hissed, unclicking her seat belt. Harvey threw open the passenger-side door.

Orville listened as closely as he could.

"Excuse me, ma'am." This was Charlie. "I regret to inform you that the Anders brothers are not available——"

"I'm one of Orville's old dig partners." This voice sent a shock through Orville. He sat up as best he could now, just in time to see Joan and Harvey descend upon Lydia, Stefan trailing behind. He thought to scream, but before he could, Harvey smiled and shook Lydia's hand. He then held his arms wide to hug Hans, who made his way slowly across the parking lot. With his arm still around him, Harvey motioned for Orville to come out, then began to apologize for the "security" people giving them a hard time.

"Can't be too careful," he said.

Orville emerged and made his way to them, feeling a terrified version of elation. To see his friends after so much time on the road issued an automatic response of joy, and yet, despite the needle not even being in yet, he couldn't fully relish it while playing this alternate version of himself.

As if to reinforce this, Joan whispered into his ear as he passed: "You know the rules. No funny business."

"Look who showed up," Harvey said. He turned back to Lydia and Hans. "The whole way down, Orville kept saying, 'I wonder if any CamperTown people are going to show up.' And I kept saying, 'It's pretty far,' and boy, do I need to eat my words now!"

"Sorry it took me a minute." Orville motioned to the van. "Just trying to get a quick nap in."

Hans and Lydia nodded and smiled awkwardly, in unison.

"We know you're busy," Lydia said. "And we didn't get tickets beforehand, so we won't be able to make the show, but we just wanted to see you and——" She reached into her canvas bag. The two henchmen stiffened, but Lydia produced only a flyer. "To invite you. To something."

She handed it to Orville. It read *Camper Retirement Ceremony*, then a date and time: the following day at five P.M.

"People have been breathing down my neck about that camper, your camper," Lydia went on. "But to me, it's like a historical landmark. Still, it is taking up some space. So I thought—we thought"—she motioned to Hans, who nodded—"why don't we retire it? You know, do a little ceremony, take some photos, and then drive it away. Maybe sell it to a museum. I know you're keeping a schedule, but it would sure mean a lot to all of us in CamperTown if you could swing it."

"It wouldn't take more than an hour," Hans added.

Harvey took the flyer from Orville. "That is just a wonderful idea! I'll tell you what, we're going to take a look at our schedule and see if we can make this. How does that sound?"

Lydia smiled gracefully. "That would be wonderful." She looked to Hans for a long moment. It reminded Orville of early on in the tour, when he had struggled to remember each line. A meeting like this was bound to be weird, but not this weird. They seemed to know not to ask too many questions.

"Well, we better get back on the road," Hans finally said.

They turned to leave, but Lydia stopped short. "Oh, sorry, one other thing." She reached into the canvas bag once again and pulled out two Christmas sweaters. "You left these behind, and I thought you might be needing them." She handed them to Orville. "It's not the season yet, but it's coming."

Orville took the sweaters and stared at them. "I have been wondering where those went," he said. He could barely breathe and his voice registered as little more than a whisper. "Thank you."

Lydia looked Orville in the eye and nodded, then she and Hans left.

On their way across the parking lot and into the greenroom—stopping briefly to address the stage crew— the members of the Cartel argued in hushed tones.

Joan took the Christmas sweaters from Orville and looked at them suspiciously. "I thought you two cleaned his camper," she said to the henchmen.

Stefan looked at Charlie, who cleared his throat, surely ready for an argument about both his cleaning abilities and adherence to directives. Orville spoke first. "I probably left them in hers." This satisfied them, and him: he'd always wondered why they'd never made any mention of the rifle.

"Well, we're not going," Joan said. "There's something odd about the whole proposal."

"If you mean how they were acting, it's not so odd," Harvey said. "It can be difficult to talk to someone, even someone you knew so well, after they find fame. It's not something I'd expect you to understand."

Joan's grip on the sweaters tightened. It struck Orville as almost funny, her white knuckles gripping something so cheery and colorful. "Really?" she said. "After last time, you want to go?"

"They invited us back to where it all began. Do you understand how bad that would be for publicity if it got out that we'd turn our backs on our roots like that? Besides, we don't have a gig tomorrow." He patted Orville on the back and grinned. "And anyway, I didn't get a good look around last time. Really would be good to see where my dear brother spent all those months looking for me."

Joan stared at him with pure hatred but said nothing.

"Good," Harvey said, "so when we call Strom tonight, we'll tell him that we're going."

This discussion all came before Joan set Orville's needle. He practiced his breathing so she couldn't tell how hard his heart was beating. He would have a bad show, he could feel it. He was too distracted. They likely wouldn't let him talk to Bernard tonight. But he couldn't get himself to focus. In his mind, the same words repeated over and over again.

They know, they know, they know . . . something.

FROM *THE LATER YEARS:*

ENTERTAINMENT

*Few in Los Verticalés had televisions. Our world was so far re-
moved from the outside that we didn't care to follow their pro-
gramming. At one point, an entrepreneur floated the idea of
starting a closed-circuit station local to the Vert, but planning
didn't get very far. First, there was the issue of scheduling for
an asynchronous city. Moreover, the majority of the population
relied on UV screens as windows; the idea of more screens was
not particularly appealing. Yet we needed some form of entertainment, and thus Los Verticalés became, over time, home to a
booming theater scene.*

    *Occasionally we invited traveling companies to perform
classic plays in the amphitheaters. Attendance was strong,
but the companies almost never came back after their run was
through. More offensive to them than the "strange" performance schedule were the requests issued by event organizers.
In one instance, the director of a thespian troupe was appalled
when asked to rewrite certain scenes in* Othello *so that Iago
insinuated Desdemona and Cassio had taken an elevator ride
to the parking garage together. They'd eventually obliged, but
made sure to deliver the new lines coldly, and so they could not
hide their anger when the audience reacted with audible shock
and delight.*

    For this reason, most of our theater came from within our

walls. Some of the plays employed a traditional structure: a one-off story between an hour and three hours long, with an intermission. Many more followed the pattern of a television series, with new installments coming each week for two or three months at a time. The performances themselves charged no admission fee; instead, they were sponsored by local businesses, mostly restaurants, who paid for props and provided actors with meals during the production. This meant there were no professional actors, and so we were never surprised to see our friends, neighbors, and coworkers onstage.

But even if we didn't recognize any of the cast members, we always recognized the drama. All the plays focused on life in the Vert. Some used it merely as a backdrop, a way to ensure the audience's engagement. Others sought to comment on our collective lives. This could be controversial, and sometimes affected the show's success. For example, a long-running comedy series like Condo President & Condo Resident—*concerning a set of identical twins: one a bumbling idiot, whose actions were often wrongly attributed to the other, the condo president— was allowed to use a heavily trafficked community room due to its inoffensiveness. Meanwhile,* The Skyward Imperialist, *a drama concerning a power-hungry entrepreneur turned real estate developer, could manage to secure only a tiny public conference room and lasted just a single season, despite receiving strong reviews. "The dialogue is sharp," stated one. "It's a shame nobody could actually see the actors deliver it." This spoke to the key issue* The Skyward Imperialist *faced in attracting an audience: due to "inexplicably important" wiring work, the electricity to the conference room had to be cut for an hour each week, and each week that hour just happened to coincide with the performance.*

Perhaps the most innovative and successful show was a thriller called Moss. *Performed in the stairwell, with the audience crowding to watch it from above and below, the story centered around six survivors of an unexplainable disaster:*

The entirety of the Vert had been overtaken by a mossy fun-
gus. Simply breathing in its spores turned one into a violent
creature serving only to spread the moss further. Somehow it
had not managed to enter the stairs, nor had the moss's zom-
bielike foot soldiers thought to check there. So the six survi-
vors lived in fear, scheming about how to get back into the
Vert to secure food and supplies, forming alliances, and turn-
ing against one another. We in the audience left each week
in shock, walking from the stairwells back into the hallways,
half expecting them to be empty. We stopped and examined
any discoloration on the wall, staring at it long after we'd
determined it to be a simple scuff.

It ran four seasons. By the final season, most of the survivors
had gone mad and tried to return home, so that there were only
two left. One died in the penultimate episode, leaving the other
unsure of how she would go on. The series ended on this note of
tragic uncertainty.

Occasionally, someone would question why they didn't
simply take the stairs to the ground level and leave through
the emergency exit, but for most of us, this was not a question
at all. It was not a plot hole. If anything, it was a strength.
It made the characters admirable. They could have left, but
they did not. They never even discussed it. We took this as
evidence of their devotion to Los Verticalés, proof that they
loved the place with a passion that matched, if not exceeded,
our own.

A BUMP IN THE ROAD

ORVILLE HADN'T slept well for two reasons. For starters, the visit from Lydia and Hans, and the coming disruption of their schedule, left him both energized and terrified. He'd done just about as poorly as he could onstage—fumbling lines, forgetting cues, speaking too loudly into the mic—but surprisingly, Joan hadn't punished him. She'd blamed it on Harvey trying to work some new material into the script. It was charitable, but it didn't feel like it. Orville's mind raced as Bernard stammered on about the darkness. He knew Hans and Lydia knew something, but how much? And what did they have planned?

"You sound distracted," Bernard had said.

Orville wanted to tell him everything, but Charlie stood watch in the doorway separating the motel rooms.

"I'm just thinking about what you said that time. About how maybe I should pretend he's you." It was a lie, or maybe it wasn't. He had thought about Bernard's suggestion, but he still didn't consider it an option. At any rate, Bernard seemed relieved to hear this.

"That's good, Orville," he said. "I'm glad to hear you're giving it some thought. You deserve this. You really do."

That was only one of the reasons Orville slept so poorly, the excitement. The other was that the Cartel had left the needle in. They hadn't forgotten. Before he'd even talked to Bernard, when Stefan and he sat down to remove it while Joan spoke to Strom, Harvey said, "Let's wait on that." They were going into CamperTown, where there might not be a greenroom or equivalent. Joan would have to put it in before they got on the road the next morning, and wouldn't that just hold things up? In truth, it would save them only about five minutes total leaving it where it was, but this had nothing to do with efficiency. Harvey, Orville gathered, simply wanted to feel like he had some say in things after the way Joan had dressed him down on the ride south.

"But I have to sleep," Orville said.

"You'll be fine," Harvey said. "Just don't roll over, or you could stab yourself in the heart."

He'd spent the night on his back, practicing stillness. On the way to CamperTown, Orville tried to catch up on sleep, but then the van hit a bump on one of the poorly paved county roads. Suddenly, he felt wide awake.

THE LAST FLYER

THOUGH THE preparation for the ceremony was stressful—though it had all been stressful, these last few days—Lydia realized she was, if not happy, at least not as unhappy as before. The work gave her that rush she'd been looking for: the satisfaction of executing a plan on a strict deadline without sacrificing precision. She might even admit that, while it obviously had been concern for Orville that had set this in motion, it was this feeling more than anything that buoyed her now and would continue to keep her afloat throughout the difficult day ahead.

Before making the trek with Hans out to the theater yesterday, she'd gone to a cubicle building and found the Interdepartmental Form Distribution Department. All she wanted was to print the Camper Retirement Ceremony flyers. It had not gone well. There was a smug discussion between a few workers about whose computer might be most easily given up, the subtext of which was: Who works the least? Thus nobody had been willing to cede their workstation, as doing so would hinder their ability to complain later about being overworked. She eventually found an empty cubicle—someone was on break—and was able to put the flyer together quickly. *Celebrate a piece of CamperTown history!* it read.

The printer posed another issue: it looked to be about twenty years old and took about two minutes to print each flyer. As it slowly chugged away, Lydia noticed several small gatherings of the cubicle workers in her vicinity. They spoke, without looking at her, about paper allotment. One massaged her forehead and bemoaned a forthcoming migraine brought on by "the noise." Lydia had worked in offices before, and thus knew that the word "migraine," when spoken in an environment such as this one, was not the specific condition as defined by medical professionals but a term of general discomfort encompassing everything from dehydration to hunger to mild fatigue. She managed to tune out the complaints while the printer made its slow but steady progress. After a few minutes, though, a man came and turned it off, emphatically citing an ink-use protocol that, he made sure Lydia understood, he was tired of seeing abused. Lydia had left with only four flyers (one of which she'd given to Orville) and as she wouldn't be returning for a repeat of the same ordeal today, she had to triage how best to use her remaining three.

She would set up the ceremony on the trail along the Heap. That would get the Dig Hands' attention. And the cubicle people already knew, so they would be there. She placed one flyer at the café and another in the little enclave of picnic tables where Assistance Sector workers often ate their lunch. For the final flyer, Lydia had an idea. She went to the Displaced Travelers' camp. It had been some time since she'd visited. These days, reading *The Later Years* only made her yearn for an opportunity to put her vision for CamperTown into practice, and besides, they'd been writing less and less.

Stepping into the courtyard for the first time in months, Lydia felt her whole body tense up when she saw the man with the glasses and the mustache, sitting at a café table near the entrance. He seemed surprised to see her too, in his own understated way, sitting up straight and brushing off his shirt. His hair looked disheveled, his glasses crooked, his mustache a little uneven and sloppy.

"Lydia." The man tried to smile. "It's been some time. How's life as the chairperson? Everything you dreamed of?"

This last question caught Lydia, but she would not be victim to his ominous all-knowing bullshit again. She composed herself quickly, stepped forward, and held out the flyer. "In fact, yes. And I'm here to cordially invite you—all of you—to a very special event we're putting on later today. We're hoping the Anders brothers can make it, and perhaps even say a few words."

The man studied the flyer. "This is cute," he said, after some time. "But what about the bigger picture? What about CamperTown's future? Have you been able to talk to Peter about that?"

This question Lydia could not sidestep so easily. Her mouth hung open for a moment as she tried to form some diplomatic nonresponse. "No," she said. "But he's very busy."

"When I put you on that tour," the man said, "it was because I had the sneaking suspicion that you idolized Peter, and I wanted you to see for yourself what kind of person he really is. I thought that if you met him, you might realize he's a hack and set your sights higher. Of course, I forgot what people always said about him, about how charming he can be. I've never met him personally, so I wasn't prepared for him to be as persuasive as he seemed from afar."

"Excuse me? When *you* put me on the tour?" Lydia said.

"You think it's impossible, that something you worked on for weeks I could achieve in an afternoon, but I have a way of doing things," the man said.

"A way of doing things," Lydia repeated.

"I once orchestrated a four-floor riot to distract from the dismal opening weekend of a condo board member's Mexican-hibachi fusion venture. Turning Gil was no trouble. And once I'd done that, it was easy as delivering the message. Peter and his people were already here. I did it for you, Lydia. I wanted you to know the truth. About him. About all of this. You deserve better."

Lydia felt the excitement of her morning alchemizing into nervous impatience. "I have to be honest, I'm not following."

The man too seemed to be growing angry. "People said Los Verticalés was a social experiment for years. They were right, but only partly. It was an experiment, but not a social one; it was a financial one. And so is this place."

"So is what place? Here?"

The man nodded.

"So it's all some big diabolical plan," Lydia said. She didn't know what to do with her hands, so she kept them straight at her sides. "Build a giant building, knock it down, hire a bunch of folks to clean it up, and somewhere in there you make money? That's ridiculous."

"No!" The man nearly shouted. When he spoke again, he managed to affect a calm demeanor. It was thin. He seemed to be trembling. "What is actually ridiculous is your assumption that it must be either good or diabolical. It's neither. Peter Thisbee makes bubbles. The bubbles he makes are so enormous and so shiny that you forget they're empty. This is where the perceived measure of Peter's talent matches reality. He knows just how to build something—a tower, a community—that will keep you from asking the more difficult questions, from seeing just how fragile and careless it is beneath the surface. That's what I'm saying. It's a test of carelessness. This part isn't about making money off of it. The Vert was to make money. Whatever comes next will make money, I'm sure. This part is about not losing it."

Lydia motioned to CamperTown behind her, to the Heap somewhere beyond that. "This," Lydia said. "You don't think he lost any money on this."

The man shook his head. "No. I don't."

"He bought the wrecked condos back!" Lydia was losing her cool, but she didn't care.

"He didn't pay back the condo dues, though. He didn't pay us back for the utilities, the access to which he controlled. And the few construction companies and tradesmen we all used for remodeling and basic handy work, who set their prices as high as they wanted—you don't think they paid Peter to enjoy a near monopoly? And now he pays you all almost nothing and enjoys the profits from the Sale."

"You should've run for condo president," Lydia said, "since you seem to know a lot about every little thing."

The man sneered at this. "I had my own power. I knew everything because it was my business to know everything. I had no title, I signed no contracts, but I worked for Peter as much as anyone. I was a fixer. I built the image of Peter Thisbee as both benevolent overseer and shadow dictator. I was one of the measures he took to keep people from realizing just how simple and combustible it all was, how easily the bubble could burst."

"And how, might I ask, would you do that?" Lydia asked.

"I changed some details about a drunken accident to turn it into a story of unexpected love born out of an attempted suicide. I consulted with a local parking magnate about expanding her business into illicit realms. I spread countless rumors about emergency preparedness drills. Any of that sound familiar?"

Whatever retort Lydia had been constructing suddenly dissolved in her throat. She let the man continue.

"I made it so the stories we told were internal to us, communal. I made sure that we saw our way of life as so unique, so complex, that we wouldn't consider the basic questions any rational person on the outside might have asked: about stability, about gravity, about when perhaps we'd exhausted the limits of our upward conquest."

"So you did it all, huh?" Lydia said.

"Not all of it," the man said. "There were more of us. We didn't know each other. We didn't coordinate. But I had a hunch there were others doing what I did. And perhaps I'm just being paranoid, but I have that same hunch now."

"That's ridiculous," Lydia said. "Have you seen this place? It's too simple for all that. Thisbee said so himself. There are no distractions here." It occurred to Lydia then that she was in the middle of dealing with a distraction on a massive scale, but this was not what the man seemed to be implying, so she kept it to herself.

"You could be right," the man said. "I have no information beyond a gut feeling. But I also wouldn't assume that the simplicity of this place isn't a distraction of its own kind. Doesn't it keep you from asking questions about things like the Sale, or the monument? What do you think about that?"

"I think you're full of shit." Lydia hoped by saying it she might believe it.

The man sighed and relaxed into his chair. "How about this one," he said in a tone that almost sounded sedated. "That last part rarely gets discussed: the monument Peter promised. The tribute to Los Verticalés. What do you think it will be?"

"Like you said, it's not discussed."

The man held up a finger. "But I have a theory," he said. "It's going to be another Los Verticalés. What better tribute to the giant tower than an even bigger tower? What could be more brazen and fearless than that? And you know what? If no one challenges him, it will probably fall down too. But again, that's just my theory." He tapped the flyer on the café table in front of him. "Thank you for dropping this off. I'll be sure to tell the others. It seems like a lovely event."

CALISTHENICS

LYDIA HAD too much to do. She could not afford to be short-circuited. She forced herself to walk with exaggerated purpose and determination through CamperTown, and yet she walked nonetheless alone, without any exterior mechanisms to clear her mind of the static.

Her initial thought was outright dismissal. She'd met Thisbee, spent hours talking to him. He did not come across as some con man who built husks, let others fill them in, and then took credit for them as proof of his genius. Thisbee, like Lydia, was someone with vision, someone who wanted to build a community the right way. He wasn't just some asshole trying to see how little he could do without suffering financial consequences.

Lydia often thought about the day of the tour to combat the impatience she felt while she waited for the potential of her role within CamperTown to be realized. But revisiting it now didn't help as much as she hoped. If anything, Lydia could hear echoes of what the man had said in Thisbee's words. He'd admitted that he didn't have a concrete list of goals at the outset of Los Verticalés. He'd spoken about loosening his grip, letting things run wild. This confession was a good sign, Lydia thought, because it meant he wasn't trying to cover his tracks. Although, maybe speaking of it openly was just a way of controlling her perceptions in regard to his tracks. Which was maybe another way of covering his tracks?

Lydia could feel this thread attached to something deep within herself, and she feared pulling it further might unravel everything—all she'd done since coming to Camper-Town, and all she had yet to do. But she was in luck. She'd arrived at her destination, the Large Coveted Object Moving Rentals building, meaning the time for reflection had passed. Now there could be only action. And there was more good news: they still had only one operational mover, but this time it was available.

"Careful with the steering," the old man said as he handed her the keys.

After that, she grabbed Hans and his camera and they went in search of a good backdrop. They found a place where the path around the Heap widened, allowing for two things: a nice shot of the camper with the Heap looming in the background, and end-of-day bike traffic to make up for the marketing she had forgone.

"Need me to drive it?" That was what Terrance asked when Lydia pulled him off the Dig to help her move Orville's camper to where it needed to go. She'd stashed the case with the disassembled rifle in it behind the seat, and the last thing she wanted was to answer Terrance's questions about that, so she told him just to hitch it up.

Terrance looked disappointed, but helped anyway, because he was Terrance.

After pulling the camper to the chosen spot, there wasn't much time left to do anything but go home, put on her old overalls—she and Hans had decided to dress in their old working gear, all part of the show—and grab a couple of spare ConductionSens shovels from boss.

Back at the camper, she found that Orville and his escorts had arrived. Orville and his supposed brother wore blazers and khakis, but the others dressed in almost suspiciously casual clothes, as if they feared standing out.

"The ceremaney will be happenang here, no? Will there

be a macrophane?'" asked the pale woman, who seemed to be
their tour manager. Lydia hadn't heard her speak the night
before. She sounded foreign, and probably would sound foreign anywhere in the world.

"Microphone," said the man purported to be Bernard.
"She's asking if there's a microphone."

"Unfortunately, no," Lydia said.

Bernard smiled. "No bother. I can project. By the way,
we parked in the big lot out back. Do we need a permit or
anything for that? Orville said it's new so we weren't sure."

It took Lydia a moment to realize what he meant. "That's
the used car lot. No permit required." A thought occurred
to her. "Those cars were all excavated from the garage. You
should take a look and see if you recognize any of them.
Maybe yours is out there."

Bernard, still smiling, nodded but said nothing.

"You guys got a special dedication ready or anything?"
Orville asked. He made firm eye contact with Lydia and she
realized that he wasn't asking for a direct explanation of how
they planned to extract him, but just to know they had a plan
of some sort. She also realized that even though extracting
him was the very reason they'd lured him here, they hadn't
exactly thought that far ahead.

"No big plans," Lydia said. "We'll just see how things go."

Panic flashed across his face, but just as quickly disappeared. "Great," he said. "Keep things loose. That's the right
vibe for around here." Then, after a moment: "Speaking of
loosening up, what do you say we do our old pre-dig calisthenics routine? I know I'll look silly in my suit and all, but
humor me, won't you?"

"Of course," Lydia said. And they began: first with jumping jacks. Then jogging in place. Then a series of stretches.
When Hans arrived, Orville encouraged him to join in and
he did without hesitation, gritting his teeth through the pain
that certain exercises caused him.

Bernard laughed but turned down Orville's offer to follow along. "Don't want to get too sweaty," he said. The woman and the security detail were too busy scoping the place out to pay them any mind. Lydia and Hans did their best to keep up and keep quiet. They'd never had a pre-dig calisthenics routine.

54

FROM *THE* LATER YEARS:

HOLIDAYS

Los Verticalés' municipal holiday decorations were not, like those in other cities its size, confined to streetlamps and the occasional trees. Hooks were installed in the ceilings for ornaments and webbed lights, and ribbons of various colors could be stapled to the walls. At the outset of a holiday season—a specific date determined by the condo board—each resident would find a box of appropriate decorations outside their door. They would have forty-eight hours to decorate their area of hallway. Late decorators would be fined. Also fined were those who did not use every decoration provided for them, and as the boxes often overflowed with cheap knickknacks, this turned our hallways into tunnels of festivity, the quality of which varied based on the care and creativity of individual residents.

Christmas, not surprisingly, garnered the bulk of this celebratory momentum. It was the only holiday to earn the use of the hallway PA system that was usually reserved for emergency announcements, and so a constant onslaught of Christmas music accompanied our everyday walks. Engineers streamed vistas of snow-covered pine trees to the inner residents' UV screens. A large Christmas tree was mounted in the park on the third floor. Children grew obnoxious, bristling with anticipation of both the holiday itself and their three allotted snow days. Even QuinCare hung mistletoe from each rearview mirror.

During this time, some enterprising residents converted their extra bedrooms into "neutral zones." Using soundproofing panels to keep the music out and decor of only muted blues and grays (no greens or reds), they created small cubes of anti-cheer. They then rented these spaces out at hourly rates to residents, usually parents, who could not forgo decorating each room of their own units and thus required occasional escapes from the Yuletide spirit. If there was anything charitable about holidays in Los Verticalés, it was that, just as the season had a defined first day, it also had a defined end, with fines again for those who neglected to clean up on time.

For all the effort, this cheer always felt imposed upon us. To an outsider, the holiday seasons might appear magical, but for us, a chore-like indifference contaminated them. They were satisfying in the way that it can be satisfying to step back and look at the empty sink, the teetering pile of dishes on the drying rack. What we truly celebrated were those days specific to life inside the Vert, such as " furniture week." Twice each year we could place up to four unwanted (but still functional) pieces of furniture into the hall outside our front doors. An appraiser determined the value of this furniture and provided us with a certain number of colored tokens, which we could then use to "purchase" others' unwanted furniture. The color corresponded to the quality of our furniture, and thus the kind of furniture for which we could shop. The furniture itself received a colored sticker indicating as much, and some of us left these on, even after the furniture was in our condos, in case our refinement be questioned.

More fun than the shopping itself, though, was the communal effect. We accepted that, until its purchase, any piece of furniture might be used by passersby for its intended purpose. Comfortable chairs became way stations on a particularly long walk home from work. Friends, upon seeing each other for the first time in a long while, might sit on a couch and catch up. A Ping-Pong table might be unfolded for a tournament that lasted until security could shut it down.

These were the sorts of holidays we enjoyed most: not the ones that felt like the celebrations that could happen in any city, augmented and redesigned for our particular layout, but the kind that only we could have, and only we could truly enjoy.

55

THE CAMPER RETIREMENT

CEREMONY

SURE ENOUGH, just as Lydia had hoped, the end of the workday brought with it a massive crowd. Mostly Dig Hands at first, stopping to see what was going on, then staying. Soon, the Assistance Sector workers wandered over. Then the Displaced Travelers came en masse to stand right in the front, murmuring to each other about Bernard, telling anyone who'd listen about how this was their first time seeing him in the flesh, that in Los Verticalés he'd never made public appearances.

As the crowd formed, the manager and the two members of their security detail disappeared into it. Their casual clothes—which Lydia could now confirm were disguises—worked perfectly. Nobody paid any attention to them. Everyone was too busy trying to get a look at Orville and Bernard.

Lydia grinned at the turnout, then smiled fully as she posed with Orville, Bernard, and Hans for a photo. The photographer was a newb.

"Gear assholes," Hans whispered through his teeth. "They buy a nice camera and think that's all it takes."

"This angle," the newb said, getting on his knee. "The framing." Then he made a sort of whistle noise, as if to imply the framing was a thing that he lusted after.

"Psst."

Lydia turned to see Terrance at the front of the crowd, still in his dig gear, shovel in hand. He made a motion to see if he could join the photo. Lydia shook her head.

Finally, the newb had gotten enough. The crowd swayed, ready for more ceremony. Bernard stepped forward into the semicircle of path between the camper and the crowd, a makeshift stage.

"Hello, CamperTown!" he shouted. "As I'm sure you can understand, being back here is a bit emotional for my brother, so I'll be the one saying a few words today. I don't have the same attachment to this place as he does. In fact, I don't like it here at all." People looked at one another, confused, uncomfortable, but then the man smirked. "Sorry, it's nothing against you all. It's just that, the year or so I spent here was a real dark time in my life."

The tension broke. The crowd laughed and cheered.

THE DECISION had been made on the drive—Orville wouldn't speak. They scripted it on the way. It wasn't enough time for an amateur to memorize a part. Harvey would deliver the speech, which was "Something something the camper is a capsule, something something its leaving signifies a change in the reality of CamperTown and the Heap."

He hadn't listened to it very closely at the time because he couldn't stop wondering what Hans and Lydia had planned. And he didn't listen now either because he was basking in a feeling of freedom. It gathered at his left oblique, at the belt, beneath his blazer. It was his needle. With its weak day-old tape, it had been loosened by the bumps in the road to the Heap, then worked free by jumping jacks and shifted out of view with a side-bend stretch.

Orville felt like a new man, standing there in front of everyone, but not like in the glistening-newborn sense. No, he'd been carved, whittled down to a sleeker, bolder, more cunning version of himself. The last time he'd taken action, when he'd stolen Harvey from a hole in the desert, he'd learned the dangers of the head-down-and-run approach. He would wait patiently for the right course of action to present itself this time.

Harvey appeared to be wrapping up. "Truth is," he said, "I would have gone absolutely out of my mind if I didn't know you all were up there, digging for me." The Dig Hands hooted. Harvey kept going. "Don't get me wrong, I was definitely sweating your arrival. I mean, metaphorically speaking. Not like *you* guys were sweating." Harvey waited for a laugh. None came. "Me, I was practically in air-conditioning down there!" A few people snickered. Mostly they appeared confused. Harvey forced a smile. "Well, anyway, thanks so much for coming out."

Everyone clapped and cheered as loudly as they could, as if Harvey hadn't just botched the end of his speech, as if they weren't standing around waiting to watch a drab old camper pulled away by an object mover that looked like it should've been taken off the road decades ago. And sure, maybe it was just because they rarely got much of anything like a show down here. Maybe they'd marinated in their own boredom for so long that their standards for excitement had been lowered to one-level-up-from-infant and they were just a few years of backward evolution away from entertaining each other on Saturday nights with a couple of rousing rounds of peekaboo. But Orville didn't see it that way. No, to Orville's mind, these people cheered so loudly for a slapdash speech without stage or amplification because that was the right and respectful thing to do.

These were good people. He'd missed them. He'd taken them for granted before. The rah-rah enthusiasm of the early Dig Hands had made him uncomfortable. It'd felt unacceptable to give himself over to their excitement, and also unacceptable not to. Still, they worked hard. The Dig Hands who remained today were not as driven. Not the newbs. Orville couldn't speak for them. But the ones who had been here all along? They could be outright lazy. Yet they knew this place. They might get bogged down in the ins and outs of their jobs, but they respected Bernard, which meant, by proxy, they respected him. Orville had tried to remain outside of them, to give them as little as possible beyond the vague mythology of his existence. But it was like Nina and the Cartel: try as he might to deny it, he'd always be one of them. It was time to let them in. He got into this mess in the first place because he hadn't trusted a single one of them to help. He would get out by relying on all of them gathered here.

"Hell, maybe I will say a few words," he called out. The cheering, having just settled, erupted once again, providing enough cover for Harvey to grab him and whisper, "What the hell are you doing?"

Orville shrugged him off and stepped forward to another wave of cheers. He held up his hand and the crowd shushed. "I've gotta be honest. It's great to be home." He scanned the crowd, looking for the Cartel. Without the added altitude of a stage, it was difficult, but he saw Joan, peeking through a gap between two men a little ways back. He made note of her location, then let his gaze wander. "I first came here to the Heap with a goal, and I dreamed so long of achieving it. But now that I've been gone, I only dream of one thing: coming back here and showing that big pile out there who's boss!" The Dig Hands howled at this. The Ass workers joined in, too lost in the moment to be ashamed. The Displaced Travelers remained silent, but nodded in a knowing way. "But let me be clear: I say this not just out of love for this place, but out of hatred for the road. Every other night, Bernard and I are in another place where we don't know anyone." He returned his gaze to Joan now. Their eyes locked. "Hell, sometimes it feels like we don't even know each other."

She reached into her pocket. Orville heard a tiny buzzing noise from his left side, felt a slight vibration as the needle shot forward into nothing, spraying poison against the back of his shirt. The crowd waited for what he would say next. Orville winked at Joan and her eyes went wide. She turned left and mouthed something to Stefan, who began to push forward in the hushed crowd. Orville had them just where he wanted them.

He pointed straight at the henchman and shouted: "Look out! That guy's got a gun!"

A HIDEOUT

SOMEONE SHRIEKED and then it seemed like everyone was shrieking. Lydia watched as the Displaced Travelers, without discussion, locked arms, forming a human wall. The man Orville had just singled out—one of the men he'd been traveling with—didn't make it to them. The crowd collapsed on him. He cried out in anger or pain as they wrestled him to the ground. It was high-pitched and almost birdlike.

The other two captors struggled to free themselves from what now could only be categorized as a mob. Lydia threw the door to the camper open. Orville motioned for her to take Bernard. This confused her, but she did it: holding up her shovel and pushing him in, making it look like a rescue, not a hostage-taking. She watched to make sure Orville had gotten into the object mover with Hans and took one last look at the crowd as they grabbed and kicked at the downed man, before shutting the camper door.

"Oh, thank god," the impersonator said, struggling to catch his breath. "Oh, that really was a close call."

Lydia couldn't believe it. This asshole was trying to keep the show going.

"You might've just saved my life!" he cried. Then he fell suddenly silent. As in: he fell suddenly, when Lydia knocked him hard over the head with her ConductionSens, and was silent, shifting only a little bit on the floor as the object mover rumbled to life and they lurched forward. Lydia sat at the dinette and kept a close eye on him.

This feeling of movement was something she'd have to get used to, she realized. In one moment, all her goals and ambitions—all her dreams of building the perfect community—had been rendered into dust. Their lives now would be in constant motion. Orville obviously had a bone to pick with the fake Bernard, then they'd dump him and it would be them and only them, on the road, never stopping, sleeping with one eye open, or three eyes open, since there were three of them, or two eyes open, because maybe they would do a rotating guard-duty sort of thing. There would be no easy out for them. They wouldn't have the luxury Hal Cornish had, of hunkering down, letting the world forget about them. He'd only hired the Cartel for the wrong job. He'd never taken one of their guys. Twice. They'd want vengeance for this, Lydia imagined. The only option would be to keep moving and never stop.

At that moment, the camper stopped. Lydia heard someone get out of the object mover and approach the camper. Orville swung the door open. He'd taken off his blazer and his button-down and wore only his undershirt and his khakis now. It was likely just for comfort, but the transition seemed symbolic to Lydia. They'd freed him.

He looked in at the unconscious Bernard and nodded. "Good," he said. "That was what I was going to do." He held ties, which he used to tie the man's hands behind his back and bind his ankles.

Lydia followed him. They were still right next to the Heap, but a little ways off from CamperTown, around a bend where no one could see them. The rioting crowd continued to roar in the distance. "Are you just going to leave him here?"

"I'm taking him," Orville said.

"Where?" Lydia asked.

Orville wrestled the man over his shoulder. "I don't know. I'll find some corner of the Heap, or maybe one of those cars? It doesn't matter. He's got some information I want and it might take a minute to get it. They'll follow you, that's what I'm hoping. I need you and Hans to drive to the casino, check into a room, then get the hell out of there. Call a cab, hitch a ride, whatever you need to do. Just don't be there when they arrive. That'll keep them busy."

"Not a chance," Lydia said. "You don't need two of us to do that. I'm coming with you."

Orville sighed. "Lydia, please."

"No! Don't try that exasperated bullshit with me! You go off on your own, get taken prisoner, and end up on some wonky lecture tour. Now you're out only because we got you back to CamperTown, and you're all, 'I'm going it alone'? Unhead your ass, Orville! You need me."

Lydia trained her eyes on Orville, willing him to accept her help. He wouldn't return her gaze, but his face contorted with either exhaustion from holding the impersonator or doubt. "Fine," he said at last. "You come with me."

Lydia nodded, feeling endlessly triumphant and scared. They stepped to the driver's-side window and told Hans the change of plans.

"Where you guys going to take him?" Hans asked. "Just out to the desert?"

Orville shook his head. "We need cover. A hideout."

"The camper in the desert," Lydia said. The idea occurred to her as she spoke the words.

"That's still here?"

"It's a touchy subject," Hans said. He pulled the rifle case out from behind the seat and handed it out through the window. "You'll probably want this."

Orville stepped back, as if afraid of it. "You know how to use it?"

"We thought you did," Hans said.

"No way!"

"But when we gave you the sweaters," Lydia said, "you seemed to understand."

"I just thought it was a signal," Orville said "Like, 'we know something's up.' Look, can we get going? I can't hold this guy for too much longer."

"I can't have it in here," Hans said, "in case I get pulled over."

"How about this?" Lydia took the case from Hans and tossed it onto the Heap. "That work?"

It did. They said their good-lucks and set off, Hans toward the road, Lydia and Orville, with the unconscious impersonator over his shoulder, out into the desert.

57

ALL ALONG THE HEAP, III

BY CHANCE, at the moment Orville had pointed to him and shouted about his having a gun, the man had been pushing past Gil. Just by chance. And yet, in years to come, Gil might look at this as one of the definitive moments of his life, a moment of true change, the separator between the old Gil—deferential, nonconfrontational, a bona fide wuss in all senses, easily intimidated by men with glasses and mustaches who came to his camper uninvited—and the new Gil—a man of action, a man not afraid to get his hands and boots dirty en route to justice. These realizations would come later, though. In the moment, Gil operated only on instinct. He took the man and pushed him to the ground and began kicking him. Head, ribs, thigh. His foot heaved without discrimination. The man squawked at a pitch somewhere north of amplifier feedback, giving the others enacting similar violence pause. But not Gil. Gil kept at it. To those watching, he might have looked manic, possessed by anger, lacking any consideration of what each kick wrought, a simple machine of destruction. But internally, Gil was serene, the tight sine curves of his anxiety snapping and falling slack. When the man's squawking grew quieter and bubbly with the invasion of some internal fluids, the crowd turned from assisting Gil to restraining him. Hands took hold of his shoulders. Gil turned on them, throwing punches, connecting with chins and ears until the crowd

got hold of his arms. They wrestled him away and to the
ground, where he immediately fell asleep.

"LET ME through. I'm a doctor," called the doctor. It was a
halfhearted attempt. He barely raised his voice.

The man whom the crowd felled would need medical attention, that was a certainty. Even from his vantage point,
which really wasn't much of a vantage point—he only saw
the man, then didn't see the man, then saw a blurry commotion where the man had been (the blurriness not the fault
of the vantage point or the commotion, but of the drink
he'd invented with breakfast and enjoyed a few of throughout the day, a "Moscow mimosa," which was really just a
screwdriver)—he could tell harm had been done. So why,
then, not force his way into the melee? There was the obvious
reason, of course: sobriety, or a lack thereof. But that hadn't
stopped him in the past. Mornings when he'd woken still so
drunk from the night before that he could barely put the hospital key into the lock, carving another line into what looked
like an abstract cave painting with each miss—even on those
mornings, he still managed to set splints, stitch wounds, and
perform tests on the intact deads they found up in the Heap.
He actually worked well in this state, loose and uninhibited.
The choices he'd been trained to agonize over in med school
he made without a moment of hesitation. Difference was, in
the day-to-day, he was called upon after the dust settled and
damage had been done. He didn't need to stop the leg from
breaking, or the wound from opening, and he sure as hell
couldn't go back in time and halt the collapse. Now he had
a chance to curtail the damage as it happened, and possibly save himself work later. On the other hand, if the crowd
did enough damage, it would mean almost no work at all,
given that a DOA took as long to issue as the pronunciation
of its three syllables—especially out here, a place left to its

own devices by the enforcers of regulation. Did he feel a bit guilty for thinking this? Sure, a little, but not so much, because really, he wasn't a keeper of the peace. His job didn't require that he break up fights or protect a victim who, by the way, very well might have been marching toward his friend Orville Anders with intent to kill. He had no responsibility until the fight ended, really. "I'm a doctor," he said again, and this time he didn't even pretend to be speaking to anyone but himself, a personal reinforcement not of what he was, but what he wasn't, namely, the police.

※

IN HIS previous run-in with the Vocalist Cartel, Hal Cornish had ended up with a wire strapped to his chest and a gun to his head. Needless to say, he chose to observe the Camper Retirement Ceremony from afar to avoid a repeat of that or worse. When he saw the crowd compact around a tall figure, he remained where he stood, off a ways in the Assistance Sector, in the shadow of the café. Everyone in the crowd— and he could see the whole thing—seemed set on implosion, pushing inward toward the disturbance. Only two figures managed to wriggle free and run away. Hal Cornish recognized them. She'd been the one to put the wire on him and explain just what he was to do if he wanted to live. He'd been the one holding him down while she did it. They ran now, but not toward him nor along the Heap the way the camper had gone. They went the opposite direction, into Camper-Town. Nobody seemed to notice them, and they didn't seem to notice him. He could stand just where he was and be safe. And yet, he saw an opportunity, a chance to do the right thing. He ran, a path roughly perpendicular to theirs, weaving through Assistance Sector buildings and campers so they might not see him coming.

He managed to come out right in front of them. "Stop there!" Hal Cornish shouted, holding up his hand. They did not stop. Or they stopped just long enough to pull the knife from his stomach. He felt a stabbing pain shoot through him. It disappointed him that he could find no better way to describe the pain of being stabbed, just as it disappointed him that his act of heroism had done nothing to slow them down. Clutching his stomach, he watched them for a moment. They were already through CamperTown, out into the desert, making their way to the used car lot. He turned away when his vision became hazy and he collapsed to his knees. "Help," he called, though he doubted the crowd would hear him, not with how loud they were, and not at this safe distance.

TERRANCE BIKED the path along the Heap with his head hung low. He'd stood at the far end of the crowd for the ceremony, hoping that he might parlay his way into a nice picture with the four of them. Lydia's dismissal left him feeling raw, and when the fracas erupted, he didn't have the heart to join in. He was tired. And not tired as in tired-from-moving-debris-all-day tired. It was more of a tired-of-all-this tired. Tired of his terrible dig partners. Tired of going to The Bars alone. Tired of being asked for information but not input. Tired of being used, and worse, tired of making himself available for the using.

He was following the path the object mover had taken with the camper in tow, but he wasn't pedaling very hard and didn't expect to catch up. So it came as a surprise when he rounded a corner and saw them parked in the distance. And for all the reasons he'd taken this ride, he hung back—hid, actually—behind a clump of rubble that looked to be a faux-brick wall. He wasn't close enough to hear them or even make out their facial expressions, but he watched. Orville had his brother over his shoulder—he must've fainted from fear—and spoke briefly to Lydia, then all three of them seemed to discuss a valise that Hans had in the truck. Lydia took it from him, finally, and flung it onto the Heap. After Hans left, she and Orville—and, well, Bernard too—struck out across the desert toward . . . nothing.

Terrance waited until they were farther away before walking his bike forward, slowly approaching where they'd been. It took him a moment to find it, scanning the rubble with his eyes: the black valise Lydia had thrown—which, he could now see, wasn't a valise. Terrance, a collector, had seen such cases before in photographs from magazines, but he still didn't believe it. Why? Why would they have something like this? And why would they just leave it? *It has to be something else*, he thought. But when he clicked the latches open and lifted the lid, he saw exactly what he expected. Terrance felt a rush of something like pure Christmas.

58

ANYWHERE BUT HERE

THE OLD busted camper looked different inside from what Orville expected. He had always imagined it as a derelict version of his own—the stuffing ripped from the seats, the walls covered in graffiti. Not the furniture-less shell they found, empty save for a small round lumpy shag rug at the center of the floor.

Lydia seemed to be thinking the same thing. "I didn't even know you could strip a camper down to this," she said.

Orville put Harvey down in the corner, propped up against a wall. He'd started to stir a few moments before they arrived. Now he opened his eyes and went to rub the spot on his head where Lydia had hit him, but found his wrists bound.

Lydia moved to shut the blinds, but there were none. "It's like a fake camper," she said.

"Where are we?" Harvey asked. As he took in the scene, his eyes grew wide. "Fuck!"

Orville knelt in front of him. "First off, ditch the voice. I don't want to talk to Bernard. I don't want to talk to myself. I don't want to talk to anybody but you, Harvey."

Harvey flinched at his own name. It had been so long since even Joan had called him by it. "Fine," he muttered, his voice thin and nasal. Orville remembered it from the day he'd abducted him. It sounded so weak. Maybe it was another impression, designed to invoke pity. It didn't work.

"All I want is a number, for Strom."

Harvey sounded strangely relieved by this. "You want to get in touch with Strom?"

"That's it."

"And you don't know how?"

Orville stamped his foot and this returned the fear to Harvey's face. "Of course I fucking don't!" Orville shouted.

"I can help you," Harvey said. "Just take me somewhere else. Take me to a phone. I'll call him right up, I swear."

"Don't take the bait," Lydia said from the window. "He knows you have the upper hand here. He's trying to get you out in the open."

"It's not true," Harvey pleaded. "You get me to a phone, I'll put you through to Strom, and he'll let you talk to Bernard as long as you want. Like, fucking hours, man."

"I don't want to talk to him," Orville said. "I want him back on the air."

"You could negotiate that," Harvey said. "I bet Strom would be understanding. You'd have all sorts of leverage. You just need to get me to that phone."

"I'm not getting you to a phone," Orville said. "The deal is, you give me his number."

"I won't tell you anything if we stay here," Harvey said.

"How about you take some time to think about it," Orville said. "Nobody knows where we are. We can wait."

Harvey didn't say anything to this. He looked forward, affecting a blank expression. Orville remembered that Nina had worn a similar expression the day they came for him, though this was significantly less terrifying than hers. After a few minutes, Orville got tired of crouching there and took a seat next to him.

Lydia sat against the opposite wall. "So do you want to give me a rundown?"

"What do you know already?" Orville said.

Lydia pointed at Harvey. "I know that this guy—"

"Harvey," Orville said. "Joan's the woman. The other ones are Stefan, the tall one in the crowd, and Charlie."

"Right. So I know Harvey was hired to play you for purposes of ad revenue, that you took him hostage, and then they took you hostage."

Orville blinked. "How'd you figure that out?"

"I talked to Hal Cornish," Lydia said.

They both turned to the impersonator, curious whether this name would stir anything in him. He didn't move.

"How'd you find Hal Cornish?" Orville asked.

"He's around," Lydia said. "But I'm a little hazy on how Harvey ended up being Bernard."

"I kept him in the apartment." Orville pulled his knees to himself. It was getting cold as the sun went down. "A big Heap shift happened, buried him. I thought he was dead, but then Hans dug him up."

"And he claimed to be Bernard," Lydia said.

"The others were already there by then," Orville said. "They were with me in the camper when the siren went off. When you knocked."

Lydia's eyes went wide. "Holy shit," she mumbled.

"If you hadn't come, they were going to kill me," Orville said.

Lydia had no response to this. It fell silent in the camper.

"Anyway, you seem to be doing well," Orville said, after some time. "Or it seems things had been going well, before I came back."

"Before I *brought* you back," Lydia said. "And yes. Sort of. I thought I was doing well, then I thought I wasn't doing well, and now I'm thinking maybe I'm doing less well than I thought I was doing. I don't know, really."

Orville nodded and they fell quiet again.

Lydia broke the silence this time. "So, did you guys make some pact when you were little or something? That if one of you ever got in trouble, the other would be there to post bail, metaphorically speaking?"

"No," Orville said. "We weren't those kind of brothers."

"What do you mean?" Lydia said. "What kind of brothers were you?"

"The kind that didn't really talk about the future much. Didn't really talk much at all when we were kids. Or ever, for that matter. Maybe a little bit more in the end with Mom. But even then, we didn't share memories or feelings. It was all logistical."

"Then why do all this, if you're not even that close?" Lydia asked.

On any other day, at any other moment, the question might've offended Orville, but Lydia spoke with a calm, genuine interest that disarmed him and left no room for anger or cliché—only honesty.

"A sense of duty, I guess," he said. "If it were just a friend down there, I probably wouldn't feel the same way. Even if it were someone I was really close to, I might be out there for a few months, then quit. It would be reasonable. Even your friend would understand. If you don't succeed, you've wasted your life just to fail. If you do succeed, that's no better. There'd be no way to repay you for all the work you did. And you could say, that's not what friendship is about, but even *that* is asking for something. It's asking for the friendship to persist. It's asking them to never stop being your friend. They're indebted to you. With family, there's no debt accrual. And you can't say, 'Not my problem,' because you're the person everyone else means when they say, 'Not my problem.' It's why when you grow distant from a friend they just stop being a friend, but when you grow distant from a family member they become 'estranged.' It's got 'strange' right in the word because it's not supposed to happen."

Orville could not deny his exhaustion any longer. It slurred his words and caused him to blabber. He felt as though he had more to say, and also nothing more to say.

"Why don't you close your eyes for a little bit," Lydia said. "I'll watch him."

Harvey sat there, staring out into the middle distance, breathing through his nose.

Orville accepted the offer. He shut his eyes and nodded off.

Harvey's shifting awoke him some time later. Or maybe it was Lydia cursing. He didn't know how long he'd been out, but he knew it had gotten darker. Dusk, at least. Headlights shined in through the camper's blind-less windows.

59

ABOVE AND BEYOND

LYDIA HOPED that it was some partiers, looking to get goofy in a setting more intimate than The Bars, driven to try a new spot by the excitement of a Camper Retirement Ceremony gone wrong. This wouldn't make it easy to explain what she, Orville, and a restrained Bernard were doing out here when likely all of CamperTown had been worrying sick about them for three hours, but Lydia could handle it.

And that was exactly what she whispered to herself, "I can handle this, I can handle this, I can handle this," until she recognized the van, and saw not just two figures emerge, but three: a woman and two men, one holding the other, who looked bedraggled and beaten. This cut the thread on her muttering. "Oh, fuck," she said now, ducking under the window.

"What is it?" Orville asked. He sounded groggy and didn't stand up.

"It's them," she said. "They've got Hans."

"Christ," Orville said. "Did they see you?"

"I don't know," Lydia said.

"Stay quiet and see what they do," Orville advised.

"Hey! We're in here! Hello!"

This came from Bernard—or Harvey. He'd been so quiet they'd forgotten to gag him. Orville slapped him across the mouth, quieting him, but the damage was done.

"Get out," Joan called. "Get out here right now." She spoke with no inscrutable accent, and perhaps that was what made her words seem so sharp. She waited before speaking again. "If you come out and surrender, we promise not to take your friend's cords." It was supposed to be a concession, but her urgent tone remained.

"Cords?" Lydia whispered.

Orville touched his throat. "Like, as in 'vocal.' It's a thing they do, with a scalpel. They were going to take mine."

Lydia shivered. "We can't let them do that to Hans."

Orville nodded, stood, and grabbed Harvey, dragging him to his feet. Outside, the three of them were silhouetted by the van's headlights. The woman and the henchman had pistols drawn. Hans stood forward from the other two, swaying on his feet. A sizable gash ran along his head.

"You people are monsters," Orville called.

"We didn't do anything," Joan said. "We just found him. What you see is the work of the windshield."

"I'm sorry, guys. I tried," Hans murmured. "I took a turn too hard and ran off the road."

"Enough talk," Joan said. "I'll need you at least fifty feet away from the camper. Now."

They moved forward, as told.

"You two stop," she said, motioning with her pistol to Orville and Lydia. "But let Harvey go."

Orville released Harvey's arm. His legs still bound, he hopped the rest of the way. "You aren't supposed to call me Harvey," he said when he reached them.

"Shut the hell up and get in the van," Joan said.

"You aren't going to untie me?"

Joan huffed, hesitated. "Okay, fine," she said finally. "I will. Charlie, shoot these three. Start with the driver."

"All three of them?" Harvey said. "But what about the tour?"

"I think, if this whole ordeal has taught us anything," Joan said, turning Harvey around to work on his wrist ties, "it's that we're not cut out for live theater. We need to get back to what we're good at."

Harvey nodded. "Bernard's return to radio. I like it. We probably want to avoid going near Sundial again. Seems risky to keep doing things right under their nose. Not to mention, what if our old contact resurfaces?"

"I wouldn't worry about that," Joan said. "And don't get too excited. We haven't worked the casting out."

"But, the people have grown so used to me," Harvey said. "To my version."

"We'll discuss it after we clean all this up," the woman said. She struggled with the ties. "Give me a minute." She left Harvey standing there and went into the van.

Meanwhile, the goon, Charlie, had forced Hans into a kneel. Lydia could run, but she knew it would be futile.

"What the hell!" Orville cried. "You said you wouldn't kill him if we came outside."

Charlie, holding the gun to Hans's head, paused and looked to Orville. "No. That is simply incorrect. Once again, just as on the first day we met, you have been caught asserting something inaccurate. The promise was that, in return for your exit from the camper, we would not take his vocal cords. There were no prohibitions placed on any other potential means of death. Perhaps"—and he seemed to take great pleasure in this next part, his face, in the headlights' glow, taking on a self-satisfied smirk—"if you had been more careful, in listening and in other activities beyond listening, you would not find yourself in this situation."

Orville laughed. "Me? More careful? We're here because your shit-run organization can't even get the right kind of tape."

To Lydia's surprise, the mild insult hit the man hard. He lowered the gun from Hans's head to gesture with it in Orville's direction. "You must be even less attentive than I'd suspected. I have not, since we acquired the incorrect tape, been on tape duty. And I am sure you are aware that my removal from said duty was for the very reason that I expressed concern over the tape's quality. So no, sir, I will not stand here and be insulted by the implication that I had anything to do with the tape that failed to adhere the needle to your body."

"Honestly," Orville said, "all I'm hearing is someone making excuses. A truly great worker doesn't say, 'It wasn't my job.' A truly great worker makes sure the work gets done no matter what, because a truly great worker goes above and beyond."

The man seemed to clench his teeth. His nostrils flared so wide Lydia could see them from where she stood even in the dying light. Harvey, a little ways behind him, repeated to himself, "Good morning, listeners," over and over in Bernard's voice.

Joan emerged now with a bloodstained knife. She wiped the blade on Harvey's back, then moved to cut his ties, but when she glanced in their direction, she saw the three of them still alive.

"Charlie, what in the hell is taking so long?" she said. "Just shoot them."

"I would like to request a change in the order," he said. "Of the shooting, I mean. I would like to request that he be shot first." He motioned with his gun to Orville.

"Pathetic," Orville muttered, "letting your emotions get the best of you."

Joan sighed. "Sure," she said.

Charlie didn't move to Orville. He lifted his gun from where he stood next to Hans and took aim. Lydia couldn't watch. She closed her eyes and waited for the gunshot.

A DISTANT POP

IT CAME soon enough. A distant pop that surprised Lydia only in how unsurprising it was. When she opened her eyes, she looked to Hans, hoping they could share one last remorseful moment. He didn't abide by the mood. His eyes were wide and the side of his face was awash with spattered blood. "What happened?" he mumbled.

Lydia turned, saw Orville standing just where he'd been, and turned back to Hans. To his left, the man, Charlie, lay facedown in the sand.

The woman threw down the knife and drew her pistol again, crouching and looking toward the horizon. Harvey struggled to free his hands but it was no use. He hopped and ducked behind the van, where he went to work furiously trying to untie his ankles. With his hands still behind his back, his movements gave Lydia the impression of a struggling mealworm.

Orville stood completely still. Hans did not get to his feet. Lydia also found that she could not move. She remained there, shocked into stillness. The woman trained her pistol on something. A blurry silhouette in the desert. Did Lydia see a bicycle? In the moment it took for the woman to steady her hand, there came a flash, another distant pop, and a hole opened in her throat. It appeared like a magic trick.

The woman wobbled, then fell backward, raising her pistol weakly as Orville ran to her side. He wrested it from her grip, tucked it into the back of his pants, and got on his knees next to her.

"Strom," he said. "I need Strom."

"Oh, this is almost too much," the woman gurgled. "You demanding Strom when we're right here. It's a bit over the top, don't you think? We love this sort of thing, but this? It's just . . ." She began to laugh now. It sounded terrible, as though it came more from the wound in her throat than her mouth.

"What are you talking about?" Orville said, but she wouldn't stop laughing.

Lydia became aware of an approaching shadow. It stepped into the headlight's glow.

Terrance. In his hands a rifle that looked to be as long as he was tall.

"Y'all okay?" he said.

Hans got to his feet now, ran—or more accurately, hobbled briskly—to Terrance, and hugged him, pressing the rifle between them.

"Careful," Terrance said.

"Where'd you get this thing?" Hans asked, pulling away.

"I thought it was yours."

Lydia looked to the van. Harvey was no longer where he'd been a moment ago. She scanned the horizon and saw him: a figure moving in short-legged strides, falling often, struggling to get back up. The dark fuzzied the details, but it looked as if he had only been able to loosen the ties around his ankles, not free himself of them entirely. Despite his desperation, he covered almost no distance.

Lydia had escaped death. Probably she should feel elated, or reinvigorated by some newfound sense of being alive, ready to throw herself into the task at hand with a level of laser focus tapped from a deep unknowable source in her heart, corked and set aside for exactly this moment, when she, for the first time, understood that life was not something you simply had, but something given to you each moment by fate.

Really, though, she just felt tired. And the idea of running to chase down some dickwad, even one who could barely
walk, was a bit too much to handle. "Terrance," she said.
"Help me grab Bernard."

"He's probably just scared," Terrance reasoned. "He'll
come back."

"No, he won't. C'mon. And bring the gun, in case he
resists."

Terrance stood his ground. "Did I not just come here and
save all y'all's lives? And what now? A hug, a quick thanks,
no explanation of what the hell is going on? And what's more,
I'm supposed to just come along and gather up Bernard like
firewood, gun in hand, 'in case he resists'? No, I need to know
what this is all about."

"He's not Bernard," Lydia said. "He's a voice actor,
hired to impersonate Orville, but Orville captured him,
stashed him in a preserved apartment in the Heap. A shift
destroyed it, nearly killed him, so when Hans dug him out,
he talked in Bernard's voice. They   these voice actors and
their underlings, like the ones you just shot—then captured
Orville and paraded him around the country as part of a
sort of speaking tour."

Terrance blinked. "Voice actors? Like for cartoons?"

"Sort of," Lydia said. "Now let's go."

Harvey seemed too focused on himself to notice their approach. They only had to walk to catch up to him. On the
way, Lydia said to Terrance: "That stuff I just told you? You
can't talk about it back in CamperTown."

Terrance didn't look at her. "Back in CamperTown? I'm
only going back long enough to pack my things. This place
is hell."

$\wr$

ORVILLE HAD no real threat to level against Joan. Her men
were dead and she was on her way. "Strom," he said, shaking

her. "I need his number. I need it now. You don't need to tell me where he is, just what to dial."

He repeated this over and over again, but Joan met his pleading with nothing but laughter at first, then eventually a cackling series of pained wheezes. Orville let go of her at that point. He couldn't handle the idea of her dying in his arms. More accurately: he couldn't handle the idea that someone dying in your arms might be one of those human things that causes your synapses to fire off in the formation for grief. Joan's death was not one to be grieved.

Orville stood and assessed the rest of the scene. Hans was still there, but he was the only one. "Where's Harvey?"

"Harvey?" Hans said.

"Bernard," Orville said.

"Oh," Hans said. "Lydia and Terrance went after him."

"Terrance is here?"

"Yeah. He was the one who, you know . . ." Hans said, raising an imaginary rifle and peering through an invisible scope. He looked past Orville. "Terrance, would 'sniper' be an appropriate term? Or is that a capital-letter sort of thing, like you have to be branded a sniper by some sniper-certifying agency?"

Orville followed Hans's line of sight to see Terrance stepping out of the darkness. He had an enormous rifle over his shoulder and dragged Harvey behind him by the arm. The latter's hands were still tied behind his back.

"Sniper works," Terrance mumbled.

"He's actually the one who figured out the phone bank was shut down," Lydia said, following Terrance and Harvey into the headlights' glow. "Without that, we wouldn't have even known you were in trouble."

"Well," Orville said, "thanks."

It was not nearly enough, but Terrance still blushed. "Of course," he said breathlessly.

"Let's get this guy inside," Orville said, nodding at

Harvey. "Now that he can be sure no one's coming for him, maybe he'll be more willing to talk."

Orville led the way to the camper and opened the door, but now Harvey really struggled. Lydia came over to help Terrance keep hold of him. "I told you!" he shouted. "I'll take you to call him. But I won't talk here."

"What the hell is it about this place?" Orville said, turning around.

"Maybe he thinks it's haunted," Terrance offered.

"Christ, Terrance," Lydia muttered, but Hans, loopy with survival—and maybe a little light-headed from the blood loss—said, "Terrance might have a point. I'll make sure the coast is clear of ghosts." He pushed past Orville into the camper. He paused upon seeing the place's emptiness, before pointing to the carpet on the floor. "They could be hiding under here."

"We could go to the casino," Harvey called. "We could get a room. I'll give you his phone number. You could negotiate. You've got me. They're all dead. You know what we do. You could threaten to spill it all if he doesn't put Bernard back on the radio and leave you all alone."

Orville was considering if the desperation in his voice, ratcheted up to absurdity, was affected—it sounded true, but that was what these people did—when Hans issued a loud "Huh?"

He had pulled the carpet aside, revealing something like a manhole cover in the floor. "I'll be honest, I wasn't expecting to find anything," Hans said.

Orville stepped forward. Printed on it, a sign: *Danger: Electricity. Authorized Personnel Only.* In the corner, a utility company's name: *Desert Power & Light.* Orville bent down for a closer look. The *i* in *Light* tilted just barely to the left, a tiny microphone.

"What is it?" Lydia asked. She and Terrance dragged Harvey inside. When Harvey saw Orville crouching next to the door in the floor, he ceased to protest, went so limp that Lydia and Terrance had to refocus their efforts on keeping him upright.

"It's him," Orville said. "Isn't it?" He looked to Harvey, but the man would not return his gaze. "That's why you're so desperate to get us out of here. That's why Joan couldn't stop laughing. He's down there. He's been right underneath us this whole time."

"What?" Lydia said. She left Harvey to Terrance and stepped forward to look. "Who?"

"Strom," Orville said. "He's their leader." He opened the hatch. Dusk had passed. The only light came from the van's headlights through the open door. It barely illuminated the top rung of a ladder leading down into absolute darkness. "I'm going down there. Alone."

"Orville," Lydia said, "we talked about this."

"I know, I know. But trust me. I can't have company for this." Orville had to work to suppress a quaver in his voice. "When I'm in, close this. We'll need privacy." He lowered himself and began to climb down.

"I just don't get it," Lydia said. She stood, looking down at him, in a circle of weak light. "Why would their leader be here?"

Orville had hoped not to vocalize the answer to this question, but deep down he knew he couldn't confront Strom without confronting the truth.

"He'd be here," Orville said, "for a role."

61

STROM

WHEN THE hatch closed, Orville found himself briefly in total darkness before a light turned on below, as faint as the light had been from above. At the bottom of the ladder, a small archway separated the tunnel down from another room, where the glow came from. Orville, a few rungs from the floor, let go of the ladder with one hand, drew Joan's pistol, and jumped the rest of the way down. He turned in the air so that he faced the archway, his gun out in front of him, ready to pull the trigger before Strom could.

But Strom was not poised for a fight. Short, pudgy, and bald, he crouched in the room rubbing his eyes. "Sorry, sorry," he said. His voice struck Orville as inhuman in its flatness. It sounded almost robotic. "It's been a while since I've turned on the lights down here."

The room he stood in appeared to be constructed from a buried shipping container, but piled high on all sides were cinder blocks, stones, broken televisions, junk of all kinds. Wire netting above housed more of the same detritus, creating an artificial ceiling, leaving only a short, low tunnel. The light came from a single green-shaded desk lamp, perched precariously on a protruding slab of stone. Behind Strom, a phone and a soundboard. Orville flinched at the sight of it.

Strom finished rubbing his eyes but still squinted. "Please, put that down. Look at me. I'm not one of the dangerous ones. Or not in that way."

Orville reluctantly lowered his pistol.

"Good, thank you," Strom said. "I wish I could say I knew we'd meet like this, or that I had a strange feeling about the apparent 'Camper Retirement Ceremony.' But I didn't."

"You underestimated me," Orville said.

Strom waved this off. "No. It wasn't cunning. It was luck, all of it. You lucked into some information about our existence. You lucked into Harvey. It was a trial run, the whole thing. We found a way to circulate some vague knowledge of our existence throughout Sundial. Unlikely as it might be, we didn't want them to hear about us from anyone other than us. If we controlled what they knew and what they didn't know, we could ensure they wouldn't find out about, well . . ." Strom did a flourish, to indicate everything around them. "When they reached out to us, it was a chance to try our hand at something we'd long been considering: smaller, simpler jobs that might keep us afloat during periods when the big clients didn't need us. Hence, we sent Harvey. Not one of our best. Had we sent someone of Joan's caliber from the beginning, I am certain you would not be here."

"Joan's dead," Orville said. "It's only Harvey up there who's left."

Strom shrugged. "Luck again, I'm sure. At any rate, you are here, so I guess we can talk. Trying to send you away when you've come this far would be more damaging to me and this enterprise. I'll give you answers if you have questions, but some of the things I'll say may upset you, so please, try to remain composed for both our sakes."

Orville couldn't believe it. *If* he had any questions? The questions were the only thing that kept Orville from screaming or crying or raising the pistol and pulling the trigger. He didn't *have* questions. Orville *was* questions, all questions, anthropomorphized and given a gun.

"How long have you been down here?" Orville asked.

"Have I been Bernard all along? Did your brother even survive? That's what you're really asking, isn't it?"

"I just wanted to know . . ." Orville began but could get no further. Strom's response left him feeling naked, exposed.

"I'm sorry, you're right, that was insensitive of me. I'll answer the question as you asked it. I've been here since the beginning. Is that clear enough? I arrived about a month before the Dig started, but there were preparations before that. It was my first job in some time." Strom sat on his haunches, as if preparing for a long casual chat. "I'd been focusing more on the managerial side of things, so it fell on me to prepare for the role in terms of both character work and logistics. I managed to get it done in a week. That's something nobody ever talks about: It was ten days after the collapse that Bernard came on the air. What was he doing that whole time? Our client was worried about that, but I told him: give them enough hope, give them a good story, and people don't ask questions. Anyway, by the time you started the tour, I'd gotten used to it down here, not to mention, I needed to be in character for our talks, so I stayed."

Everything Orville wanted to know, it was all right there. And yet, he didn't want to process it, not here, not with Strom watching him, this man whom he'd just met and knew so well. He didn't have any idea what to say now, only that he had to say something. Letting silence settle was not an option. Silence would crystallize everything, trap him in a potent mixture of grief and embarrassment. Orville looked at his feet, clocking the contrast of his shiny dress shoes glinting in the low light with the rough concrete floor. He forced another question to keep the conversation going: "Who's the client?" Just as quickly as it formed, its answer occurred to him. "Thisbee."

Strom nodded.

"And Bernard was?"

"Publicity," Strom said. "Nobody's going to show up just to dig some rich guy out of a nasty situation. There needed to be something more for people to get invested. So Thisbee enlisted our services and we obliged, for a meaningful sum. Suddenly, cleaning up that rich guy's disaster became an act of nobility—an opportunity to be a part of something greater than oneself, an opportunity to save a life. And honestly, though it came from a mistake, the press tour proved extremely valuable this way. It rejuvenated the Dig Effort. We didn't really make much from the performances themselves. The profit came here. Or up there."

Orville felt a fierce anger percolating inside him, but he took a deep breath and exhaled it. *Keep it together,* Orville thought, *for now.* "What you mentioned before, about controlling what Sundial knew. Do you mean that when they came to me about reading ads, they didn't know I was just talking to some voice actor buried under a fake camper?"

Strom nodded with self-satisfaction. "Exactly. That was one of the things we dealt with in the week of lead-up. A full rewire. There was power to the antenna but the wires to Los Verticalés were cut. We had to reroute them to our station"— Strom tapped the soundboard behind him—"without anyone noticing. Luckily, after the collapse, people weren't exactly too concerned with checking the connectors. So, Sundial had no idea that they were hiring one of us to talk to another one of us. When I found out about that, I just laughed and laughed and laughed."

"What do you mean, when you found out? You just said you were down here the whole time."

"My operatives called in often," Strom said. "They spoke in voices, of course, and we communicated in code. Most matters, though, I dealt with at night."

"But you were still on the air," Orville said. "I could hear you breathing."

"A recording. A day of preparing for the project was spent in an induced sleep. Twenty-four hours gave us enough noise variance that we could cut together years of sleep tracks. I'd simply queue one up, turn down the mic, and then I'd be

free to make calls and arrange whatever needed arranging."
Strom stood now, or hunched. He wasn't more than five feet
tall, and even he couldn't stand straight up in the tunnel. His
eyes had adjusted to the light. He no longer squinted. "But
Orville, I hated those times. Those moments outside of Bernard, they destroyed me. Just as I hated when I had to speak
with Harvey instead of you."

Orville, still twenty or so feet away at the foot of the ladder,
scoffed and tightened his grip on the pistol. He tried to breathe
out the anger again, but this time there was some left over.
"Could've fooled me. All that stuff like 'You've been so talkative lately, Orville,' 'Thanks for opening up, Orville.' Don't
give me this sentimental bullshit. You were having fun."

"It was only to make you jealous. I thought if I spoke to
Harvey as though I was getting closer to him than we'd ever
been, you'd consider cutting a deal with Hal Cornish," Strom
said. "But I want to return to something you said earlier. You
said you were talking to some voice actor in a fake camper.
But I think we both know it was more than that."

"You're a liar," Orville said. He felt himself cracking.
"That's all you are. You're a fake."

"No," Strom said. "I'm an incredible fake. The best fake
that ever was. I'm going to tell you a story. It might take a
minute or two, so feel free to sit down." When Orville didn't
move, Strom shrugged. "Fine, here it is: I didn't speak for
the first six years of my life. My parents didn't know what
was wrong. They contacted speech therapists, experts, doc-
tors, psychiatrists. Then, one summer, my cousin Ezra came
to visit for a week with my aunt and uncle. When he left and I
began speaking, my parents couldn't believe it. Nor could they
believe my voice. It was a carbon copy of Ezra's. They were
shocked. Yes, we were family, but still, the resemblance was
so striking, it almost couldn't be called resemblance. It was
the same voice. Later, after Ezra's voice grew deeper, I moved
on to a different one, a classmate of mine. Troy, I believe his

name was. Only then did anyone realize that I never possessed a voice like Ezra's. I'd taken it."

"What does this have to do with me?" Orville said. "What does this have to do with Bernard?"

"Everything," Strom said. "What I mean is, there was no me. There never has been. I was born with an unparalleled vocal range, and nothing else. This was why I never liked voicing commercials or dubbing over foreign films. They were only momentary escapes into being someone. I created the Cartel to satisfy my need for roles that were immersive. And then, even those roles were not enough. This—Bernard—was my dream. On a hot mic for hours, only breaking character for occasional chats at night. Orville, I was in heaven."

"I'm glad you could find such satisfaction in the role of my dead brother." Speaking the word made it true. His brother was dead, had been for quite some time. The nausea Orville had felt before making his way down here returned to mix with his anger.

"You're not understanding me." Strom rubbed his temples, annoyed. Still his voice remained flat. "I didn't enjoy playing your brother, because I didn't play your brother. Just as with Ezra and Troy in my youth, I *became* Bernard. The life I portrayed on the radio, I lived. When they delivered water rations each month, I poured half of it out, so I could know the thirst of a trapped man. And when they asked me what I wanted to eat, I told them to bring me vermin. Don't you get it, Orville? I'm just who you thought I was when we spoke every day at four. I'm your brother."

Orville had so much to say that he could say nothing. The silence, as he feared, seemed to be closing in around him. With his empty hand, he reached back slowly and touched the ladder, to make sure it hadn't vanished somehow, to make sure he still had a way out.

Strom spoke at last. "Here, I'll show you." He reached for the light and suddenly it was pitch black.

Orville raised his gun now. It wouldn't be difficult to shoot him. He knew where to point. But what if the bullet deflected off something, some block or rock or shard of metal? Not to mention, the phrase about this very circumstance, "a shot in the dark," did not imply a soundness to one's logic. For this reason, Orville, though refusing to lower the gun, did not squeeze the trigger. Or maybe he just wanted to see what Strom had planned for him.

"Orville, are you there? Can you hear me?"

The voice sent chills through him. His palms grew sweaty in an instant. The real Bernard, or at least the realest Orville had known in some time.

"Orville? Seriously, don't mess with me."

"I'm here," Orville said.

"So you finally made it," said Bernard. "You did it, just as you promised. You found me."

"I did," Orville said.

"Hey, now that I've got you here, let me hash something out with you, something I've been thinking about. When someone quits a job, what happens?"

Orville held his breath.

"Orville? Come on. You made it this far just to leave me hanging? I don't think so. So, what happens?"

"I don't know," Orville said. He would give himself over to this moment, he decided. How could he not? "They get another job?"

"No, not for them. For the company."

"They find someone else to do it."

"Exactly. They find a replacement. And when your car breaks down and can't be fixed—it's totaled—what do you do?"

Was Bernard's voice getting closer? Or was Orville just imagining it? "You get another car," he said.

"Right. You replace it. And when a cat dies, you might choose to get another cat, or if a plant shrivels up, you go to a plant shop for a new one. The word 'replaceable' is often used in a sort of derogatory way, isn't it? As if it means the same thing as 'interchangeable.' But there are a lot of important things that are replaceable in the good way. Or, replacement-worthy. As in, when they give out, you don't just move on. You don't say, 'I once had a car,' or 'We once had an engineer who worked here,' or 'I used to be a cat person,' or 'There used to be a plant over there.' You get a new one, not out of disrespect for the old one, but out of respect, out of necessity, or, in the case of the cat, out of a love that has become so strong it feels like necessity. Are you following?"

"Yes," Orville whispered.

Bernard's voice too had grown softer, but louder, closer, nearly spoken directly into Orville's ear. "Then why are families finite? A father, mother, sister, brother—they provide something that no other person or pet or service can give you. But for some reason, we only get as many family members as we're born with. And when they die or when they go away, we don't get to replace them. You can say to your friend, 'You're like a brother to me' but you wouldn't say, 'You are my brother now.' Doesn't that seem wrong? Don't you think that we should be able to replace the family members we lose? It'd be symbiotic: they give you a reason to keep going, and you give them an identity. Doesn't that just seem fair?"

Orville didn't want the conversation to end, but he saw where Strom was going with this, and he didn't feel right letting it get much further. "I don't know, Bernard."

Two things happened next: a hand took hold of the pistol, and a forehead crashed against Orville's nose. He felt a splintering pain in his head. His grip on the pistol slipped and he let it go, stumbling back against the ladder. Strom was on him in an instant, pinning his left arm to the wall with one hand. Orville reached out, found his other arm in the darkness. Strom was trying to push the pistol toward the sounds of Orville's breathing, but Orville held it back.

"Just let it happen, Orville," came the voice, still Bernard, and despite the obvious struggle, still calm. "You trust me, don't you? This is what's best. Do you really want to go on, knowing what you know now?"

"I'm not here alone," Orville wheezed. "You wouldn't make it up the ladder."

"This might sound mean, but I'm not worried," Bernard said. Strom leaned in close, so close Orville felt his nose brush up against his chin. "Those people, whoever they are, are amateurs."

It was true. They were amateurs and so was Orville. But he wasn't weak, and more than that, he'd lost his patience. Every night onstage or in the motel, every day in the back of that van, he'd wanted this to be over—not just the tour, but everything. He was tired of trying to make things happen only to get swept up in some new terrible undercurrent. He was tired in the constant rejiggering of what was true and what was a lie. And he was tired of all the goddamn voices. This wasn't the end he'd hoped for, but it was an end nonetheless. He worked his hand up Strom's arm until he found the pistol and managed to get his index finger wedged in with Strom's on the trigger.

"Stop that!" Bernard shouted.

Strom tried to shake his hand loose, but Orville didn't let go. He let his left arm go limp against the wall and focused all his energy into pushing the pistol down under Strom's chin. Strom realized and threw his head back just as Orville forced down the trigger. The shot echoed through the underground compartment and for less than a second all was bright. Strom didn't fall down, but he didn't struggle either. They stood, frozen, standing and holding the gun together.

The hatch opened above them. "Orville?" Lydia called down. "Are you okay? We heard a shot."

Orville didn't answer. The faint light from upstairs illuminated Strom's face. Blood poured down his shirt from under his chin. His front teeth were chipped where the bullet had exited before burying itself somewhere in the tunnel above them.

"Orville?" Lydia called again.

Slowly they lowered the pistol together, but neither would let go, so they stood there, as if holding hands through it. Strom removed his other hand from Orville's arm. He reached into his mouth and fished out something that looked like a slug but was actually, Orville realized, the majority of his tongue, shot clean off. He held it up and stared it for a long time.

"Huh," he grunted, at last, and dropped it to the ground. He wiped his hand off on his shirt, balled it into a fist, and punched Orville in the face. Orville's head recoiled, hitting a metal rung. Quasi-concussed, he again lost his grip on the gun. Strom had it now. He could do what he wanted with it. Orville would have no time to dodge or deflect. But Strom didn't point it at him. Rather, he raised it to his own head, and without a moment's thought, pulled the trigger.

62

THE MORNING AFTER

BOSS APPEARED tired and very sober, painfully sober even, as if sobriety had attacked him from behind. He moved files—New Dig Hand paperwork, Reorganization of Dig Group Requests, etc.—off a few chairs so the three of them had places to sit. Then he sank into the chair behind his desk, where he had to rearrange more papers just to see them. The uptick in Dig interest had hit him hard.

"I know you all must be exhausted," he said.

He, of course, meant from the long walk back after crashing the object mover (in the process of which Hans sustained a gash to the head and Orville broke his nose), the attempted shortcut through the desert, getting lost, and so on. That was the story they'd given him. They said nothing about what had actually happened: about the showdown, the confrontation, about moving Joan's and Charlie's bodies down the hatch, replacing the rug, about puncturing the gas tank on the minivan, walking a safe distance away, and having Terrance issue a round into the puddle the gas made in the sand, setting the whole thing aflame. But the point stood: they were exhausted.

"I just . . . well." Boss closed his eyes tight and knocked hard on the side of his head in an attempt to coax the words. He was hurting. "There are a few things I wanted to talk to you about. So, Bernard . . . you said he jumped out of the camper, driving down the road?"

"That's right," Lydia said.

"And did he say why?"

Lydia shook her head. "Nothing I can remember. He excused himself into the bedroom area at one point, and drew the curtain. I thought maybe he needed to lie down after everything that happened, so I gave him his privacy. He was back there for a while, crying, I think. I heard him sniffling real loud." Lydia made what was clearly a snorting noise to illustrate. "When he came out, he seemed, I don't know, nervous? He started to ask where we were going, and when I told him we just needed to get to a place where we felt safe to stop, he laughed, said something like, 'Yeah, right,' then opened the door and dove out. I tried to get Hans's attention to pull over but there was no way."

Someone with more training in the art of interrogation might've noticed just how scripted Lydia's speech sounded, but not boss. He wrote a few notes down before shaking his head and putting his pen away, too distraught to form words.

They waited for more questions. When none came, Hans spoke.

"I feel terrible," he said.

"No, Hans, I feel terrible." This was Orville. "I didn't want to tell you guys before, but here, in front of boss, I just can't lie anymore." He turned to boss. "See, Bernard had, over the course of our tour, how do I put this? He'd developed a few habits."

Boss, a man understanding of habits, nodded.

"After so much time underground, he just had no restraint," Orville said. "He got in with a bad crowd, often spent all the money we made on god knows what. After a while, he bought more than he could afford. He owed money to a few people. We never stayed long in one place, so he figured he wouldn't run into anyone who had it out for him. But a few nights ago, Bernard swore he saw one of them, someone from thousands of miles away, waiting outside the venue. I didn't believe him until, well, you were there, weren't you, boss?"

"The man in the crowd at the ceremony?" boss said. "That was one of the guys? That Bernard owed money to?"

"I believe so," Orville said solemnly.

"What happened to him?" Hans asked.

"He's in critical condition, last I talked to the doctor," boss said. He seemed wistful mentioning his drinking buddy, as if they'd been separated for years, not an afternoon and a morning. "Not sure he'll make it."

"I'm really sorry," Orville said. "With everything that's been going on with Bernard, I shouldn't have taken you all up on the invite to come back here. But believe me, when he turns up, I'll be sure to get him the help he needs."

Boss hung his head. "Well, actually, that's just the thing. Orville, we found your brother late last night. By that busted camper. Benjamin, old guy who works the gate—he said he saw a fire out there, so a few of us went out to check it out and they found him, propped up against the camper door. He'd— he'd been shot."

"Oh, no," Hans said.

"Five times," boss added.

"Just awful," Lydia added.

Boss paid no attention to them. "Orville, I'm really sorry."

"It's okay," Orville said. "Or, it's not okay, but, you know, it was starting to feel like I lost Bernard a long time ago. With the drugs and all."

Boss's eyes began to tear up. "No, I just mean . . . I'm sorry. I could've saved him."

Hans and Lydia looked at each other. Orville scooted his chair forward and took boss's hand across the desk. "Boss, there was nothing you could do."

"That guy, the gate guy, he was being such a pain in the ass while we were over there checking the logs, trying to fig- ure out who the guy in the audience was, or if it was maybe someone from outside who stabbed the other guy—"

"Someone was stabbed?" Lydia said.

Boss looked up, wiped his eyes with his free hand. "Did I not mention that? Only been here a little while. Got his paperwork somewhere. Kyle something."

"Eckles?" Hans said.

"That's it," boss said.

Lydia looked at her feet.

"Anyway, this old guy at the gate, he's saying, 'Check the logs.' That's it. But the logs, they don't say anything. Only visitor is 'the Anders brothers.' And so I'm trying to ask, did he see anyone? But nope. Just check the fucking logs, he said." Boss had himself all worked up. Orville squeezed his hand, but it didn't help. "So, later he comes up to me bitching about some headlights out there at the busted camper, and I told him to give me a break, and he's all, 'Who would be out there at a time like this?' And you know what I told him?"

"To check the fucking logs?" Hans offered.

Out-and-out crying now, so hard he couldn't even muster the words, boss nodded.

"You don't know that you could've saved him just because there were some headlights," Orville said.

Boss choked off the last sob, closed his eyes for a moment to compose himself. He let go of Orville's hand and took a deep breath.

"Maybe you're right. But I'll tell you what I do know: I'm not going to risk making another mistake like this. You have my word on that, Orville. I'm going to interview everyone at that ceremony, I'm going to figure out who those assholes were, and you know what else? I'm going to take an object mover out there into the desert and drag that piece-of-shit camper away this afternoon."

Lydia spoke up now. "I'm sorry, boss, and I mean no disrespect here, but your position is to oversee the Dig, correct?"

Boss looked at her. His wet eyes took on a squint of either confusion or annoyance or maybe both. "What does that have to do with this?"

"That just doesn't seem Dig-related to me," Lydia said. "Seems more of a CamperTown issue."

"You weren't here," boss said.

"I'm here now," Lydia replied. "You've done great work. Really. But I can handle it from here. I'll get Thisbee's people to pick up the camper tomorrow."

Boss grunted. "It's been out there since anyone can remember. You think you've got the magic words that will get them to come take that thing away in a day?"

"Actually, yes," Lydia said.

Boss shrugged. "Be my guest." He turned to Orville. "Hate to make you do this, but the doctor's got Bernard. You mind IDing the body? Just to keep things official."

"Of course," Orville said. "I'll go there right away."

The three of them stood.

"Oh, and Orville," boss said, before he could leave. "We didn't really get to see you off last time, so if this is goodbye . . ."

"Don't worry about that," Orville said. "I'll be around."

As they stepped outside and started walking toward the hospital, Hans asked, "That true?"

"Where else am I going to go?" Orville said.

"I could make a position for you," Lydia offered. "Something to keep you out of the sun. You're a big name around here, whether you like it or not. Might be tough to be out there digging with everyone else."

With all that had happened, Orville hadn't even thought about the actual Heap. He looked out now and there it was. What parts of it reflected light glistened in the morning sun. He could see a difference. They'd made progress, but there was still work to do. It would take some time, perhaps years.

He was back. He was free of the Cartel, and moreover he was free of something he hadn't, until the night before, even realized he was trapped inside—a large-scale untruth that had dictated the entirety of his recent existence. Sure, fragments of it remained. He had, all through the night and even this morning, experienced tremors of residual anxiety. One shook him now: Shouldn't he be doing something to restore Bernard to the radio? Orville stopped and took a breath. Bernard had not been on the air for a long time, long before he'd arrived.

Lydia and Hans also stopped and waited without speaking. They already knew not to ask if he was okay, which he was, but also wasn't. In some ways, this whole thing, as messy as it had been, had prepared him to grieve his brother in a way that felt true to their relationship. The days immediately following the collapse, when he'd imagined Bernard dead, had been rife with confusion. He'd felt the need to mourn, but only intellectually. When Bernard came on the air, it didn't so much cut the process short as elongate it. It wasn't a closed case. It gave Orville time to think about how they'd been as brothers, and how they might be.

The truth about Bernard—about Strom—meant he no longer had any obligation to this place. But it was too late. He couldn't go back to who he'd been prior to the Dig. His decision to come here, to leave his previous existence behind and try to forge a new relationship with his brother, layers of grit and debris be damned—that alone had severed his past life irreparably from his life now. Hans and Lydia might be the only two people who knew him here—and God knew, Orville could do a better job at making himself available—but that was two more people than he could name beyond the gate.

What Lydia offered was further compartmentalization. He could assume an administrative role and remember those months on the press tour as something vague, more like a movie he'd seen than a life he'd lived. He'd be insulated. But he'd also be insulated from the time before then, on the Dig, in the same way. He'd have to tell his story and tell it often, and each time he told it, it would become more abstract. Did he even want that? Did he want to start over?

Did he want to learn to live a new way? Just the idea of it made Orville weary. It wasn't an option. He'd rather live the lie out there on the Heap with everyone else than tell it from some office. Because if he lived the lie long enough, he might eventually come to terms with the truth. He could be happy that way. And Orville deserved to be happy. Bernard had told him so.

Orville started walking again. Hans and Lydia walked with him, toward the shipping-container hospital, where Orville would look at a man who was not his brother and say, yes, that was him.

"Think about what kind of position you'll want," Lydia said when they'd reached their destination.

Orville had his hand on the door, but he paused. "You know, I appreciate the offer, Lydia," he said. "But I had a job as myself for a little while and I didn't like it much. I think I'll stick to digging."

63

FROM *THE LATER YEARS*:

EMERGENCY DRILLS

A rumor that seemed to be constantly making the rounds involved an emergency drill, though it wasn't a single rumor, really. There seemed to be endless variations, without any formula. Only a few characteristics remained steadfast. For example, the drill always took place in a part of the Vert far from where the story circulated. The outer units of the 115th floor spoke of a mock evacuation among the 21st-floor inner units. The 21st-floor inner units spoke of an alarm going off on the 73rd floor. The 73rd floor was sure it had happened on the 200th floor. Save for this distance—which conveniently rendered the rumors almost impossible to verify—each apparent drill was unique.

Most often, we heard some version involving orderly lines proceeding down stairwells with a murmur of fear and excitement. Sometimes they employed the sledding inflatables to expedite their descent. Occasionally we heard something truly wild: that security shut down an elevator and forced the residents of a certain area to parachute through the shaft. Or that they once loaded the residents of a high-up floor into a gondola-cum-hang-glider and sent them soaring to the ground below.

None of these were corroborated. Nobody had seen anything fly by their window (nor, of course, on their UV screen).

No one had experienced a strange elevator delay. No one who lived close to the stairwells ever heard echoes of a procession. But we didn't speak of the incongruities.

Why? That is something we think about often now. Some of us choose to take it as evidence that we knew true danger lurked in our future, that these unconfirmed drills were more premonition than gossip. From time to time, we've even caught ourselves positing that our respective reasons for leaving the building immediately before the collapse were all born of a subconscious notion of coming doom, even when those reasons were outside of our control. In truth, it's likely the opposite. We believed in our safety so wholeheartedly that our intuition for danger could only exercise itself through fantasy. Or, to put it differently: just as real drills remind a population of the worst potential danger, we felt so safe that we needed reminding of the worst potential drills.

Of course, it doesn't matter now. No drill likely would've helped. We debate often about how long it took for Los Verticalés to come down. Seconds? Minutes? Hours? We're constantly disappointed that nobody called in and asked Bernard. We thought of doing so ourselves, but we could never summon the nerve. We should know the answer ourselves. But we don't. We weren't there.

Unearthed Corpse Raises Questions Regarding Operations of Los Verticalés Dig Site

UNINCORPORATED LAND—Confusion erupted at the Los Verticalés Dig Site on Tuesday afternoon when an identity test for a recently unearthed body returned a curious result. The match was Bernard Anders, esteemed radio personality and the only known survivor of the Los Verticalés collapse.

Among the most confounded was the site's doctor, who asked to remain unnamed. "I just don't get it," the doctor told reporters. "Things around here, they can be a little ramshackle, but I'm a doctor. I know what I'm doing. Only thing I can think is the test must be flawed. In which case, we can chuck just about the whole [expletive] Victims Log."

"I had Bernard in here," the doctor added. "I mean, right the [expletive] there on the examination table. We got a positive ID and everything."

The doctor was referring to Bernard Anders's death nearly one year ago, a mere four months after he was discovered alive in the wreckage of Los Verticalés. It was an event not without its own controversial circumstances, Orville Anders waited nearly two months before announcing that his brother had died and been buried in a private desert funeral service. The living Anders claimed he needed time to process his brother's passing and that he had planned to reveal it eventually, but some believe he only shared the news after a number of venues across the country threatened litigation over his and his brother's failure to fulfill their speaking engagements.

Orville Anders, working once again at the Los Verticalés Dig Site, refused to answer questions from reporters on this recent twist.

"I think my grief has been complicated enough," Anders said before retreating into his camper.

Lydia Olin, friend and former dig partner of Anders, did not shy away from giving her opinion. Currently serving as the Supervisor of CamperTown Life, a position she was able to create and assume with an outcry of public support from Anders and other CamperTown heavy-hitters, Olin sees herself as less of a politician and more of a "societal engineer." The test results, in her opinion, are part of a bigger problem.

"The population here is skyrocketing," she told reporters. "New recruits arrive in droves just about every day. They choose to come because they think the singular sense of purpose will make for a simple life, a brief escape to do some good. But they only choose to stay when they learn that the opposite is true."

Olin sees parallels between life at the Los Verticalés Dig Site and the massive condominium whose ruins they now work to clear. "Like it once was in Los Verticalés," Olin told reporters, "life here may be sparse, but not in a way that makes it simple. It is both familiar and entirely foreign, reminiscent of the outside world while standing so completely apart from it."

To Olin's mind, the recent results raise an issue of respect. "As Supervisor of CamperTown Life, it's my job to build support structures to keep this unique community exactly that, unique, while also streamlining and simplifying all necessary policies and procedures," she said, growing particularly heated. "But, at the end of the day, we've got the resources of a glorified summer camp. That's what these test results prove: we've never been given what's required to fully do our jobs and live our lives.

"We need support," Olin continued. "We need to be fairly compensated for the work that we do, and not just in terms of our volunteer stipends, but with a willingness to invest in our community's infrastructure. Maybe that means looking to Mr. [Peter] Thisbee and his partners for more of a commitment, or maybe it doesn't. Maybe our reliance on them has been the problem all along; maybe they need to be working to please us, and not the other way around. After all, Thisbee may have organized the Dig Effort initially, but we're the ones living here. We're the ones doing the work. And we're the ones who built this community. We are the Dig Effort."

At press time, Peter Thisbee could not be reached for comment.

Acknowledgments

I'D LIKE to thank everyone who helped make this book possible. I couldn't have done it without:

- My family—Mom, Dad, Brian, and Seamus, who were always supportive and pushed me to take on creative endeavors.
- My generous first readers—Kris Bartkus, Ben Bush, J. M. Holmes, Alex Madison, and Frank McGinnis, whose feedback and encouragement motivated me to follow this thing through to the end.
- My agent and my editor—Kent Wolf and Nate Lanman, respectively, who turned what could've just been "a fine attempt" into "a real actual thing I am proud of."
- My wife—Emma, who read even the earliest drafts that were just me rambling on about scene ideas when we could've otherwise been enjoying dinner, and moreover whose love and support buoyed me throughout this process (and also before it, and also after it).
- My dog and my cats—Harold, Chandler, and Toby, whose complete and utter lack of concern not just for my book but also for the world of literature as a whole provided some much-needed perspective throughout the writing and editing process.

About the Author

SEAN ADAMS is a graduate of Bennington College and the Iowa Writers' Workshop. His fiction has appeared in Electric Literature's recommended reading, *The Magazine of Fantasy & Science Fiction, The Normal School*, Vol. 1 Brooklyn, *The Arkansas International*, and other publications. He lives in Des Moines, Iowa, with his wife, Emma, and their various pets.